TRUE NORTH

MARIE FORCE

Marie Force
Copyright 2011 by HTJB, Inc.
Published by HTJB, Inc.
Cover by Kristina Brinton

ISBN: 978-0615824499

All characters in this book are fiction and figments of the author's imagination.

marieforce.com

The editor who famously said, "No one wants to read about a super model," thank you. Thank you, thank you, thank you. A million times over, thank you.

CHAPTER 1

On anyone else the dress would have looked ridiculous. Pink bows of all sizes, tulle, a puffy peplum, and the full, swinging skirt that, all combined, made up the most hideous bridesmaid dress Travis North had ever seen. Chuckling, he imagined the reaction of the exquisite creature wearing the dress when she saw it for the first time. *What women did for their friends…*

Travis had worn Armani so he would blend in with the guests as he kept tabs on his well-orchestrated staff while they served filet mignon to five hundred guests under a massive white tent overlooking Narragansett Bay. The sun was setting in a blaze of summer color, and so far, there had been no major crises. Travis did a quick check of the elaborate ice sculptures, sparkling white lights, shimmering candles, forty thousand dollars worth of flowers, thirty-piece orchestra, and seven-course meal as the scene played out from his vantage point on the sidelines.

All his careful planning, obsessive attention to detail, and unwillingness to leave a single thing to chance was paying off. Anything less than a complete success was unacceptable to Travis, who had an enormous amount riding on this evening. He had bided his time waiting for the right premiere social event to elevate North Point, the country club and marina he had built over the last three years on the northern coast of Aquidneck Island, home to the high-society city of Newport, Rhode Island.

When Edith St. Martin and her homely-as-sin daughter Enid came calling nine months earlier, Travis had known he had a winner. The St. Martins were old Newport money, and Enid's wedding would guarantee a tent full of the very people who would ensure North Point's success. Travis couldn't pay for the kind of P.R. this lavish wedding would generate. That's why he'd personally seen to every detail, and now, as he watched it unfold, he was annoyed to realize he was focusing far too much attention on the stunning dark-haired bridesmaid and not enough on the delivery of petite filet mignon.

"Sam." He waved one of the waiters over to where he stood amidst the shrubbery that lined one side of the tent.

"Yes, Mr. North?" the young waiter asked with the earnest desire to please that had convinced Travis to hire him.

"Do you know who she is?" Travis nodded toward the bridesmaid seated next to the bride at the head table. "I feel like I've seen her somewhere before."

Sam raised an eyebrow. "You're kidding, right?"

Travis glanced over at him. "What do you mean?"

"You really need to get out more, boss. That's Liana McDermott."

"Who?"

"Hello? *Sports Illustrated* swimsuit model of the year, 2008, 2009, 2010." Sam counted off the years on his fingers. "Portsmouth's most famous ex-resident?"

Travis took another look at the stunner, mentally removing the ugly dress and replacing it with a thong bikini. Before his sex-starved body could react to the image, he returned his attention to Sam. "What the hell is she doing here?"

"Horse Face's first cousin." Sam referred to the nickname the staff had given the bossy bride. "Maid of honor."

Travis rubbed his clean-shaven chin absently, knowing he should reprimand Sam for the use of the name, since Horse Face was going to be a cash cow for North Point.

"It's hard to believe they share the same DNA, isn't it?" Sam asked, settling into the conversation.

Travis snapped out of his daze. "Thanks for the info. Go on back to work."

"Yes, sir," Sam said with a salute.

Liana McDermott. Travis watched the delicate beauty share a laugh with her cousin. Her long, raven hair cascaded over creamy white shoulders, and the silly dress seemed to have been cut to highlight her full breasts. She was too far away for Travis to be able to tell what color her eyes were, but even from a distance he could see they were almond shaped and topped with extravagant lashes. Suddenly, he was far more interested in finding out what color her eyes were than he was in supervising the cutting of the wedding cake.

Travis watched with interest as she scanned the tent, her brows knitting with concern.

Probably looking for her date, he thought as he wondered what kind of man might accompany a woman like her.

Oh, this ugly dress is so itchy! Liana squirmed in her seat in a failed attempt to sooth her irritated skin. Why she had ever agreed to wear such a hideous excuse for a dress she would never know. Actually, she hadn't agreed to it. She had been too busy on an extended shoot for *Vogue* in Milan to come to Rhode Island for a fitting and hadn't seen the monstrosity until it was too late to object.

Lesson learned.

Never leave such an important thing to chance, not that it was likely she would be a bridesmaid again any time soon. Despite Enid's over-the-top social climbing, she was the only close friend Liana had—and the only person she would have worn this dress for.

Now where in the world is Mom? Liana scanned the room yet again. When she arrived the night before she had been startled by the change in her mother. A little bit of forgetfulness on her last visit a year ago had blown up into something much more serious. After the wedding Liana planned to have a long chat with her Aunt Edith who was supposed to be keeping an eye on her sister in Liana's absence.

Enid reached for her hand. "Come with us to cut the cake," she said, her dull gray eyes dancing with excitement.

Poor Enid. Liana shuddered again at the unfortunate wedding dress her cousin had chosen. The thing had to weigh at least forty pounds, and the fine sheen of sweat on Enid's face was a testament to the effort it took to carry the concoction around. But the dress did cover up a world of sins on Enid's pear-shaped body. Her equally unattractive groom, Brady Littleton, gazed at his wife with such unabashed love that Liana was struck by a sharp wave of longing. For all her supposed beauty, no one had ever looked at her like that.

As she got up to follow Enid, Liana took one last visual trip around the tent in search of her mother. She didn't find her mother, but she did catch a handsome man in a tux checking her out. Thick dark hair, strong jaw, well built, and devastating in the formal attire, his eyes crinkled at the corners when he smiled and nodded at her.

"Enid," she whispered.

Her cousin turned back, and the huge bustle on the back of her dress caught Liana like a punch to the stomach.

Protecting her midsection from her cousin's dress, Liana asked, "Who's the wallflower in the corner?"

Enid made no attempt to be discreet as she leaned around Liana's shoulder. "I don't see anyone."

Liana turned and was disappointed that he was gone. "Oh, well, he was there a minute ago."

"Enid," Brady said. "They're waiting for us, honey."

Still wondering where the heck her mother was, Liana took the arm of Brady's pimply-faced best man—who had already made several flagrant passes at her—and went to watch Enid and her husband cut their cake.

Somehow Liana managed to get through the required dance with the best man, who acted as if his three minutes of smashing her toes was the highlight of his life.

Ugh! Liana was so sick of men panting after her like dogs in heat. If they only knew how boring and predictable they were. Not one of them was different—same old boring lines, same old boring compliments, same old, same old. Just because they had seen her in a few skimpy swimsuits they thought they knew her and worse yet, they thought she owed them something.

When the dance finally came to an end, Liana broke away from the befuddled best man, determined to locate her missing mother.

Looking around the crowded tent, she wasn't watching where she was going and collided with a broad chest and a bow tie.

He grabbed her arms, which was the only thing that kept her from falling.

"What the . . ." she muttered, glancing up at the strong, handsome face she had spotted earlier. "Oh. It's you."

With the amused lift of a dark eyebrow he went from handsome straight to rakish. "Have we met?"

"No, but I saw you looking at me before."

"I would think you'd be used to that."

"Would you please excuse me?" She tugged her arms free of his hold.

"Is there something I can help you with?"

Another line, Liana thought with exasperation until she looked up to find genuine concern on his flawless face. She wondered if he had ever modeled. "I can't find my mother."

"When was the last time you saw her?"

"Right after the wedding party arrived. She waved to me when we were having photos taken on the lawn, but I haven't seen her since."

"You're sure she's not in the tent?"

"I've checked every table, but I don't see her."

"What's her name?"

"Agnes McDermott. She's wearing a navy gown and has short gray hair and my eyes."

"Violet eyes," he said, offering his arm. "Come with me. Let's see what we can do."

"Thank you, Mr. . . I'm sorry, I didn't catch your name."

"Travis." He led her from the tent to an office in the clubhouse and gestured for her to have a seat on the sofa.

"Mr. Travis."

He laughed. "No, just Travis. That's my first name."

"Oh, I'm sorry. I'm just so worried about her. She hasn't been herself lately, and I'm worried she might've wandered down to the water."

Travis sobered and went into management mode. Reaching for the inside pocket of his tuxedo jacket, he withdrew a wireless headset with a built in microphone. "Beck, it's Travis."

As Liana sat on the sofa and tried to get comfortable in the scratchy dress, she watched Travis take charge, intrigued by the authority he projected.

"We have a missing guest, and her daughter is concerned she may have wandered down to the shore. Can you send some men down there to check? Yes, Agnes McDermott." He covered the microphone to ask Liana, "How old is she?"

"Sixty-three."

"She's sixty-three, gray hair, violet eyes, wearing a dark blue evening gown."

A moment later, a young woman wearing a headset knocked on the office door. "Travis, I saw the woman you're looking for about an hour ago. She left in a cab. I recognized her from your description."

"Never mind, Beck," Travis said into the mike.

Liana rose to her feet. "Where was she going?"

"I'm not sure, Ms. McDermott. I can call the taxi company and find out if that would help."

"That would be great, thanks," Liana said.

"Thanks, Niki," Travis said before he turned back to Liana. "You're welcome to wait here."

"Is this your office?"

"Yes."

"Are you the manager?"

"Something like that."

"May I use your phone?"

"Of course." Travis lifted the receiver and punched a button to get her an outside line. He handed her the phone and gestured for her to make herself at home behind his desk.

She dialed a number and chewed on her bottom lip while she waited for someone to answer. Dejected, she set the phone down a minute later. "I thought maybe she went home."

Niki came back with a slip of paper. "They dropped her at 242 McCorrie Lane fifty-five minutes ago."

"Thank you very much," Liana said.

"Do you know that address?" Travis asked.

Liana nodded. "It's her house. I wonder why she didn't answer the phone."

"Is there a neighbor or someone you can ask to check on her?"

She brightened at the suggestion and dialed a number from memory. "Mrs. Zito? This is Liana." She sighed with exasperation. "Yes, I'm here for the wedding. Two weeks. I know. I wish I got home more often, too. Listen, I need a favor. Can you run next door and check on Mom for me? She left the wedding without telling me. Sure, I can wait." Holding the phone to the side, she asked, "Am I keeping you from something?"

"It's fine," Travis said with a glance toward the tent. "Take your time."

"Oh," Liana said with a sigh of relief several minutes later. "Thank you so much, Mrs. Zito. Yes, I'll be over to see you. I have to get back to the wedding now. Okay, bye." She set the phone down and turned to Travis. "Crisis averted. She was asleep in bed."

"Why wouldn't she tell you she was leaving?"

"Something's going on with her. I'm not sure what to make of it."

"Well, I'm just glad she's safe."

"Me, too. I'm sorry for the trouble. Thank you so much for your help."

"My pleasure. May I?" He held out his arm to escort her back to the wedding.

Liana looked first to his outstretched arm and then up to meet his dark brown eyes. "Yes, please." She hooked her hand through his arm. "Do you know what time this thing is supposed to end?"

"Midnight. Why?"

"How many more hours is that?"

He checked his slim Phillippe Patek watch. "More than three."

"I'm going to die in this dress before then."

Travis laughed. "It does make quite a statement."

"Don't say a word, do you hear me? Not one word."

"I'll do my best to refrain from comment."

As they entered the tent, Enid rushed over to them. "Oh, there you are, Liana. I see you've met Mr. North, the owner of this beautiful place."

Liana glanced up at him. "Owner?"

"Guilty," he said with a small smile.

"I'm so glad you've met because I've asked him to take you home," Enid said.

"You did?" Travis asked, perplexed.

"Remember the final revision to the contract where I added the addendum about my special guest?"

"I assigned that to my chief of security, Mr. Beck."

"I'd like you to see to it personally."

"I can find my own ride home, Enid," Liana said.

"No need. I'm sure Mr. North will be happy to take care of it himself."

"Of course," Travis said with a charming smile. "It's no problem."

"In the meantime, why don't you ask her to dance," Enid said.

"Is there anything else I can do for you, Ms. St. Martin?" Travis asked.

"It's Mrs. Littleton now, and no, that'll be all." She scooted them along to the dance floor with a delighted gleam in her eye.

"I think I'm being handled," Liana said, amused by her cousin's flagrant matchmaking. "She wants everyone to be as happy as she is tonight."

"They do seem well suited to each other," Travis said as he led her around the dance floor while keeping an eye on the goings on in the tent.

"They're madly in love," Liana said, glancing up at him. "You're released from obligation. I'm sure you have better things to do than baby-sit me."

"Actually, it seems my very capable staff has everything under control. We've both got a few hours to kill, so why don't we kill them together?"

Since that was a line she definitely hadn't heard before, Liana smiled. "Why not?"

CHAPTER 2

"Isn't he dreamy?" Enid asked hours later as Liana helped her change from her wedding dress into an equally ghastly going-away outfit. The girl needed some major fashion advice, but Liana had given up on that years ago.

"Who?" Liana asked. "Brady?"

"Well, *of course* Brady's dreamy."

Dreamy wasn't the word Liana would have used to describe Brady.

"I meant Travis North," Enid said with a sigh. "The day I met him I said to Mummy, 'wouldn't he be perfect for Liana?' Mummy totally agreed. He's so James Bond-the-Pierce-Brosnan-years, isn't he?"

"Thus the addendum to the contract," Liana commented as she zipped Enid into her dress.

"You didn't seem to mind dancing with him for the last couple of hours."

"Dancing with him kept every other man in the place from badgering me."

"Oh, it's so hard to be you, isn't it?" Enid joked without a hint of jealousy. "How *do* you stand it?"

If you had any idea . . .

"I knew you'd never bother with him if I didn't help you along a little," Enid said with exasperation at the old argument. Despite the disparity in their looks, Enid had had twice as many boyfriends as her much more exotic cousin.

"I don't have time to bother with anyone," Liana said with equal exasperation.

"I'm only here for two weeks, and then I'm working in Europe for the rest of the year. What do you picture happening between me and Pierce Brosnan?"

"White picket fences and very pretty babies," Enid said without hesitation.

"You're high on wedding cake and love! I just met the man, and to pacify you I'm allowing him to drive me home. How do you get picket fences and babies out of that?"

"All right then, how about some sweaty sex?"

"Enid!"

Enid grabbed Liana's arm. "When was the last time you had sweaty sex?"

Never. Liana tried to remember the last time she'd had *any* sex. "I don't keep track of such things."

"If you don't know, then it's been too long."

"I'm not having sweaty sex or any other kind of sex with Travis North," Liana said, even though the idea wasn't exactly repulsive. She shook her head to rid herself of salacious thoughts about the very sexy Mr. North. "I have other things to be focused on over the next two weeks. I thought you and your mother were keeping an eye on *my* mother."

"We were," Enid said. "We *are*, but she doesn't make it easy."

"What do you mean?"

"She's very evasive and secretive. Mummy goes over there at least once a week and everything is always in perfect order, but Auntie Agnes never has much to say to Mummy."

"Do you think she has Alzheimer's?" Liana asked, expressing her deepest fear.

"I really don't know, Leelee. I've been so busy with the wedding I haven't spent as much time with her as I should have. I'm sorry about that."

Hearing her childhood nickname and seeing the genuine regret on her cousin's face made Liana go soft with sentiment. "You have nothing to be sorry about. She's my mother. I need to spend more time with her." Liana zipped the wedding dress into a garment bag and turned back to Enid. "You look beautiful."

"No, I don't," Enid said in her typical matter-of-fact way. "You've got the market cornered on beautiful. But Brady doesn't care. He loves me just the way I am. I want you to find that, too, Liana. There's nothing quite like it in the world."

"I'll have to take your word for it. Come on, your husband's waiting for you."

"*He* wants to have sweaty sex."

Liana laughed. "Enid! Really! Spare me the details."

"Maybe I should *share* the details so you'll want some of your own."

"I'll pass, but thanks just the same."

"Your loss," Enid said with a breezy wave of her hand. "But if I were you, I'd jump all over that sexy Travis North. Have a little fling while you're home. What could it hurt?"

"I'm not the fling type," Liana reminded her.

"And that's your problem. Take my word for it—a sweaty fling exactly what you need."

"Thanks for the advice, Dr. Ruth. Now, let's go."

On the way out the door, Enid stopped Liana with a hand on her arm. "I want you to have what I have with Brady. I know your career is important to you, but don't be so focused on your work that you forget to have a life. I love you, Leelee. I want you to be happy."

Liana hugged her. "I love you, too, and I'm delighted to see *you* so happy."

"Thank you for coming so far to be with me tonight."

"There's nowhere in the world I'd rather be," Liana said sincerely.

Enid and Brady ran through a shower of rice to the vintage Rolls Royce Liana's Uncle Charles had rented to transport his daughter and her new husband to Boston where they would spend the night before leaving on their European honeymoon. After they left, the tent began to empty out.

Liana was still wiping the tears from her eyes when Travis came up behind her, offering his handkerchief.

"Thank you." She dabbed at her eyes in a practiced move that protected her makeup.

"Are you ready to go home?"

"Don't you have to supervise the cleanup?"

"Hell, no. That's what I'm paying all these fine people to do. I have appointments this week with seven of your cousin's guests who want to discuss having their events here," he said with a satisfied grin as he tugged off his bow tie and released the top button of his formal shirt. "My work here is finished."

"That's wonderful. With such a beautiful place I have no doubt you'll be very successful."

"Too bad not all the locals are as generous."

"What do you mean?"

"Let me drive you home, and I'll tell you about it."

"Would you mind terribly if we didn't go right home?"

He tilted his head to study her. "What do you feel like doing?"

She shrugged. "I'm just wide awake and full of energy. Must be all the excitement of the wedding."

"Do you have a change of clothes with you?"

"No," she said with a frown. "I guess I'll just go home after all."

"We could go to my place right over there." He pointed to the ten-story building at the other end of the sweeping lawn. "I could loan you a T-shirt and a pair of shorts."

Her captured her bottom lip between her teeth as she sized him up and tried to gauge his intentions. "Is that a line?" she finally asked.

He tossed his head back and laughed. "I guess it kind of sounded like one, didn't it?"

Wow, that smile is devastating. "Sort of."

"Well, let me put your mind at ease. I meant it only as an offer of more comfortable clothes."

She contemplated the situation for another moment, remembering Enid said she could trust this Travis North. "In that case, I accept. Thank you."

He offered her his arm. "Right this way."

Accompanied by a chorus of crickets and the bay rolling gently to the shore, Travis and Liana walked the short distance to the newly constructed condo tower, the tallest building between Newport and Providence. In the elevator, he inserted a key to the penthouse.

The doors slid open into a dark room. He took her hand to help her from the elevator. When he reached for a lamp, she stopped him.

"Let me see your view first." The moonlight drew her to the wall of windows overlooking the bay. To the left she could see the Newport Bridge lit up in the distance. To the right were the Mount Hope Bridge and the Providence skyline. "Oh, Travis. This is amazing."

"I'm glad you like it," he said, reaching around her to open the door to a sweeping patio.

Liana stepped outside for a better look. "I've always wanted to live on the water."

"So why don't you?"

She shrugged. "I don't really live anywhere. I have an apartment in New York, but I haven't been there in months."

"That seems like a tough way to live."

She flashed him the smile that had made her millions but isolated her from regular people. "And yet my job sounds so glamorous, right?"

"It does have that reputation. Can I get you a drink?"

"Do you have white wine?"

"Sure do. I'll get that and the clothes I promised. I'll be right back."

Liana turned back to enjoy the tranquility. Far below she could see the workers cleaning up after the wedding and heard the faint hint of reggae music coming from the tent. She wondered if Enid was having sweaty sex yet. *Stop*, Liana, she told herself, but she couldn't deny her cousin had struck a nerve with her comments about Liana's austere lifestyle. Maybe it was time to shake things up a bit. *If*—and that was a very big *if*—she was to have a sweaty affair, Travis North would certainly make an intriguing candidate—a very sexy candidate.

"Liana?"

She jumped, startled out of her scandalous thoughts.

"Sorry, I didn't mean to frighten you."

"You didn't," she said, breathless from the current of electricity that raced through her at the sound of his voice. He had changed into faded jeans and a T-shirt that confirmed what she'd discovered while dancing with him—sculpted pecs and biceps along with what appeared to be six-pack abs. She licked her suddenly dry lips and watched his eyes follow the progress of her tongue.

He handed her the glass of wine. "I left a couple of options on my bed." He gestured toward the one room in the sprawling penthouse that was lit. "Use whatever you need."

"Thank you." She took a sip of the dry wine, put the glass down on a table, and brushed past him on her way inside. His bedroom was tastefully decorated with a king-sized bed, marble-topped tables, and a small sitting area by the full-length windows. The room, like the man who slept here, was masculine but elegant. Liana was further intrigued after being allowed into his private sanctum.

At the foot of the big bed, he had left several T-shirts and two pairs of gym shorts with drawstrings. Suddenly frantic to get out of the itchy dress, Liana reached for the hook at the back of her neck and pulled, but it snagged. Working to free it, exasperation began to mount along with a burning need to be free of the hideous dress. She whimpered as her arms fell to her sides, exhausted from the struggle. Realizing she was hopelessly stuck, she went back to where he waited for her on the patio.

He turned when he heard the swish of her long skirt. "Didn't fit?"

"I, um, I need some help."

He chuckled. "Is that a line?"

"*Please,*" she pleaded. "Get me out of this thing!"

"With pleasure." He led her into the bedroom to make use of the light.

She gathered her thick hair and pulled it to one side, giving him access to the wayward hook.

"What would you have done if you were alone?"

"I would've gotten a big pair of scissors and cut the thing straight down the middle."

He laughed as he worked to free her.

His breath was warm on the back of her neck, and she suppressed a gasp when his fingers brushed against her sensitive skin.

"I think I've got it. Do you want me to do the others?"

She swallowed hard. "Sure. Thanks."

As he worked his way down her back, Liana told herself the slight shiver was from the cool air hitting her irritated skin, not because a sexy man was all but undressing her in his bedroom. *God, he smells good.* When he disposed of the last hook, Liana began to turn around.

He stopped her with his hands on her shoulders. "Wait."

Her heart pounded with anticipation, and her skin heated under his hands. She jolted when his lips brushed the sensitive spot where her neck met her shoulder while his finger grazed the straight line he'd uncovered down the middle of her back. "Travis," she gasped, tilting her head to give him better access.

"What?" he murmured against her neck.

"Don't."

He ran his tongue lightly over her ear, making her shudder. "Why not?" he whispered as he moved around to face her.

"Because."

He took her hands, brought them to his shoulders, and went back to work on her neck. "Because why?" He caressed her back inside the dress.

"Because," she said, leaning into him as her protests became less and less convincing.

With a disarming smile, he brought his hand to her face, tilting it to meet his kiss. His lips were soft and undemanding, but they electrified just the same. At the exact moment when she thought she would go mad from wanting more of him, his control snapped and he plundered. All she could do was hold on for the ride as he ravaged her mouth. *Never,* she thought, in her one moment of lucidity before she ceased to think at all. Never had she been kissed quite like this.

Held prisoner against the hard wall of his chest, Liana buried her hands in his hair and met the thrusts of his tongue with her own, eliciting a groan from deep inside him.

Only when he lowered her to his bed and came down on top of her did Liana snap out of her passion-induced fog. She pushed against his chest and twisted to break free of his kiss. "No," she gasped. "Stop."

Travis rolled to the side and lay flat on his back, breathing heavily with an arm covering his eyes.

Liana sat up and tugged her sagging dress back up over her shoulders. Tears burned her eyes. *Why can other women be so cavalier about these things? Why can't I just take the pleasure he offered and enjoy it?* Probably because she never had figured out how to tell the difference between men who were out to nail a supermodel and men who wanted to make love to *her*—Liana, the girl from the small town in the smallest state who also happened to be an international celebrity. She had yet to meet anyone who fell into the latter category. Apparently, the man panting next to her on the bed wasn't going to be the exception.

His expression full of regret, he sat up. "I'm sorry."

"I said I didn't want you to do that," she snapped.

"You were as into it as I was," he said, clearly making an effort not to snap back.

Liana got up, keeping a tentative grip on what was left of her dignity as she held her unbuttoned dress closed with one hand over her shoulder. "I'd like to go home now, please."

His eyes narrowed into an expression that could have turned water instantly to ice. "Get changed, and I'll take you." He stalked from the room and slammed the door behind him.

Liana sank to the bed and tried unsuccessfully to curb the tears.

CHAPTER 3

Travis went straight for the bar and poured himself a tall shot of whiskey, which took his breath away when it burned all the way through him. *You deserve to hurt, you idiot.* The wounded face, the tears, the dress, the whole picture was more than he could bear to remember. *Goddamn it! Why did you have to be exactly what she expected you to be?*

Oh, but that kiss, that feeling of having finally found the missing piece . . . Would he ever be able to forget how perfectly she fit against him, the satiny feel of her skin, the mysterious scent that belonged only to her, and those violet eyes that gave away her every emotion?

Damn it, she had kissed him back! He had done enough kissing in his life to be able to gauge when his partner was reciprocating, and Liana had done a hell of a lot more than reciprocate. He could almost still feel her fingers in his hair, for Christ's sake! Despite her claims to the contrary, he had *not* read the signals wrong. No way.

The bedroom door opened and she came out wearing his Stanford T-shirt and shorts that were so big on her she'd had to roll the top down a couple of times to anchor them to her slim hips. She drew the puffy dress from under her arm and held it against her middle like a protective shield.

Travis finished the last of his whiskey and put the glass down on the granite bar. He ached when he saw her tear-stained face, and it was all he could do to resist the urge to take her into his arms and hold her, to sooth away the tension that had gathered in her forehead, to kiss away the sadness radiating from her. That surge of tenderness for someone who had treated him the same way she might treat Jack the Ripper astounded him.

She flinched when he brushed past her on his way into his bedroom.

He came back with his keys and crossed the room to the elevator without a word. Punching a button on the wall, Travis kept his back to her while he waited. The doors opened, and he held one side open for her.

In the elevator Liana fixated on a light in the corner. She seemed smaller next to him than she had earlier, and Travis realized she was barefooted when he noticed the stiletto heels dangling from her fingers.

The elevator deposited them into the parking garage in the basement of The Tower, and he walked to his burgundy Jaguar without so much as a glance over his shoulder to see if she had followed him. He opened the passenger door for her and went around to slide into the driver's seat. Only when he heard her seatbelt click into place did he turn on the car.

She had bunched the dress onto the floor, so when he turned to back out of the parking space he got his first look at her long, smooth legs and high, firm breasts outlined in all their plump perfection by the seatbelt. *Oh God, what that horrible dress had hidden!* He cringed when his body reacted with embarrassing predictability.

With tremendous effort he tore his eyes off her and navigated the car through the small garage. Once they had emerged into the sultry summer night, he continued to try his best to ignore the desire that beat through him as her scent filled the small space. Suddenly in need of air, and lots of it, he pushed a button to open the driver's side window.

"Do you know where you're going?" she asked in a soft, quiet voice.

She sounded so defeated he wanted to pull over and give her whatever it was she needed, but he knew she'd never take it from him. "I know where McCorrie Lane is, but you'll have to show me which house it is."

Turning to look out her window, she didn't say another word as he drove through the sleeping town of Portsmouth. On their way from the west side of the island to the east, they passed everything from million-dollar homes to shacks. Ten minutes later, he pulled onto McCorrie Lane, which wound down a hill that ended at the shores of the Sakonnet River. About halfway down the hill, she pointed to a neat white ranch house with royal-blue shutters. A light over the front door cast a glow on the well-tended flower gardens that lined the shrubbery and walkway.

Travis pulled into the driveway behind a tan sedan.

Liana reached for the door handle. "Thank you for the ride."

As it occurred to him that he might never see her again, a sudden wave of desperation hit him. "Liana."

She turned to him.

"I'm sorry."

"So am I."

Surprised, he asked, "For what?"

Her cheeks flamed with embarrassment. "You were right."

"About?"

"I did kiss you back," she whispered.

Reaching for her hand, he closed his fingers around hers. "Liana, I want to see you again. Give me another chance." He brought her hand to his lips. "Please."

With what seemed to be great reluctance she took back her hand. "There's no point. I'm only going to be here for two weeks, and I have to take care of my mother."

"I'm only suggesting dinner. Surely you can squeeze in one dinner in the next fourteen days."

She drew in her lower lip as she held his gaze and appeared to be weighing it all out. "I'm sorry," she said, finally looking away after a long moment of silence during which neither of them seemed to breathe. "I just can't. Thank you again for the ride home." Before Travis could reply, she bolted from the car.

In that moment of indecision he had seen in her a hint of longing—for what he couldn't be sure. But he had little doubt that she had wanted to say yes to him.

So he would have to change her mind. He waited until the porch light went off before he backed out of the driveway.

Travis North had developed a few skills that had gotten him where he wanted to be in life. Liana McDermott would soon discover that persistence was the greatest of all those skills.

Liana dumped the dress and her shoes in a lump on the sofa and tiptoed through the quiet house. She peeked into her mother's room and was relieved to find her sleeping. *Where did I think she would be?* Liana leaned against the doorframe and remembered crawling into that bed in search of comfort during thunderstorms and bad dreams. She had always found exactly what she needed in the arms of her mother. How she wished she could crawl into that bed right now so her mother could tell her everything would be all right.

Instead, she went into her own room, which remained just as she had left it ten years earlier when she'd moved to New York two weeks after graduating from Portsmouth High School. Her diploma and Portsmouth Patriots pennant sat next to her cheerleading megaphone on a shelf where her mother had placed a framed copy of her first *Vogue* cover.

Liana ran a finger over the frame as she studied the girl in the stylized photograph. Had she ever really been that young and naïve? If she had known then what she knew now about celebrity would she still have wanted it so badly? And what was it exactly that she had? A fat portfolio, a handful of people she trusted to manage her life and her career but no close friends, no husband, no children, and nothing but the next assignment to look forward to. And when was the last time she had gotten excited about an assignment? She had been to almost every exotic location in the world but had rarely taken the time to enjoy any of them. Trading on her beauty, she had built a career that was the envy of millions, but she had begun to spend more time lately thinking about how empty and shallow it all was.

Thanks to her acclaim, she couldn't even spend time with a handsome man without being wary of his ulterior motives. She had learned the hard way to be cautious as one relationship after another failed under the glare of the spotlight, the pursuit of paparazzi, and the disingenuous motives of the men she had dated. So she no longer trusted her own judgment, even when it was telling her she had nothing to fear as it had earlier with Travis.

Sinking down onto the narrow twin bed, she relived the embarrassing encounter with him. He probably thought she was a tease, and was there anything worse you could say about a woman? *Well, I suppose there is, but there's nothing worse you could say about me.* She cringed when she recalled the way she had treated him, as if he had tried to rape her or something.

You're a freak, a total freak. Any other red-blooded woman would have jumped all over a hot guy like him without a second thought. *Hell, he probably has women standing in line for the opportunity you turned down tonight.* He had seemed so, well, different was the only word that came to mind. Despite what had happened between them, she honestly believed he hadn't brought her to his home with that in mind. She couldn't deny it had happened so naturally and hadn't felt at all like a practiced move. And if anything, he had been even more rattled afterward than she was.

Liana reclined on the bed from her childhood and gazed at the mementos from another lifetime. As she looked around the room, she tried to remember what she had dreamed about while growing up here. All she recalled was the desire to be rich and famous. Well, she was both those things now, but money and fame were funny things—for all their supposed glamour, they didn't hold you during a thunderstorm, they didn't comfort you after a bad dream, and they sure as hell didn't keep you warm at night.

Her thoughts wandered back to Travis North and how incredibly sexy he had been in the Armani tux. He had worn the suit like a man who belonged in it. Oddly enough, he had looked just as at home in a T-shirt and jeans. Liana never would have expected to meet a man like him in little old Portsmouth, Rhode Island. In Paris or Milan, yes, but not in Portsmouth.

We're both single. At least I think he's single. Surely Enid would have confirmed an important detail like that before pushing Liana to have a fling with him.

A fling.

Had she ever had one? Not that she could recall. Relationships? Yes. Doomed relationships? Several. No one would be harmed if they indulged in a little fling, right?

Liana sighed. How she wished she could be that kind of girl, but she wasn't about to become that kind of girl in the next two weeks. So it would be best if she just forgot about him and how his lips had devoured hers, how his hands had felt on her bare back, his muscular body stretched out on top of hers . . . *Ugh!* She rolled her heated face into the pillow. No *way* would she forget that.

CHAPTER 4

In the morning Liana found a note from her mother and freshly baked blueberry muffins on the kitchen table. "Good morning, honey! I had an errand to run, but I should be back by eleven. Coffee is ready to go. See you soon. Love, Mom."

Liana wondered what kind of errand her mother had to do early on a Monday morning when her only child was home for the first time in a year. Unfortunately, such things were becoming the norm where her mother was concerned. Missing their regular phone calls, sounding distracted when they did manage to talk, telling her the same story two weeks in a row, and forgetting to pass along important messages from Enid were just a few of the things Liana had noticed lately. The evidence was pointing to a medical problem, and Liana had begun to wonder if her mother had Alzheimer's disease.

But as she nibbled on a muffin and sipped her coffee, she couldn't deny the house was immaculate. Every knickknack shined, the stainless steel appliances Liana had bought her a year ago gleamed, every surface was dusted, and the kitchen showed no sign of the baking that must have occurred early that morning. From everything she had read about Alzheimer's, Liana would have expected more disarray in the house. If anything, the opposite was true. *Puzzling*, she thought, vowing to spend as much time as she could with her mother while she was home to hopefully figure out what was going on.

With nothing to do until eleven, Liana decided to take a walk. Since she was always concerned about attracting attention, even in Portsmouth, she wore dark sunglasses and pulled her long ponytail through the open back of an old Red Sox hat she found on the closet shelf in her bedroom. Leaving a note for her mother so she wouldn't worry if she got home first, Liana set off down the big hill that led to the river.

Along the way, she saw people she knew but didn't stop to talk to any of them. So far she had managed to elude the paparazzi on this trip, but she had learned the hard way that no one was above selling her out to earn a quick buck.

Mr. Duckworth was pruning his roses when Liana walked by his house. His daughter Meghan had been a childhood friend of Liana's, and she had spent many an hour in that house. By the time they reached high school, though, Meghan and most of Liana's other childhood friends had distanced themselves from her as her staggering beauty set her apart from the other kids.

The coaches hadn't had much of a choice about allowing Liana onto the cheerleading squad because she'd been an outstanding gymnast and athlete, but the other girls had gone out of their way to exclude her from the fun they had away from school. Even her teachers had treated her differently, something Liana had never understood. So she was pretty. Why did everyone care so much?

Only many years later did it fully register with Liana that by the standards of the rest of the world, she was a whole lot more than pretty. And while her face had opened doors for her, it had kept others firmly closed. Being at home never failed to stir up memories of those lonely high school years when she had craved a few good friends and a boyfriend who cared about *her*—not how she looked. Ten years later, she had yet to find any of those things.

After a short walk along the pretty river, she trudged back up the hill, which was much steeper than she recalled. By the time she reached Mrs. Zito's house next door to her mother's, she was panting and sweating. She stopped short when she saw the burgundy Jaguar parked behind her mother's car in the driveway. *What's he doing here?*

Liana debated whether to turn around and head back down the hill until he gave up on her and left. Unfortunately, his very presence here today told her he wasn't one to give up easily. *Damn it! I don't feel like dealing with him right now.* He had stirred up feelings and longings in her that were better left dormant. She couldn't afford to want the things he made her want.

After a full minute spent staring at the shiny Jag, she lifted the ball cap to wipe the sweat off her forehead. *Let's see what he wants and get rid of him as fast as possible.*

The first thing Liana heard when she went in through the front door was her mother's laughter. Liana had forgotten that wonderful sound and realized she hadn't heard it very often in the seven years since her father died.

"Oh, Travis, that's just *so* funny," Agnes was saying when Liana walked into the kitchen.

Her mother wiped away tears from laughing so hard.

Travis leaned back in one of the kitchen chairs—something Liana had never been allowed to do—with a cup of coffee and a muffin on the table in front of him. He wore a faded green T-shirt, khaki shorts, and black flip-flops. His jaw, which had been clean-shaven the night before, now had a layer of stubble that only added to his already overwhelming appeal.

An adorable yellow lab curled up at his feet was the only one who seemed to notice Liana. The dog raised her head, gave a perfunctory sniff of the air, and returned her head to her paws, as if getting up to greet the newcomer was too much trouble.

"So," Travis said, finishing his story without so much as a glance at Liana, "I just rowed harder and faster trying to catch up to Dash before she reached the beach, but by the time I got there she had invaded two picnic baskets and knocked over a toddler with her tail. I made her apologize to the child, but I don't think she learned anything from it. Then, we get back out to the boat, and she pees on the deck."

"Stop it." Agnes held up her hand as a new fit of laughter overtook her. "I can't take any more."

"What are you doing here?" Liana asked, unable to stay quiet for another minute.

"Liana, don't be rude," her mother said.

Travis took a long sip from his coffee cup. He still hadn't bothered to look at her. "I was just having a lovely visit with your mother," he said with a smile for Agnes.

Oh, that smile! He should have it registered as a dangerous weapon.

"Travis came by to see if you'd like to go sailing today," Agnes said to Liana.

"No, thank you."

"I told him you'd love to go," Agnes said as if Liana hadn't spoken. "You work too hard and don't have nearly enough fun."

"But, Mom—" Liana sputtered.

Agnes held up her hand to stop her daughter. "Enid spoke so highly of Travis, Liana. He was wonderful to them when they were planning her wedding. You wouldn't want to be rude to a friend of Enid's, now would you?"

Liana fumed when she realized she was being manipulated again.

Travis watched the proceedings with what seemed to be growing amusement.

"I was planning to spend the day with you, Mom."

"Oh, go on, now. We've got two weeks to spend together. When was the last time you had a man as handsome as Travis ask you out, honey?"

Ignoring that question, Liana said, "Why did you leave without telling me last night?"

"I was tired and bored. Now, go get your bathing suit on, and find a different shirt. That big T-shirt does nothing to show off your cute figure."

Travis cleared his throat as if to stifle laughter.

Liana glared at him before she turned on her heel and stalked down the hallway to change. She took her time and returned ten minutes later carrying a tote bag with a change of clothes and a sweatshirt.

He polished off his second muffin, unfolded himself from the chair, and reached for Agnes's hand. "Thank you for the muffins and coffee," he said, brushing a kiss over her knuckles.

Liana rolled her eyes. *Could he be anymore ridiculous? Does he honestly think he can use her to get to me? Well, she is the only reason you're going with him today. Damn him!*

"I enjoyed our chat," Travis said. "I hope you and Liana will come to the club for dinner while she's home. My treat of course."

Utterly charmed, Agnes gazed at him. "We'd love to. You two have a nice time and don't worry about getting her home too early. She doesn't have a curfew anymore."

"Honestly, Mother," Liana said.

Agnes kissed her daughter and all but shoved them out the door.

Travis opened the back door of the car for the dog and the passenger door for Liana. When the dog seemed to get all of a sudden that Liana was coming with them, she paused to give her a full sniff.

"Dash, this is Liana." Travis squatted down to make eye contact with the dog. "Make nice."

The dog gave Liana a look that said, "Don't mess with my man," before she leaped onto a blanket in the back seat.

"Whew," Travis said when the dog was settled. "Dash says you can come with us."

"That's a big relief," Liana said dryly. She wanted to giggle at the way he treated the dog like a person but didn't wish to encourage him.

He laughed as he closed her door and walked around to the driver's side. They reversed the route they had taken the night before on the way to the marina.

"After meeting your mother I can see where you come by your good looks."

"She's not giggling at you like a foolish school girl anymore, so you can give your whole phony baloney act a rest." Liana edged as far to the right of the passenger seat as she could get without falling out of the car.

He glanced over at her. "I won't bite, you know."

"That's what you said last night, and we both know how that turned out."

"I don't recall using the word 'bite' at any point last night."

She shot him a "very funny" look, which she hoped sent the message that she didn't appreciate his pathetic attempt at humor. "Why aren't you at work?"

"We're closed on Mondays and Tuesdays, so I'm all yours."

"My lucky day."

"All that money your mother wasted on charm school. Such a pity."

"I didn't spend five minutes in charm school for your information," she retorted.

"Well, that explains it."

Furious at herself for walking into his trap, she asked, "Explains what?"

"Oh, nothing," he said with a smug grin.

"You're annoying me."

"At least you're talking to me."

"I can rectify that."

He pulled into a parking space at the marina and turned off the car. "What do you say we strike a truce and enjoy this spectacular summer day in peace?" he said with one of those lethal smiles.

She nibbled on her bottom lip for a moment before she shook his outstretched hand. "Okay. Truce."

He brought her hand to his mouth and left a lingering kiss on the back of it.

"That might work on my mother, but it does nothing for me."

He turned her hand over, and the flutter of the pulse in her wrist made a liar out of her. "Nothing at all?" he asked, pressing his lips to the throbbing spot.

She tugged her hand free. "I thought we had a truce."

"You didn't say it was a 'no touching' truce."

"It is."

"All right. We'll do it your way. For now."

The loss of his touch left her bereft, and Liana was already sorry she had made such a big deal out of it. The more she pushed him away, the more she wanted him close. Why that was would be something she'd mull over later when she wasn't using all her energy and wit to resist him.

CHAPTER 5

The small sailboat had a tiny cabin and even tinier bathroom. Dash hopped aboard and made herself comfortable on the V-berth in the cabin.

"Have you sailed before?" Travis asked as he prepared the sails.

Liana ran a sunscreen stick over her ivory complexion. "Not in years."

"It's just like riding a bike. It'll come back to you." As she took a good look at the North Point property in the daylight, Travis took advantage of the opportunity to study her when she wasn't paying attention. She had worn a sleeveless top in a buttery tone that complemented her natural glow. Her endless legs were on full display under a denim mini-skirt. He noticed a bathing suit tied in a bow at her neck and couldn't wait to see if it was a bikini.

Travis had never met a more beautiful woman. He supposed it would be easy to get so caught up in the stunning face that discovering the woman inside became secondary. Perhaps all the other men in her life had made that mistake. The more time he spent with her, the more he wanted to know who she was behind the flawless façade. He wanted her to trust him with her dreams, her hopes, her desires, and the passion that lurked just below the surface of her carefully cultivated disdain. He yearned to know it all, and that frightened him more than anything had in a long time.

"Do you approve?" he asked, gesturing to the sprawling country club, marina, golf course, condo tower, and the luxury homes under construction on the south end of the property.

"It's amazing. You've really created something special here."

He was more pleased by her approval than he cared to admit. "I'm trying. We're finally starting to get some legs under us after a lot of years of planning, building, promoting, and fighting."

"Fighting?"

He cast off the last of the lines and sailed the boat out of the slip into the bay. Just a smattering of boats dotted the water between Portsmouth and the north end of Prudence Island. "I've had a few issues with some of the locals who've been less than welcoming to an out-of-towner with grand plans."

"You'd think the town would appreciate the tax revenue a place like yours will generate."

Impressed by her astute assessment, he nodded. "You would think so, but it's been quite the opposite. I had to take them to court to clear the zoning board, had to repave the access road—which the town owns—had to pay a hundred phantom fees and taxes, and have had to fend off vandals who decided to take the law into their own hands when their legal avenues were exhausted."

"What kind of vandals?"

"Oh, mostly harmless stuff that's just really annoying. Sprinklers redirected toward golfers, windows broken in the new construction area, tires flattened in the parking lot. That kind of stuff."

"That's terrible! What do the police say?"

"They've ramped up patrols in the area, but they haven't caught anyone." He shrugged. "I'm here to stay, so I'm counting on them to lose interest after a while. I'll admit, though, I was relieved when the wedding went off smoothly last night."

"I'm sorry you've had to deal with that, Travis. This is enough of an undertaking without having your property damaged."

"Thanks." He appreciated that she understood the magnitude of what he'd tried to do at North Point. Living his dream hadn't been without its challenges.

She tipped her face into the sun. "This is so peaceful. I don't think I've been on a boat for pleasure since I left here ten years ago."

"What do you do for pleasure?"

Her eyes came down from the sky to give him a measuring look. "I read."

He snorted. "You're kidding."

The subtle lift of her eyebrow told him she wasn't kidding.

"You read. How... interesting."

"How *relaxing*," she corrected. "It's what I enjoy."

"How do you, you know . . ."

"What?"

"Let off steam."

"I don't have any steam to let off."

He laughed. "Please, Liana. Try telling that to someone who hasn't kissed you. I know better."

She blushed, which he found completely disarming.

"Why are you staring at me like that?" she asked.

"Am I staring?"

"You know you are. Stop it. Right now."

The more flustered she got, the rosier her cheeks became. "Is that no touching clause still in effect?"

She swallowed. Hard. "Why?" she asked in little more than a whisper.

"If I were allowed to touch, I'd want to brush a finger very lightly over that sweet blush on your cheeks."

"I don't blush," she said with indignation, exacerbating the color.

"Oh, sweetheart, trust me. You do."

Her violet eyes were full of vulnerability as she worked over her bottom lip. "I want to trust you."

Travis felt a curious twist in his belly that was all new to him. "You *can* trust me, Liana." He kept his right hand on the tiller to steer the boat and lifted his left arm to invite her to move closer to him.

After mulling it over for an endless second, she scooted across the bench to sit next to him and managed not to flinch when his hand landed on her shoulder.

"I love how you do that thing with your lip when you're considering something."

"What thing?"

"This," he said, demonstrating it for her.

"I do?"

"Uh huh. I've never been so jealous of someone else's teeth."

Shocked, she turned to him and found his face a mere inch from hers. "Travis," she sighed.

He let go of the tiller to caress her face as he'd longed to since the blush first appeared. Without his guiding hand the boat soon floundered. The sails whipped in the breeze, but Travis did nothing about it. "I want you, Liana," he whispered. "And not just because you're the loveliest creature I've ever seen. I want to know you. I want to be with you. I want to talk with you. I want to make love with you, but not until you want to." He almost stopped breathing when she reached up to drag a finger over his unshaven jaw.

"I can't decide whether I like you better with the stubble or without."

"Let me know when you make up your mind, and I'll either shave every hour on the hour or every three days."

She smiled, and Travis felt himself falling. To where he didn't know, but the sensation of falling was unmistakable.

He closed the small distance between them. "I'm going to break the truce."

"I wish you would."

He kept the kiss easy and light, and it would have stayed that way if she hadn't sent her tongue to look for his. His mind went blank with lust as he hauled her even closer to him so he could explore her sweet warmth while his hands moved over her back.

Dash began to bark, and Travis reluctantly pulled back from Liana. "She doesn't like it when I let the sails flap in the breeze," he said with a quick kiss before he reached across the boat for the main sheet to bring the sails under control. As the boat began to move through the water again, Travis put his arm around Liana and leaned in for another kiss. "Are you hungry?"

"Kind of."

"We can drop the anchor and take lunch into the beach."

She raised a surprised eyebrow. "You brought lunch?"

"Sure. You can't be out here all day without food."

"You were pretty confident I would come."

He shrugged. "Dash and I were going anyway. We're glad you decided to join us."

She looked up at him. "So am I. This is fun."

He steered the boat toward a sandy stretch on the north end of Prudence Island. When they got close to the shore, he dropped the sails and tossed the anchor overboard.

Feeling the boat come to a stop, Dash came up from the cabin to see where they were.

"Stay," Travis said with a look of warning.

Dash appeared to smile at him before she leapt over the side and began swimming to shore.

"Goddamned disobedient bitch," he muttered.

Liana laughed. "I can see who wears the pants in this family."

Travis shot her a dirty look. "I could've made her stay if I'd really wanted to."

"Yeah, okay. If you say so."

When he went below to retrieve the cooler he had brought, Travis pulled his shirt over his head and tossed it onto the bunk. "Ready?"

"How do we get to the beach?"

"We swim." He lowered a ladder over the side of the boat.

"And how do we get the cooler there?"

"Don't you worry about that. Dash and I have a routine."

She glanced at the beach where Dash frolicked in the sand. "Apparently." Standing up, she pulled her shirt over her head and dropped her mini-skirt.

Travis went dumb when he saw she was, in fact, wearing a bikini, and it was every bit as spectacular a sight as he had hoped it would be. Reminding himself that he was trying not be predictable, he kept his eyes on her face rather than her breasts as he offered her a hand over the side.

Once she was down the ladder and in the water, Travis followed her and reached back for the cooler. Propping it on his head, he used one arm to swim to shore.

"Very clever," she said, watching him as she floated on her back.

"I think I would've made a good refugee," he joked.

She laughed and swam the short distance to shore.

Travis landed a minute behind her and carried the cooler as Dash danced around his feet. "All right, girl. Just a minute."

"What does she think you have in there?"

"She knows I always have something for her."

Liana put her hands on the dog's pretty face and kissed her head. "You're a very spoiled girl. Do you know that?"

Dash barked in agreement.

"Oh, she's so cute!"

"She's a terror," Travis said.

"Where was she last night?" Liana asked, blushing at the memory of being in his apartment.

Travis ran his finger over her rosy cheek. "With Beck, my security chief. I didn't want her causing any mischief during the wedding." He reached into the cooler and withdrew something wrapped in foil.

Dash went nuts.

Travis unwrapped a meaty bone and gave it to the dog. "Now scram."

Dash galloped off with the bone.

Reaching into the cooler again, Travis pulled out a sheet, and Liana helped him spread it out on the sand. Next, he withdrew a bottle of sunscreen and handed it to her.

"Thank you."

"That skin of yours doesn't look like it sees a lot of sun."

"It doesn't." She lathered on the lotion. "Yours, on the other hand, looks like it sees too much."

"I've never had a sunburn in my life."

"You should still use sunscreen or you'll have wrinkles at forty."

He laughed. "So what?" Her look of horror made him laugh harder. "Sweetheart, I couldn't care less if I have wrinkles. They tell the world you've lived a little."

"I can't imagine not caring about wrinkles."

He found two bottles of beer in the cooler and opened them. Handing one to her, he leaned back on an elbow to watch Dash wrestle with her bone. Snorting with laughter, he glanced at Liana and found her staring at his bare chest. "What?"

"You're very sexy."

Travis hid his surprise at the unexpected compliment. "Thank you, I think," he said with a grin before he took a long drink from his beer.

"I want to have a fling," she said in a rush of words.

Travis choked on his beer.

Liana reached over to pound his back. "Are you all right? Travis? Can you talk?"

He coughed. "Yes," he croaked. "You need to give me some warning before you say something like that."

"I'm sorry. Forget I said anything."

"No way. I won't forget it."

"I'm no good at this," she said in a small voice.

Travis reached over to tip her chin up to force her to look at him. "No good at what?"

She shrugged. "All the things other women seem to find so easy: flirting, flinging, casual sex."

He swallowed hard. "There's nothing casual about you, Liana."

"I know! That's the problem. I want to be casual. I want to feel free to make love with a sexy man if I want to, but I can't."

"Why not, sweetheart?"

"Because."

"Care to elaborate?"

"Nothing is ever simple for me. My every move is usually recorded in the press, every man I've ever been involved with has disappointed me—usually by kissing and telling—and I never have any idea who I can trust."

Listening to her, Travis was filled with sympathy.

"Enid said I can trust you and that I needed to have sweaty sex. So I thought maybe . . ."

Travis lay back on the sheet as all the oxygen left his body in a long exhale. "I feel like I've just dialed a 1-900 number."

"If you're going to make fun of me, Travis . . ."

He rolled onto his side so he could see her. "I'm not making fun of you, believe me. Tell me about this fling you want to have."

She pushed at the sand with a toe tipped with bright pink polish. "It was a dumb idea."

"Liana . . ."

"What you said before about how you want to know me and be with me. No one's ever said that to me before. They're usually so caught up in how I look that no one ever cares if they know me or not."

Travis sat up to cup her face. "I meant it when I said I want to know you. I really do. But I love looking at you, too. I can't deny that, Liana. I'm not going to tell you how breathtakingly beautiful you are because you've no doubt heard it a thousand times and in every possible way there is to say it. So just because I don't say it doesn't mean I'm not thinking it. I want to be honest with you about that."

"I guess that's fair enough."

"How about you define what you mean by a fling, just so we're on the same page here."

Her cheeks flamed with embarrassment as she cast her eyes down. "You know . . . Sex. Sweaty sex if you're up for that."

"Hmm, sweaty sex. That's quite an offer, sweetheart. I'm going to have to give it some thought."

Her eyes whipped back up. "You are?"

Amused by her surprised expression, he said, "Well, I wouldn't want you to think I'm easy."

Liana erupted into laughter. When she had finally caught her breath, she was still wiping at the tears in her eyes. "You're too much. Who writes your material?"

"My own original work," he said with a chuckle. He opened the cooler and withdrew sandwiches and chips. "Let's eat. I can't think on an empty stomach, and I'm sure you're going to want an answer to this very nice offer you've made me."

"You're going to make me squirm, aren't you?"

He raised an eyebrow. "By the time I'm done with you, I'm fairly certain you'll be squirming—at the very least."

Her hand trembled as she accepted the sandwich he handed her. "So does that mean you're done thinking?"

He ate his sandwich and contemplated her question. "Let's just say I agree to this sweaty fling you're suggesting—hypothetically, of course."

"Of course."

"Are we talking strictly missionary, or would I be allowed to branch out?"

He watched as she attempted to swallow the bite she had taken from her sandwich. "Define 'branching out.'"

"No."

"No?" she squeaked.

"No."

"How can I answer your question if I don't know what you mean by branching out?"

"Either I can branch out or I can't. It's up to you."

She ate in silence for a few minutes before she said, "Fine. You can branch out, but nothing kinky."

He smiled with pride at the courage she was showing by even having this conversation. "Define kinky."

She sighed with exasperation. "You know what I mean."

"Do I?"

"This was a bad idea." She shook her head. "Let's just forget about it. Really. I'm in way over my head here."

He reached for her hand. "I'm only having fun with you, Liana. You don't have to define kinky, okay?"

She nodded. "I'm sorry for being so uptight. I've never done anything like this before."

"I know." He kissed her hand and gave it back to her so she could finish her lunch. "Let's talk duration."

"Two weeks," she said. "I'm leaving in two weeks."

"What if you decide you like me and don't want it to end then?"

"Two weeks," she said more emphatically this time. "I'm not interested in a long-distance relationship, so you can't have any feelings for me. This is a sex-only fling."

He wondered if she really thought she was capable of such a thing.

"I don't want you to get hurt," she added.

"What about you? What if you fall for me?"

"I won't."

"How do you know? You haven't slept with me yet."

"You're pretty confident in your abilities."

He shrugged. "I know what I'm doing between the sheets." Baiting her was turning out to be as much fun as talking about their sweaty fling.

"You've had so many lovers?"

"A few." He bagged their trash and put it back in the cooler. "What about you?"

"A few."

He moved closer to her and nudged her ponytail aside. As he dropped hot kisses on her neck, he whispered, "Have any of them made you scream?"

Her breath hitched in her throat. "Travis . . ."

"Hmm?"

"What are you doing?"

"Kissing your neck."

"Does this mean you've decided?"

"Nope. I'm just taking a sample so I know what I'd be getting if I agree to this fling of yours."

She pushed him away. "You've already had a test drive," she reminded him.

"Oh yeah," he said with a grin.

"I guess it wasn't very memorable."

"It was *very* memorable. You know, you never answered my question."

Her eyebrows knit with confusion. "What question?"

"Have any of them made you scream, Liana?"

"No," she said softly. "No, they haven't."

He reached for her and brought her down across his chest. "I think," he said with a lingering kiss, "that's going to turn out to be their loss."

CHAPTER 6

Liana could barely breathe. Kissing Travis was, without a doubt, the most carnal experience of her life. She couldn't imagine what making love with him would entail.

He rolled her under him on the beach and the feel of his chest hair brushing against her sun-kissed skin made her breathless with longing.

As he trailed kisses down her neck, between her breasts, and over her belly, Liana writhed beneath him. "Travis . . ."

"Hmm?"

"Does this mean our fling is on?"

He nibbled on her hipbone, causing her to cry out.

"I haven't decided yet."

Liana couldn't seem to breathe. "When do you plan to decide?"

He kissed his way back up to her lips. "Soon."

She decided if he could test out the merchandise, so could she. Sliding her hands over his back, she ventured further south and discovered he had muscles everywhere.

His gasp told her she had his attention. "Liana . . ."

The sound of a speedboat caused her to panic. She pushed him off her and sat up.

Startled, he asked, "What is it?"

"Paparazzi."

"Huh?"

"Reporters, Travis. If they catch me rolling around on the beach with you the photos will be all over the Internet in an hour."

He took a good look at the boat. "That's Tommy Boyle. I'd know that boat anywhere."

"Photographers could've hired him. They've done it before."

He whistled for Dash. "Let's go back to the boat."

They packed up their picnic, folded the sheet, and waded into the water.

Liana welcomed the coolness of the water after the heat of the beach. She hadn't been exaggerating when she'd told Travis she was in over her head. *Suggesting a fling! What had come over her? This was all Enid's fault.* She hadn't found her life to be lacking anything until Enid had pointed out what she was missing. And now she was dying to know exactly *what* she'd been missing. What if Travis said no? Would she ever have the courage to offer it to anyone else? Probably not. She reached the boat a minute ahead of Travis and Dash. Climbing the ladder, she tried not to think about the view he was getting from behind her.

When he caught up to her, she leaned over to retrieve the cooler and caught the quick glance he gave her breasts in the skimpy bikini.

He lifted Dash onto the boat with a warning for Liana to watch out for the shake the dog launched into the moment her paws hit the deck. Travis climbed up after the dog and brought the ladder in with him. He put it away and ordered Dash to stay on the bench seat.

Unaccustomed to his sternness, the dog lay down with a whimper.

Travis looped an arm around Liana's waist and urged her into the cabin.

"Where are we going?" she asked.

"To where your imaginary reporters can't find us."

"And what are we going to do there?"

He pushed her back against the V-berth and captured her lips in a deep, lush kiss. "Practice."

"For?"

"Our fling."

"Are we having a fling?"

"I'm still trying to decide." He untied her bikini top and peeled it down. "Oh, Liana," he sighed. "You're so . . ." His lips took a slow journey from her long neck to her full breasts. "So very beautiful. I know I wasn't going to say it, but . . ."

Liana moaned when he ran his tongue over her nipple.

"Do you like that?"

She clutched his shoulders, which were still wet with salt water. "Yes," she whispered.

"Do you want more?"

"*Yes!*"

"We'll get back to that," he said as he kissed each of her ribs before he dipped his tongue into her belly button.

"Travis," she gasped. "Oh God."

He urged her back onto the bunk and stretched out next to her. "Kiss me, Liana."

She reached for his face and molded her lips to his.

His arms tightened around her, brushing her sensitive breasts with his soft chest hair. He cupped her bottom with one big hand and pulled her tight against his erection.

Soon her lips were numb and her face chafed from the abrasion of his beard, but she didn't pull away from the kiss. Skimming her hands over his back, she discovered he was now slick with sweat, and suddenly she got it. This was sweaty sex—or the start of it anyway. "Travis, *please . . .*"

"What, sweetheart?"

"I want you."

"And I want you." He kissed her throat, her jaw, her ear, and then her lips again. "You'll be glad to know I've decided to have a fling with you. Two weeks, no boundaries, no emotion. Is that we what agreed to?"

"Yes. Can we start now?"

He chuckled as he caressed her breast. "Not quite yet."

Her eyes flew opened. "What do you mean?"

"You didn't say 'no' to romance, did you?"

"Romance? What are you talking about?"

"Before we have sex, we're going to have a little romance."

"But I don't want romance," she protested. "I want sex. Sweaty sex." She pushed her hips against his erection. "Remember?"

"Yes," he hissed. "I remember. Sweaty sex is always better after a bit of romance, sweetheart. Take my word for it."

"Oh, that's right," she snorted with disgust. "You've got all kinds of experience at this."

"And you'll be the beneficiary of all that so-called experience. When you're screaming out with one orgasm after another, you'll be thanking all those women you think I've been with for showing me how to do it."

"One orgasm after another, huh?"

He kissed her breast and made her shudder. "Uh huh."

"Good luck with that."

He stopped what he was doing to her breast and looked up to find her eyes. "Don't tell me you've never . . . you know . . ."

"I have, but not easily."

"Oh," he said with a smug grin. "A challenge."

She pushed him off her and sat up, retying her bikini top. "I'm starting to think you're all talk and no action." Before she knew what had hit her she was flat on her back with two fierce brown eyes staring down at her.

"I'll show you action, sweetheart. And when we're through with each other, you'll spend the rest of your life trying to find another man who makes you feel the way I'm going to make you feel."

Liana felt a tremble go through her entire body as she studied his handsome face. Reaching up to caress his cheek, she brought him down to her for a kiss. With his soft lips gliding over hers, Liana's heart began to race with fear and excitement as she realized she might have just made a deal with the devil himself.

The sun was setting in brilliant pinks and oranges by the time they returned to the marina. Dash sprinted from the boat the moment it landed alongside the floating dock.

"Will she be all right?" Liana asked.

"Believe it or not, she knows where she's allowed to go." Travis tied the last of the lines to a cleat. "She's gotten better about not peeing on the boat."

"How long have you had her?"

"She's been my best girl for four years."

"She's got you wrapped right around her paw."

He faked offense. "I don't know what you're talking about."

Liana reached for his hand, and he stopped what he was doing with the sails to focus on her. "Thank you," she said.

"For?"

"A wonderful, relaxing day. I haven't had this much fun in a really long time."

He kissed her hand and then her lips. "That's too bad. We'll have to see what we can do about that over the next two weeks."

"I have to spend *some* time with my mother," she reminded him.

He laughed. "Sweetheart, as much as I'd love to spend the next fourteen days in bed with you, I do have a business to run."

Liana rolled her eyes. "When exactly is the 'in bed' portion of our fling going to begin?"

He shrugged as he secured the bright blue sail cover over the boom. "I don't have a schedule."

Liana nibbled on her bottom lip and stared at the colorful sunset.

Travis sat down across from her and reached for her hands. "Don't stress out about it, Liana. It'll happen when it happens. And when it does, I want you to enjoy it. If you don't feel like you can trust me—really trust me—you won't enjoy it." He pressed a kiss to each of her hands. "I already know you well enough to know that. Since this isn't something you do every day, I want you to enjoy it. So let's take our time, get to know each other a little, and see what happens, okay?"

Liana sized him up, trying to decide if he was for real. He surely seemed to be, but she had learned to question her judgment in such things. "All right."

"Why do you still look stressed?"

"There's just one other thing we didn't talk about, and it's kind of a big deal . . ."

"What's that?"

"You can't tell anyone you're . . . seeing me."

Travis sat next to her and put his arm around her. "You can trust me. And you can trust the people around me. You're not going to read about us in the papers—not because of me, anyway."

She studied his earnest face.

"You've heard that before haven't you?"

She nodded.

"This time you can believe it, Liana. I promise you. I won't tell anyone."

"Hey, Trav!" A tall blond man came bounding down the dock with Dash trotting behind him. A walkie-talkie was attached to the belt of the cargo shorts he wore with his burgundy North Point polo shirt. He took in the scene on the boat—Liana wearing her denim skirt with her bikini top and Travis still shirtless. "Um, we had a little trouble today."

Liana watched as Travis tensed. She wanted to reach out to him but didn't.

He stood up. "What happened?"

"More flat tires. This time in the parking garage at the tower."

"How many?"

"Thirty tires on twelve different cars."

"Son of a bitch," Travis muttered. "Did you call the cops?"

Beck nodded. "And the garage. They've all been replaced."

"Thanks. Did you notify the tenants?"

"Taken care of."

"Good job, Beck. Thanks. Oh, this is Liana McDermott. Liana, Peter Beck." She nodded to the other man. "Nice to meet you."

"You, too. Well, I'll let you get back to enjoying your evening."

"Thanks for taking care of things today," Travis said.

"No problem." Beck shook his head with frustration. "I don't know how the bastards keep getting past us, but I'm having cameras installed in the garage tonight."

"Good idea. I should've done it before now."

"I'll talk to you tomorrow, Trav. Nice to meet you, Ms. McDermott." He patted Dash on the head and went back up the dock.

Travis fixed his eyes on the condo tower as a muscle twitched in his cheek.

Liana stood up and looped her arms around his waist. "Are you all right?"

"Yeah." He leaned back to kiss her cheek. "I'm sorry."

"Why?"

"For letting work invade our relaxing day."

"I can't believe there are people in this town who would do this to you. It's horrible."

"So far it's only a nuisance. I worry they're going to ramp up their game one of these days and someone's going to get hurt."

She watched him make an effort to shake off his worries and return his attention to her.

"Let's have some dinner," he said.

"I'll understand if you need to go into work, Travis."

"Beck's got everything under control. There's nothing I can do that he hasn't already done."

"You're lucky to have him." She nibbled on her lip as she glanced at the clubhouse.

"Now what are you stewing about?" he asked, smiling as he tapped his finger on her abused lip.

"He won't tell anyone he saw me here, will he?"

"He's not just my employee, Liana. He's my best friend. We go back almost twenty years. I'd trust him with my life."

"I'm sorry. I don't mean to be such a freak show."

Travis offered her a hand to help her off the boat and then went back for the cooler and to lock up. When he stepped onto the dock, he hoisted the cooler to one shoulder and reached for her hand. "What's happened with you and the press?"

"They're relentless. So far, they haven't found me here, and I'd like to keep it that way. I hired a private plane to fly me here from Milan so Enid's wedding wouldn't turn into a media circus. They poke their noses into every aspect of my business, making it almost impossible for me to have any sort of personal life."

Travis opened the back door for the dog and stashed the cooler in the trunk. "Tell me the rest."

Astounded by his ability to read her, she looked up at him. "There was this guy once," she said softly. "He wasn't like the others. He was decent, and I liked him. But before we'd even had a chance to see what would develop the media had ripped his life apart. They interviewed his kindergarten teacher, for God's sake. It was a nightmare, and it didn't take him long to realize I wasn't worth it."

Travis trapped her against the car, which was still warm from the sun. "So let me get this straight. You're afraid if the media catches wind of this I might run away before we have sweaty sex?"

She blushed. "Something like that."

He captured her mouth in a hard kiss. "Not a chance, sweetheart."

"You say that now . . . Talk to me when they're interviewing your kindergarten teacher. If you've got deep dark secrets, they're bound to find them."

Something resembling fear skirted across his face. Then he rebounded with one of those devastating smiles. "Bring it on. I've already decided you're worth it."

"You're a very nice man, Travis North."

He ran his thumb along her jaw. "Do you want to go home and get changed?"

"I brought a change of clothes, but nothing fancy. Just a sundress."

"Good." He held the car door for her. "I'm taking you to Chez North. It's a fabulous restaurant that no one knows about, and the dress code is very casual."

He drove them the short distance across the property from the marina to The Tower. In the parking garage, two police officers were finishing their investigation.

"Evening, Mr. North," the older of the two officers said when Travis stepped out of the Jaguar.

Travis nodded to the cop. "Sergeant. Did you find anything?"

"Nothing we can use. Another clean job. I'm sorry about this. I know it's aggravating."

"It's starting to go beyond aggravating," Travis commented as he helped Liana from the car.

"Hey! You're that model! Louie come see. It's Liana McDermott."

"Listen guys," Travis said. "Ms. McDermott's trying to have some R&R without the media finding her. Do you mind keeping it quiet that she's in town?"

"No problem," the older cop said. The younger one all but panted as he stared at Liana.

"Give me your cards, and I'll send you a photo," Liana said, "to show my thanks for your discretion."

The cards were produced, and Travis reached for them, shaking the hands of both cops. "Thanks, guys. Let me know how the investigation unfolds." He escorted Liana into the elevator and handed her the cards. "From your adoring public."

"Thank you for thinking fast. I hope they keep quiet."

"What about all the people at the wedding?"

"I've known most of them my whole life. They wouldn't dream of selling me out. Besides I'm old news to them by now."

"I'm sorry you have to live like this."

"The alternative is worse, believe me." She shuddered just thinking about how crazy the media could get when they got their hooks into a big story.

They arrived in his apartment, and he held the elevator door for her. "Has it always been this way?"

"It wasn't so bad at first. But the whole celebrity culture has just exploded in the last few years with more tabloids, news shows, the Internet, and they're all out to get the big scoop. It's so out of control."

"You're imprisoned by your celebrity."

"Yes," she said, impressed by his insight. "Most people don't get that. They say 'Poor you, it must suck to be you.' Well, sometimes it does suck to be me."

"I can see what you mean."

"I had this friend in New York," she said sadly. "A girlfriend. I don't have a lot of them, and I liked her. She sold me out to one of the tabloids for ten thousand dollars. She told them I was in town and a couple of other things I'd confided in her. Nothing earth shattering, but it was personal. Anyway, the media frenzy drove me out of town, out of my own apartment."

Travis put his arms around her. "I'm sorry, sweetheart. That must've hurt."

"It did," Liana whispered. "It still hurts to even think about it. I've kept my distance from other women ever since."

"Why don't you have security?" he asked as he released her to open a bottle of wine.

"Because I *refuse* to live like that. I'd rather take my chances than have an entourage."

"But if it meant your safety . . ."

"So far, I've never felt physically threatened by it. I suppose if that day comes, I'll have to make some changes. I'd hate that though."

"I'd hate to think of you in danger. You should talk to Beck while you're in town. He knows a lot of people in the security business and could hook you up with someone good."

She shrugged as she accepted a glass of wine from him. "I'll think about it. It just feels like I'd be crossing a line if I hired security, like I'd be letting them win or something. I'm not sure if that makes sense."

"It does." He studied her for a long intense moment.

"What?"

"Do you ever think about giving it up and doing something else?"

"All the time, but it's the only thing I know how to do. I never went to college, and I'm no good at anything else."

He took her by the chin. "This face is a multi-million-dollar enterprise, sweetheart. You're already sitting atop a pretty big business. You'd be selling yourself short if you think you couldn't parlay those skills into something else that would allow you to have a more normal life."

"You really think I could?"

"Of course I do," he said with a lingering kiss. "Do you want to wash off the salt?"

"I'd love to."

"You can use the bathroom in my room. I'm sure you remember where it is."

Liana blushed even as she looped her arms around his neck. "I think I can find the way."

"The towels are in the cabinet. Use anything you need."

"Okay, thanks." She could tell she startled him when she slid her tongue along his bottom lip. "Want to join me in the shower?"

He devoured her lips, and before long her knees were weak from wanting him.

"Is that a yes?" she asked, using her best sultry voice.

"Remember when you said you were no good at flirting?"

"Yes."

"You were wrong—very, very wrong. Now, go take a shower like a good girl while I make us some dinner." He peeled her arms from around his neck and turned her around, giving her a nudge toward his room.

She cast one last coy look over her shoulder. "You don't know what you're missing."

He fell face first onto the sofa. *Are you* serious, *North? What the hell is wrong with you? Liana McDermott—the supermodel—just invited you to take a shower with her and you said* no? *Are you out of your freaking mind?* As Travis lay there and thought about why it was he had said no, he began to worry. He acknowledged he already cared about her and wanted to treat her right. Furthermore, he wanted to be different than what she expected him to be, so that meant proving to her he wasn't just after the body she had offered to him more than once that day.

Despite her earlier bravado, she wasn't a one-night stand kind of girl. And from the sound of it, she'd never had a man who treated her like a lady. He wanted to be the first. Was there anything wrong with that? Was there anything wrong with waiting until he felt she was ready for what she wanted from him? *As long as you don't fall in love with her in the meantime...*

In the shower, Liana replayed every minute of her day with Travis. She was starting to believe he might be different from all the others. In a way she was almost glad he had said no to joining her in the shower. He had proven to her that he had meant it when he said he wanted to get to know her better before they jumped into bed.

She had to admit it was refreshing to be with someone who seemed to like talking to her as much as he liked kissing her. *I could get used to being treated the way he treats me. I like him, more than I've liked anyone in a long time—maybe more than I've ever liked anyone. You just met him last night, Liana. Don't get ahead of yourself. Well, since you've offered him a fling and are currently standing naked in the man's shower, I'd say you're already ahead of yourself. I should be ashamed of myself for the way I acted with him today, but I'm not. It felt good to be a little shameless with a hot guy.*

She thought about what he'd said about making a life for herself outside of modeling. He seemed convinced she could do it, and clearly he knew something about business. *I'll give it some thought,* she concluded, as she turned off the shower and wrapped herself in one of his thick towels.

He's special, she decided. He's thoughtful, considerate, fun, successful, sexy as hell, and so handsome he could've been a model himself. *All together that makes for quite a package.* She used her towel to wipe the steam from the mirror. *I feel safe with him. When was the last time I felt safe with anyone? Not since I lived at home with my parents.* The realization was almost startling. "Just don't be stupid and fall in love with him. You're leaving in two weeks. There's no sense risking your heart over something that can't go anywhere." But even as she whispered the words to her reflection in the mirror, she accepted that her heart was already in play.

CHAPTER 7

Liana emerged from Travis's bedroom and was greeted by soft lighting and music. She could make out his silhouette on the patio where he tended to the grill, and Liana felt a sinking sensation in her belly as she took in the romantic scene. Falling in love with a man capable of this would be far too easy. *Just a fling,* she reminded herself as she made her way through the spacious living room to the patio.

"Did you make out all right in there?"

"It was great, thanks." She noticed his hair was wet and that he had shaved. "How did you manage to shower and do all of this?"

He held out a hand to bring her close to him.

Oh, he smells so good!

"I used the guest shower, and I marinated kabobs this morning in the hope of luring you to Chez North tonight." He closed the lid on the grill. "They need a few more minutes."

"You surprise me."

"Because I can cook on a grill?" He laughed. "I've lived alone for a long time, and I like to eat, so I know enough to be dangerous in the kitchen."

"I've never had a man make dinner for me before," she confessed.

"Never?"

She shook her head.

"You've missed out on all the simple things living that glamorous life of yours, haven't you, sweetheart?"

"I'm beginning to think so."

"We'll have to see what we can do about that." He reached into the pocket of the black cargo shorts he had changed into and withdrew his cell phone. "Want to check on your mom?"

Touched by his thoughtfulness, she took the phone from him. "Thank you." He went back to the grill while she dialed her mother's number.

"Oh, hi, honey," Agnes said. "You just caught me."

"Are you going out?"

"Just down to Aunt Edith's and Uncle Charlie's. They're feeling blue since the wedding's over and invited me for Chinese takeout."

"They're probably blue over the bill," Liana said.

"No doubt," Agnes said with a chuckle. "Are you having a good time?"

"We've had a lovely day."

"He's a very nice man, Liana."

"Yes, he is."

"You know, if you wanted to stay out all night, I'd never know . . ."

"Mother! What's come over you?"

"Don't be absurd, Liana. You're twenty-eight years old. If you want to spend the night with a nice, ridiculously handsome man that your cousin hand-picked for you, don't let your mother stand in the way."

Liana felt her cheeks burn with embarrassment. "I can't believe we're having this conversation."

"You're all grown up, honey. You work harder than anyone I've ever known, and you owe it to yourself to enjoy your life more than you do."

"I want to spend some time with you tomorrow, Mom. We've hardly seen each other since I've been home."

"Oh, honey, I volunteer at the Senior Center on Tuesdays. I'll be gone all day."

"Wednesday then?"

"I'm free Wednesday afternoon. We can go to lunch and get a manicure."

"I'd love that. Have a nice time with Aunt Edith and Uncle Charlie. Tell them I said it was a lovely wedding."

"I will, honey. You think about what I said."

"Yes, Mother." She ended the call and crossed the patio to return the phone to Travis.

"How's my friend Agnes?"

"She's been abducted by aliens."

"Why? Because she said you're old enough to spend the night with me if you want to?"

"How do you know she said that?"

He laughed. "I could hear the horror in your voice."

"That conversation was definitely a first. The mother I used to know would've put her hands over her ears and cried 'lalalala' at the mere mention of the word sex."

"Maybe she's gotten a sex life of her own and it's loosened her up."

"No way! You're crazy."

"She's a beautiful woman, Liana. Why do you find it impossible to imagine her with a man?"

Liana took a sip of her wine. "Because."

He used tongs to remove the kabobs from the grill. "Because why?"

"She was so heartbroken when my father died. He'd had cancer for years and had been doing really well, so when he died suddenly, it was such a shock to her. To both of us. I can't imagine her with anyone else."

"How long ago did he die?"

"Seven years."

"That's a pretty long time. I wouldn't rule out the possibility that she has someone else."

"Why wouldn't she tell me if she did?"

"To spare you from worrying about her, to preserve your memories of your father. Who knows?"

Liana nibbled on her lip as she considered what he had said. He could be right. A boyfriend certainly would explain a lot about her mother's recent behavior. It was a better explanation than Alzheimer's, that was for sure. The thought made Liana giggle.

"What's so funny?" he asked as he led her inside to eat.

"I've been thinking maybe she has Alzheimer's, and she probably just has a boyfriend."

"My grandmother had Alzheimer's, and after spending an hour with your mother today I can pretty much guarantee you she doesn't have it. She's sharp as a tack."

"You made quite an impression on her."

"The mothers always love me," he said with a smug smile.

Liana laughed. "I'm sure they do."

He held a chair at the dining room table for her. "I never thought to ask if there's anything you don't eat."

"I eat everything. I've never had to watch what I eat. I keep waiting for that to catch up to me, but so far it hasn't. Other models I've worked with are always horrified by my eating habits."

"I'm sure you've been horrified by some of theirs."

"Ugh, it's so awful the way some of them treat their bodies."

He served her a healthy portion of rice along with the kabobs and a tossed salad.

"I'm very impressed. This is fabulous."

He refilled their wine glasses. "I'm glad you like it."

"So you know all about me, and you've told me nothing about you."

"What do you want to know?"

"You said you were from out of town, right?"

"Uh huh. Allentown, Pennsylvania."

"Is your family still there?"

"My parents, five of my six siblings, and my grandfather still live there, along with assorted nieces, nephews, aunts, uncles, and cousins."

"Did you say *six* siblings?"

He smiled. "Yes, I did."

"Wow. That must've been so cool."

"It was chaotic. My father worked in a factory, and there was never enough money, never enough of anything. It sucked."

"That must've been tough for you."

"I was the oldest, so a lot fell to me. Luckily, I had a talent that got me out of there."

"What was that?"

"Football. I was an all-state quarterback. Brought home the state championship my senior year, which got me a full athletic scholarship to Ohio State and later an offer from the Arizona Cardinals."

"The NFL," she said with amazement. "You played professional football?"

He shook his head. "I said no. I wanted to go to business school."

"The shirt you loaned me last night . . . You went to Stanford?"

"For my MBA."

Amazed, she studied him with new appreciation. "You gave up a chance to play in the NFL to go to Stanford and get an MBA?"

"I did, and my father was so mad about it he didn't speak to me for a year. There's no doubt it was a gamble, but it's paying off—finally. I'm doing what I've always wanted to do by building something lasting. Football was my ticket out of Allentown. That's all it ever was to me."

"Wait." She held up a hand. "I remember reading about you. It was in the papers, wasn't it?"

He grinned sheepishly. "I caused quite a firestorm. I guess there aren't too many people who turn down the chance to play pro ball."

"I wouldn't think so. How did you end up here?"

"When I was in college I started playing the stock market. I invested heavily in Silicon Valley and got out before the high-tech bubble burst. I worked on Wall Street for seven years after I finished at Stanford. Then I used some of the money

I'd made in the market to improve my parents' circumstances and poured the rest into this place. To say I have a lot riding on its success would be an understatement."

"How did you settle on Portsmouth?"

"I looked at ten other properties on the East Coast, but this one spoke to me. It felt like home. Do you know what I mean?"

"No," she said sadly. "I've never had that feeling. Not since I left my parents' house, that is. You're lucky to have found it here."

"I know." He took their plates into the kitchen. "That's why the vandalism bothers me so much. They think they're just affecting my business, but they're taking aim at my home. My place."

When he came back, Liana reached for his hand and brought it to her lips. "You have to stay strong. They'll get tired of it when they realize you're here to stay."

"I hope you're right." He gave her hand a gentle tug. "Dance with me?"

She got up to follow him.

Once he had her in his arms, he nudged her thick dark hair out of the way so he could whisper in her ear. "I think I'm going to enjoy this fling even more than I thought I would."

"Why do you say that?"

"Because I like talking to you as much as I like doing this." He raised her chin and found her lips.

Liana tightened her arms around his neck and fell into the kiss.

When he finally drew back from her, he found her eyes. "I'm going to take you home now, Liana." He brushed his lips over hers. "But I'm going to see you tomorrow." Another kiss. "And the day after." More kisses. "And the day after that."

"But—" Liana protested.

He silenced her with another deep kiss. "Trust me, sweetheart."

Liana awoke late the next morning to rain pinging against her window. After the glorious sunny day she'd enjoyed with Travis yesterday, the rain came as a surprise. She stretched and then burrowed deeper into her warm bed. *Travis,* she thought with a sigh. *I can't wait to see him today.* Her skin tingled as she remembered his passionate goodnight kiss at her mother's front door. He had promised to call her as soon as he finished with his morning meetings.

Since her mother had probably already left for the day, Liana gave significant thought to going back to sleep for a while. Then the ringing of the phone urged her out of bed as her heart kicked into gear at the hope that it might be Travis calling.

"Hello, darling."

Liana wanted to groan. "Hi, Artie," she said to her agent. His fake British accent was too much for her before she'd had coffee.

"Am I getting you up?"

She yawned. "I was awake. What's going on?"

"I got an urgent call from Milan yesterday. They want you to come back ASAP to redo a few things that didn't come out exactly the way *Vogue* wanted. How soon can you get there?"

"Two weeks. Not one minute before."

"But, darling, they're having a cow. You can't hold them off that long."

"Watch me."

"Liana . . ."

"I haven't had a long vacation in five years, Artie. I'm not going back to Milan. If they want to send someone here, I'll give them half a day. But that's it."

"They can hold you in breach of contract—"

"I fulfilled that contract down to the letter. It's not my fault their two-bit photographer couldn't get it right the first time."

Artie sighed dramatically. "All right, darling. I'll let them know."

"Don't you dare give anyone this number, Artie. Do you hear me?"

"You made that perfectly clear before you disappeared."

"Anything else?"

"There's an intriguing little tidbit floating around that I'm not quite ready to tell you about, but it's something that'll definitely interest you. I'll call you as soon as I know more."

Liana couldn't have cared less about the intriguing little tidbit. She was on vacation. "That's fine."

"Listen, Liana. . . there's a situation I could use your help with."

"What's that?"

"Do you remember Jessica Stone? You worked with her on last year's swimsuit issue? Goes by Jessie?"

"Sure. She's a sweetie."

"Yes," he said, sounding relieved. "She is. She's run into some trouble."

"What kind of trouble?"

"She's got a seriously over-zealous fan. The cops are involved now and everything."

"That's too bad. I hate to hear that."

"I knew you'd understand, since you've had a few crazies in your time. So here's the thing: she could really use a place to lay low for a while until this blows over."

"What's that got to do with me?"

"You've never had any trouble with the press up there in Little Rhody. Do you know of anywhere she could hide out up there? Just for a couple of weeks to give the police the chance to nab this guy?"

Liana thought of Travis and North Point, but he had enough on his plate with the vandalism. He didn't need a troubled model on the property to add to his worries. However, she knew if she asked him, he'd find a place for Jessie.

"She can't go home to her apartment in New York because the guy has turned up there, and she's estranged from her family. Wherever I send her, I'd like her to have *someone* there she knows—"

"I'll make a phone call," Liana said, exasperated. "That's the best I can do."

"Thank you, darling," he said, sounding relieved. "I told Jessie you'd help us out if you could."

"*You already told her you were asking me?*"

"Well, um, I had to do something to reassure her. She's been a total wreck since the creep started showing up at her house."

Liana held back a groan. How could she *not* help the other woman now? "I'll get back to you."

"You're the best. I'm sorry to have bothered you on vacation, darling. I'll wait to hear from you."

Liana hung up the phone and tried to shake off the stress that came with hearing his voice. Any time she heard from him it meant more work. Struggling models would love to have her problems. She knew that. But after ten years of the breakneck pace she had kept, she was too tired to care what Artie or anyone else thought of her. She had earned this break, and nothing was going to cut it short. Especially since she was in the midst of a fling with the sexiest man in the world.

The thought made her giggle with nerves and anticipation and excitement. Checking her watch, she realized Travis would still be in his meeting so she decided she'd talk to him about Jessie when she saw him.

She brewed a pot of coffee, ate a container of strawberry yogurt, and perused the morning paper before she took a long, hot shower. She took extra care with her hair and applied the tiniest bit of makeup. Her body hummed with tension when she wondered if this might be the day. Surely, he wouldn't keep up this resistance act for much longer when he knew they only had two weeks. Or would he? His unpredictability made him that much more appealing to her.

With another nervous giggle she put on some of the sexiest underwear she owned even as she wondered if he would see it. She tugged on a floral skirt along with a button-down sleeveless top and slid her feet into pink flip-flops. By eleven she was ready and sat down to watch a TV talk show. She stared at it without seeing much of anything because a tall, dark, handsome man occupied her every thought. *Wow. I should be so afraid of what I feel for him, but I'm not afraid. I'm excited.*

He called at noon to say he was on his way to pick her up.

"Where are we going?"

"How about a walk in the rain?"

"I'd love that," she said, surprised to realize it was another thing she'd never done with a man.

"I'll be there in a few minutes."

He came to the door ten minutes later wearing shorts, flip-flops, and a burgundy North Point jacket.

When she opened the door for him, he handed a second jacket to her.

"What's this?"

"Your own North Point jacket. I can't have you catching a cold and ruining your vacation, not to mention our fling." He pressed her against the wall to kiss her. "I've been waiting for that all morning," he said when he finally pulled back from her. "I thought those meetings would never end. All I could think about was you."

Her heart pounding with excitement and desire, she ran her hands over the light stubble on his face. "I couldn't wait to see you either."

His eyes became even darker as he dipped his head for another kiss. With what appeared to be enormous effort, he finally stepped back from her. "Do you have a hat or sunglasses or something you could wear to hide your face? I want to take you into Newport, but I don't want to blow your cover."

"I can wear my Red Sox hat." She went into her room to get it. By the time she had donned the hat, pulled her ponytail through the back of it, and put on the jacket he had given her, she hardly resembled one of the world's top models.

"Very cute," he said with a smile.

"Before we go, I have something I need to ask you. It's a big deal, but I don't want you to feel obligated—"

He stopped her with a finger on her lips. "What do you need, sweetheart?"

She told him about Jessie and the trouble she was in with a stalker. "She's a really nice girl, a Southern belle type, but a sweetheart. I hate to think about her being afraid in New York."

Travis held her gaze as he reached for his cell phone. "Hey, Beck," he said. "A friend of Liana's needs a place to hide out for a week or two." His face curled into a smile. "Yes, another model. Jessica Stone." Laughing, Travis said, "No, I'm not messing with you. What've we got available in The Tower?" He paused to listen. "Can you ask housekeeping to get it ready? I want you to handle this personally.

Whoever's giving her grief is not getting near her on our watch." Pausing again, he said, "Thanks, Beck. Keep me in the loop." He stashed the phone in his pocket and returned his attention to Liana. "All set."

"Thank you." She looped her arms around his neck and kissed him softly.

Against her lips, he said, "Any friend of yours. . ."

"This is the last thing you need with everything that's going on at North Point."

"It's no problem. Beck will take care of it. I'm sure he's over there reveling in the 'other duties as assigned'—babysitting a supermodel."

Liana snickered. "Let me just call my agent to tell him it's all set."

"Give him Beck's cell number." Travis wrote it down for her.

After giving a relieved Artie the good news, she followed Travis to his car. "Where's Dash today?"

"Home with Beck. I can't trust her to behave in public."

The rain came down even harder as they drove into Newport. He glanced over at her. "Is this too much of a downpour for you?"

"It won't last. By the time we get into town, it'll be a light rain."

Sure enough they stepped out of the car into drizzle. The humidity was thick, the cobblestone streets slick, and the sidewalks largely deserted of the usual crowd of tourists.

He pulled her hood up over her head and took her hand. "Looks like we've got the place to ourselves."

"Fine by me."

They wandered through the quaint, colonial City by the Sea, stopping to look into shop windows, venturing into a few stores, and enjoying a lone guitarist performing under an awning in Brick Market.

"How about some lunch?" he asked after they'd wandered for an hour.

She pursed her lips thoughtfully and then ran her tongue over her bottom lip. "New England clam chowder."

Fixated on her mouth, Travis nodded in agreement. "Whatever you want, sweetheart."

"Oh, you *know* what I want," she smirked.

With his hands on her face he replaced her tongue with his.

When he showed no sign of ending the kiss, Liana pushed gently on his chest to remind him of where they were. She smiled at the expression on his face.

"Sorry," he said with a sheepish grin. "Lost my head for a moment there. That's what you do to me." He hooked an arm around her and crossed the street to find her some clam chowder.

After lunch, they strolled back toward the car. When they reached Washington Square, he tugged at her hand and led her to the box office at the Opera House.

"The matinee has already begun, sir," the ticket agent said.

"That's all right." He slid a twenty across the counter. "We'll take two."

"Travis, what're you doing?" Liana protested. "We missed the beginning."

He didn't answer her as he pushed open the door to the darkened theater and guided her into the back row ahead of him.

Except for another couple sitting close to the front, they were the only people in the theater.

Travis took off his jacket and then helped with hers.

"It's freezing in here," she shivered against the chill of the air conditioning.

He grazed her breasts. "So it seems."

She swatted his hand away from her sensitive nipples. "Stop it," she whispered with a nervous giggle.

"No," he said against her ear, sending a shiver through her. Unbuttoning the top two buttons of her blouse, he slid his hand straight into her bra and muffled her gasp with a deep, probing kiss.

The action film was loud otherwise the other people in the theater might have heard her moan when he pinched her hardened nipple between two persistent fingers. He reached down to open the front clasp on her bra along with another button on her top.

"Travis," Liana warned, grabbing his hand.

He dipped his head to lave at her exposed nipple.

"Oh my God," she whispered when she felt his hand on her thigh. Before she had time to wonder what he would do next, he tugged at her panties.

"Lift up, sweetheart," he whispered against her neck.

"No!" she hissed.

"Yes," he insisted, pulling harder at the scrap of fabric as he plunged his tongue into her mouth to quiet her protests.

As if she were outside herself watching someone else, Liana lifted her hips and felt her panties travel down her legs.

With a victorious grin, he twirled them around one finger before he pushed them into his pocket and went back to kissing her.

Liana thought she would go mad wondering what he planned to do with what he had uncovered, but he appeared to be in no rush as he kissed her senseless and played with her bare breasts. "Travis, come on," she whispered franticly. "Let's go to your place if you want to do this."

"It's more fun here."

"*No*, it's *not*."

He rendered her mute when his hand returned to her thigh, this time easing her legs apart.

"*Travis...*"

"You said I could branch out."

"Not in public!" she snapped.

He glanced around them. "Who's looking?"

"But—"

"Shh," he whispered as his fingers explored her. "Relax."

Liana's mind went blank when he stroked her and kissed her with long, deep thrusts of his tongue that mimicked the movement of his fingers. As her body began to quicken with excitement, her face went hot with shame over how much she was enjoying it. When she came apart against his hand he kept his mouth tight against hers to stop her gasps from escaping into the suddenly quiet movie theater.

Still breathing hard, Liana uncurled her toes and relaxed into him.

"I thought you said that doesn't happen easily for you," he whispered.

"Usually it doesn't." She glanced at him and then pushed him away from her. "You don't have to look so smug."

"Who's smug?"

"Give me back my underwear."

"No. I like knowing you're naked and ready."

"Ready for what?"

"Whatever I think of next."

"I can't walk around without underwear."

"Sure you can." He buttoned her shirt, grabbed their jackets, and took her hand. "Come on, I'll show you."

In the lobby, she pulled free of him and went into the rest room. Her image in the mirror was startling—red face, swollen lips, and abraded cheeks where his whiskers had rubbed against her sensitive skin. She looked like a common trollop, but she felt *divine*. That was the only word for it. Refastening her bra and straightening her clothes, Liana shivered from the air conditioning and the sensation of being naked under her skirt.

"You wanted a fling," she whispered into the mirror as she attempted to restore order to her hair and face, knowing she would never forget the most erotic encounter of her life. And their fling had only just begun.

Standing before the men's room mirror, Travis splashed cold water on his face. "Who do you think you're kidding?" he asked his reflection in the mirror. *You're not going to last another day without her in your bed.* He took a deep breath to calm his agitated body. After putting all his efforts into pleasing her, he pulsated with unfulfilled desire that could only be spent on her.

In three days, Liana had managed to invade his thoughts, fill his dreams, and fire him with a kind of passion he'd never imagined he possessed. For all his talk about other women, there had never been another one he wanted the way he wanted her. Maybe it was time to shift this fling into high gear.

CHAPTER 8

On the ride back to Portsmouth, Travis glanced over at her and saw her working on that poor lip. "Hey, are you mad?"

"What?" She seemed startled. "Why would I be mad?"

"Oh, I don't know. Maybe you didn't like what we did in the theater?"

Her cheeks turned red, and he had to remind himself to watch the road.

"I liked it," she said softly.

He reached for her hand. "It's okay if you didn't."

"I was terrified we were going to get caught," she confessed.

"Why do you think I sat on the aisle?"

She looked at him, brows furrowed. "What do you mean?"

"So I could shield you in case anyone came in. From the aisle no one would have seen you—or anything."

"You really thought of that?"

"Of course I did. I knew what I wanted to do when we went in there. I would've thrown myself over you before I would've let anyone else see what I was seeing. Okay?"

Her eyes filled.

"Now what?" he asked with exasperation he didn't really feel.

"It's just . . ." She fiddled with his fingers on her lap.

"What?"

"I don't often feel safe . . . with men, but I do with you. In the movie theater I didn't feel entirely safe, but that made it kind of more . . ."

"Exciting?"

She nodded.

"That was the idea."

"Now that I know you had a plan, that you were thinking of me that way, it makes me feel safe. I know that must sound crazy, but it's true."

He kissed her hand. "You *are* safe with me, Liana. I'll always have a plan."

"That seems to suggest we're going public again," she said with a wary look.

He grinned. "You never know, sweetheart."

"You're determined to turn me into a nervous wreck, aren't you?"

Abruptly, he pulled off the highway into a dirt parking lot and reached for her. "I'm determined to make sure you have some fun." The kiss was gentle, but the punch of it spiraled through him. Again the sensation of falling was almost overwhelming as her hand landed on his chest. *Go easy, North. You can't fall for her. You can't.* Even as he wondered if it was already too late for such warnings, he leaned in to kiss her again. "Do you like salmon?"

Taken aback by the change of subject, Liana said, "I love it. Why?"

He pulled the car onto the road. "Let's hit the grocery store, and I'll make you some salmon."

"I can't go in the grocery store without underwear. I might . . . catch a cold."

Travis laughed. "Think of it as another new adventure."

"Come on," she pleaded, reaching into the pocket of his shorts. "Give them back."

The car swerved, and he grabbed her hand. "Watch out. You might get more than you bargained for in there."

She sighed. "You're impossible."

He parked the car at the town's only grocery store and adjusted her ball cap down over her face. "Ready?"

"Sure, my face is covered, but you couldn't care less that I'm naked under my skirt."

"Oh, I care." He pulled her into a deep, searching kiss. "That's all I'm thinking about." Releasing her, he got out of the car and walked around to open her door.

Inside, Travis carried a basket as they walked to the back of the store where fresh seafood was sold.

Liana teased him about how picky he was about which cut of the pink fish they were going to buy. He spent an equal amount of time choosing the greens for a salad. "You're a food snob."

"What's wrong with that?" he asked with mock offense as they approached the check out counter.

Liana froze. "Oh no," she whispered. "*No.*"

"Liana? What is it?"

He followed her eyes to the rack of tabloids that lined the checkout. Splashed across the front page was a picture of her in the hideous bridesmaid dress dancing with him. The headline blared "Fashion Disaster: What Was She Thinking?" with a line below it asking, "Who's Liana's New Man?" Travis put the basket on the conveyer belt, reached for the pile of papers, and walked along the row of checkout counters collecting them all.

Liana had gone mute with shock.

Travis dropped the papers on the belt along with their groceries.

The high school girl working the register looked up at him with wide eyes. "All of them?"

"All of them," Travis replied, reaching for Liana's hand. He paid and nudged her through the double doors ahead of him. Once they were outside, he jammed the papers into the trashcan next to the door.

"You didn't have to do that," she said in a small voice.

He reached for his cell phone. "Yes, I did," he said, pressing a number on his phone. "Beck, I need another favor." He told his security chief about the photo in the tabloid. "Can you find out where they got it? I suspect it was the wedding photographer. If so, get his ass into my office at ten o'clock tomorrow morning. Also, tighten security at the gate. I don't want any reporters on the property."

He paused to listen. "Okay, that would be great. Thanks, I appreciate it." Travis returned the phone to his pocket and put his arm around her.

"They'll descend on this town," she said in a flat, lifeless tone. "They're probably already digging into your life. You should let your family know."

Alarmed by the shattered look on her face, he helped her into the car. He got in and reached for her. "Hey, don't worry. Beck's not going to let them into North Point, and he's sending a couple of guys over to keep an eye on your mother's house, too. If they come, they won't bother you."

She looked up at him with tearful eyes. "With the vandalism at North Point, you don't need to be diverting security away from your place."

"Let me take care of it, Liana. You can't expect me to do nothing."

"My agent told me this morning they want me back in Milan to do a re-shoot. Maybe I should just go. You don't need this right now."

"What about what you need?" With his index finger on her chin he turned her to him. "What about our fling?"

She shrugged. "Maybe it wasn't meant to be."

He ran his hand over her thigh and was gratified by the hitch in her breathing. "You promised me two weeks, and it's only been two days. We haven't even gotten to the good stuff yet."

She rewarded him with a weak smile.

He kissed her and then started the car to drive to North Point.

Beck was at the gate when they arrived. He leaned into the window Travis opened. "I sent a couple of guys to buy and trash the rest of the copies in town. Don't worry, Ms. McDermott, we'll find out who sold them the photo."

"Thank you, Beck. And please, call me Liana. I really appreciate you helping out with Jessie, too."

"It's a terrible burden, but somehow I'll manage."

Liana laughed at his goofy expression.

"Any sign of reporters here?" Travis asked.

"Not yet. We're on the lookout, though."

"Good, thanks. No one speaks to them about me. Understood?"

"I've already put out the word."

"Are you always one step ahead of me?"

Beck smiled. "Seems that way, doesn't it? They're sending Jessica in a limo from New York. I expect her around two a.m., so I'll hang out until she gets settled."

"Great," Travis said. "Thank you very much."

"You guys have a nice evening."

They parked in the garage under the tower and took the elevator to his apartment. Liana stepped off ahead of him, and after Travis had stashed the groceries in the kitchen, he went to find her.

On the patio, she looked out at the bay. The rain had stopped, and the sky had cleared in time for a brilliant sunset.

Travis put his hands on her shoulders. "How you doing?" When she didn't answer him, he turned her around and brought her into his arms. "It's okay, honey. They're not going to bother you here. You're safe with me, remember?"

She hooked her fingers through the belt loops on his shorts and leaned her head against his chest. "I'm sorry. You'd think I'd be used to it by now. I just really wanted this time to myself at home without the intrusion."

He kissed her forehead. "And you're going to have that. I promise."

"I'd feel much better if you would warn your family they might be harassed."

"Okay," he said with a kiss to the end of her nose. He reached into his pocket for his cell phone, pressed a button on his speed dial, and held her close to him while he waited for someone to answer. "Hi, Mom. It's Travis. How's it going?" He listened to his mother's news for a minute. "Listen, Mom, I wanted to tell you that you may be hearing from some reporters. I want you to do me a favor and not talk to them, okay?"

"Are you in some sort of trouble, Travis?"

"No, it's nothing like that. I've been seeing someone famous, and the media has caught wind of it."

"Who do you know that's famous?"

"The very beautiful Liana McDermott."

Liana blushed, and he pressed his lips to her cheek.

"*The model?*"

"The one and only."

"How did you meet *her?*"

"At a wedding at North Point." Travis rolled his eyes at the barrage of questions. "So, Mom, don't talk to the press, okay? Tell everyone else to just ignore them. Will you do that for me?"

"Would we be on T.V. if we talked to them?"

Travis stiffened. "I'm asking you not to, Mom," he said quietly but firmly.

"Oh, all right, don't get huffy with me. So when are you bringing your model girlfriend home to meet us?"

Unprepared to answer such a question, Travis glanced down at Liana. "She's really busy. She's only in town for a couple of weeks and is going back to work right after that."

"It's not like you ever come home anyway."

"Mom—"

"Well, I have to go. Maybe you could call once in a while, huh?"

"Okay," he said through gritted teeth. "I'll talk to you soon. Tell Dad I said hi."

"Goodbye, Travis."

Travis stashed the phone in his pocket. "Could you hear every word of that?"

Liana looked up at him with sad eyes. "I'm sorry to be causing you grief with her."

"It's got nothing to do with you. It's her. She's miserable and has been my whole life. It's all too much for her—too many kids, not enough money. Complain, complain."

"That must've been hard to live with. You're such a positive person."

He laughed, but there was an edge to it. "I wasn't always." Running his hands over her arms, he looked over her shoulder at the view from the patio. "I had my parents up here one weekend so they could see what I was doing. Do you know what she said?"

Liana winced. "I'm almost afraid to ask."

He shifted his gaze back to her. "She said, 'It sure must be nice to have so much money.' I made sure they had everything they needed for life before I spent a dime here. Why did she have to say that?"

"I don't know. I've never understood people who have to tear others down to make themselves feel important."

"Yes," he said with a sigh of relief. "Yes. That's exactly what she does."

"She won't talk to the press, will she?"

"I don't think so. As much as she likes to whine and complain, she wouldn't do that to me."

"What's your dad like?" Liana asked.

"He's a good guy, but he drinks. A lot. I think it's so he won't have to listen to her."

"I'm sure in their own way they're proud of you, Travis. How could they not be?"

He shrugged. "I tell myself it doesn't matter."

"You've done a really incredible thing here. I'm proud of you. Not that it's the same thing . . ."

"No," he said hoarsely. "Don't qualify it. Thank you."

She caressed his face and brought him down for a soft, sweet kiss.

Travis held her close and took possession of her mouth. Filled with desire and what was starting to feel an awful lot like love, he pulled back to focus on her neck. "How did you end up comforting me?"

She rolled her head to the side to give him better access. "I don't know," she said breathlessly.

"There is one bit of good news."

"What's that?"

"She's been insinuating lately that I'm gay because I've never gotten married."

Liana pressed against his erection as she laughed. "You're definitely *not* gay."

"She won't be able to say that now that she knows I'm seeing you."

"I'm glad I was able to help."

"You did help, Liana."

"Good." She reached up to toy with his hair. "So why haven't you gotten married?"

"After growing up with my parents . . ." He shuddered. "Plus I've never met anyone I could imagine spending that much time with."

"I know what you mean. On the few dates I've been on in the last couple of years, my first thought is usually how long will it be until I can go home and get into my pajamas."

He laughed softly as he smoothed his hands over her back and bottom.

She trembled from his touch.

"Are you thinking that now?"

"What I'm thinking about right now," she said, skimming her lips along his jaw, "has nothing to do with pajamas."

With his eyes fixed firmly on hers, he took her hands and walked backwards to his bedroom.

"Where are we going?" she asked with a coy smile.

"Somewhere less public."

"I thought you liked public."

"Not for this."

"What about the salmon?" she asked, sounding nervous.

"It'll keep." He moved behind her, nudged her hair out of the way, and left soft, wet kisses on her neck as he reached around to cup her breasts.

She leaned back against him.

He unbuttoned her blouse and eased it over her shoulders. When she tried to turn around he stopped her.

"Travis . . ."

"What, sweetheart?"

"You're making my legs weak."

He smiled against her neck. "And I'm just getting started." Unclipping the front clasp of her bra, he brought it down over her arms. "Hmm, very sexy." With his other hand he drew her panties out of his pocket and held them up next to the bra. "A matching set. I like that."

Liana lunged for the panties.

He held them out of her reach. "Uh, uh, uh." He put them back in his pocket. "I've got custody of them."

"Let me turn around. I want to touch you."

"Soon." He dragged his finger from the top of her skirt, up over her belly, and between her breasts. Her sharp inhale encouraged him to do it again.

She turned around and whipped the shirt over his head.

He gasped at the feel of her breasts against his chest.

Her mouth devoured his as she pulled at his shorts.

"Hey," he protested. "You're taking over my seduction."

She unzipped his shorts and pushed them down. "You were taking too long."

"You like it fast, huh?" He backed her up to the bed and came down on top of her.

"Fast would be good."

"The last time we were right here, you freaked out on me. That's not going to happen again, is it? Because I'm almost to the point of no return here."

She sifted her fingers through his hair. "No freaking out."

"Maybe a little?" he asked with a smile as he reached under her skirt.

Biting back a moan, she clutched his shoulders while he kissed his way to her breasts.

He loved the way her back arched into him as he licked and tugged and sucked until she wiggled under him. He unzipped her skirt and pulled it down over her hips. Hooking her legs over his shoulders, he felt a tremble go through her as he dragged his lips over her inner thigh.

Liana covered herself with her hands. "Don't," she said in a voice thick with desire and maybe fear.

"Why?"

"I don't like that."

Her thigh muffled his laughter. "Then you haven't had it done right."

"Travis, really, I don't want that."

His lips kept up their northbound journey as he pinned her hands on either side of her hips. "I thought you were going to trust me."

"I do."

"Then relax." He trailed his tongue over the outline of her outer lips.

She inhaled sharply. "How am I supposed to relax when you're doing that?" she squeaked.

"Try," he whispered, releasing one of her hands. He laced the fingers of his other hand through hers and squeezed reassuringly.

Falling back on the bed, she said, "Oh, God. *Oh my God . . .*"

His index finger slid through her dampness as he sucked hard on her clitoris.

Almost as if she couldn't help herself, she raised her hips.

He looked up to find her eyes closed and her lips parted in an expression of total abandon that filled him with desire. His already painfully hard cock throbbed. When he pushed two fingers deep into her and flicked his tongue over her throbbing center, an orgasm rocketed through her.

Travis stayed with her until the last spasm passed and then skimmed his lips over her belly. "Things are starting to get sweaty," he whispered as he recaptured her nipple.

Panting, Liana tugged him up to her. "I need to catch my breath."

He wrapped his arms around her and held her against him, dropping soft kisses on her face.

She caressed his chest and drew a deep breath from him when she ran a finger down to his belly the way he had done to her. "It's no fun if only one of us is sweaty," she said, pushing him onto his back.

"Liana . . ."

"Trust me?"

"You can't use my own words against me . . ." His breath got stuck in his throat as she divested him of his boxers.

"These are mine now," she said with a grin, spinning them around on her finger.

Travis burned for her but forced himself to remain still while she took a visual inventory and seemed to like what she saw. The feel of her lips on his chest and her hair sliding over him brought a fine sheen of sweat to his skin. She caressed his straining erection, and he reached for her hand. "This is going to be over before it starts if you keep that up, sweetheart," he said in a choked voice.

"We've got plenty of time," she whispered, replacing her hand with her mouth.

Through a red haze of desire, Travis fought back the need to explode. "Liana, honey," he gasped. "Stop." But rather than stop, she became even more eager. She took him deep, stroking him with her hand as she worked him over with her lips and tongue. As he watched her and conjured up images of his fat Aunt Sarah to keep from coming too soon, he was quite certain Liana hadn't done this very often in the past. But what she lacked in experience, she more than made up for in enthusiasm.

She ran her teeth lightly over him and finished him right off. The powerful climax left him depleted in every possible way. His heart hammered in his chest as she stretched out on top of him. He buried one hand in her hair and held her tight with his other arm. "You're full of surprises," he whispered when he could speak again.

She looked up at him with a smug smile. "Why should you have all the fun?"

Filled with emotions he couldn't seem to identify, Travis swallowed the lump that formed in his throat. "Will you stay with me tonight, Liana?"

"I want to, but my mother . . ."

"She gave you permission, sweetheart. Stay with me." He captured her earlobe between his teeth. "I want to make love to you all night long."

She trembled. "I'd have to call her, or she'll worry."

"I'll let you out of bed long enough for that." She snuggled into him, and he was astounded to realize he was already aroused again. "Stay right there." He kissed her, eased himself from under her, and reached for his bedside table. In the drawer he found a condom and rolled it on. When he turned back to her, he found her looking pensive. "What's wrong?"

"You've got a ready supply, huh?"

He put his arms around her. "I bought them last night after I took you home."

Her cheeks colored with embarrassment. "Oh."

He captured her lips in a deep kiss that he hoped would reassure her. "I haven't been with anyone in a long time. I've been too busy building my business."

"I'm sorry," she said, caressing his face. "I sound like a jealous, insecure girlfriend."

"I like it," he said with a grin before he became serious again. "But you don't need to be jealous of anyone, Liana. You have my full, undivided attention." He nudged her legs far apart and kissed her gently as he entered her.

She gasped against his lips and struggled to accommodate him.

He moved slowly until he filled her.

She looked up at him with wide, violet eyes.

In those amazing eyes he could see that she trusted him, and the realization infused him with tenderness as he began to move faster.

Clutching his back, she met his thrusts with the rise of her hips.

He felt her tense the moment before she climaxed, and her cries shattered the fragile hold he had on his control.

CHAPTER 9

Beck waited in The Tower's lobby office, checking his watch every few minutes until he thought he'd go crazy if they didn't arrive soon. Earlier, when Travis asked him to help out a friend of Liana's, Beck never imagined the friend would be the object of his fantasies. Liana was a beautiful, sexy woman, and Beck was thrilled to see Travis having so much fun with her. But the supermodel who made Beck drool, the one whose photo graced his calendar year round and had him waiting for each new edition of the Victoria Secret catalog was Jessica Stone.

Thank goodness they had been on the phone when Travis asked him to help her, otherwise his good friend would have zeroed right in on Beck's fascination. Of all the women who could be heading his way in the middle of the night. . . Beck couldn't wait to meet her.

He wondered if she would be as amazing in person as she was in the many photos he had seen of her over the last few years since she bounded on to the modeling scene. The whole celebrity crush thing was new to him. He had grown up with sisters who'd had posters of pretty boys taped to their bedroom walls. Beck, on the other hand, had preferred pictures of sports heroes, motorcycles, and muscle cars.

He also was anxious to know the deal with her so-called stalker. His cell phone rang, and he pounced on it.

"Peter Beck."

"This is Roland, Ms. Stone's driver. We're entering the gates to North Point."

Showtime! Beck gave him directions to The Tower and went out to meet the three-car caravan.

A couple of beefy-necked bodyguards emerged from the first of the two black SUVs that book-ended the limo. They took a measuring look around as Beck approached them.

"Peter Beck, chief of security," he said as he received two bone-crushing handshakes. He spent the next fifteen minutes answering their formidable list of questions about building and property security while anxiously waiting to meet the main attraction.

"Impressive," one of the beefy dudes finally declared. "Mr. Dale, Ms. Stone's agent, asked us to make sure everything was kosher before we left her here."

"You have my guarantee that she'll be safe here. I'll see to it personally."

The other beefcake sized him up and down once more before signaling to the driver.

A man who Beck assumed to be Roland emerged from the limo and opened the back door. Beck held his breath as he waited for his first glimpse of Jessica Stone in the flesh. Well, not in the flesh, but close enough. The picture in his mind of a glamorous supermodel hardly jibed with the pony-tailed waif in the pale blue sweat suit who emerged from the car.

She took a long look around even though she probably couldn't see much beyond the glow of headlights from three cars. Finally, she set her eyes on him, and the impact was like a punch to his stomach. Her face lifted into a small smile as she moved toward him.

Beck was frozen. He couldn't have moved if his pants were on fire.

Extending her hand, Jessica looked up at him with big eyes that he knew from her photos were blue. "I'm Jessica Stone," she said in a lilting Southern accent, "but my friends call me Jessie."

Beck knew he was expected to respond. He was supposed to shake her hand. But all he could do was stare. Finally, he snapped out of it and reached out to take her hand. A jolt went straight up his arm. "Peter Beck," he managed to say. "My friends call me Beck."

"Nice to meet you, Beck."

For some reason he was ridiculously pleased to have been granted friend status. "We're happy to have you as our guest, Ms. Stone. If there's anything we can do for you, all you have to do is ask."

Her smile faded just a little, but he noticed. "It's Jessie, and that's mighty nice of y'all. I've only met Liana a few times, but Artie said a friend of hers owns this place."

"That's right, Travis North—my friend and Liana's." Beck didn't add that Liana was spending the night in Travis's penthouse. "He asked me to make you comfortable."

"I so appreciate that. My. . . situation. . . in New York had gotten, well. . ." Her eyes filled.

As a man who had learned from experience to avoid commitment and women who screamed forever the way this one did, it was all Beck could do not to haul her into his arms and tell her everything would be just fine. He would make sure of it. But because the beefcake brothers were watching his every move, he said, "Let's get you settled upstairs so you can get some rest."

He showed Jessie and her entourage to the apartment on the fifth floor that Travis had outfitted for guests and VIPs.

"*Oh,*" Jessie gasped after Beck flipped on a light. "This is *beautiful!*"

"Wait 'til you see the view in the morning. It looks right out on the bay."

Roland deposited her bags in the bedroom. "Is there anything else we can do for you, Ms. Stone?"

"No, thank you." To the others she added, "Y'all have been terrific. And I appreciate your discretion in not mentioning to anyone that you brought me here."

"Of course," Roland replied for all of them.

"We'll take good care of her," Beck assured the five men before he showed them to the door.

When they were alone, Jessie moved slowly around the big room, taking in the elegant, contemporary furnishings. Once again, tears flooded her big blue eyes. "It's perfect. Please thank your friend Travis for me."

"You can thank him yourself in the morning. I'm sure he and Liana will want to check on you."

"I don't really know her all that well." Jessie twisted her hands in a nervous gesture. "I was kind of appalled when Artie told me he'd asked her for help with my. . . situation. She's like the Princess Diana of models compared to little old me."

"You've gotten your share of the spotlight."

"You've heard of me?" she said with that wide-eyed expression that made him want to drool.

"Ah, yeah," he said, laughing. *If only you knew. . .* "I've heard of you."

"I'm still getting used to that. And now there's this guy. . . He keeps sending me creepy letters and showing up outside my house. But he's always long gone by the time the police get there."

"We'll talk about that tomorrow," Beck said. "What you need tonight is some sleep."

"That'd be nice. I haven't been sleeping too well worrying about him showing up at my door."

"That won't happen here. I promise you'll be safe." He couldn't get over how tiny she was in real life. Her photos made her look much taller. The photos had, however, done justice to her curvy, hourglass figure and flawless complexion, marred now from crying. While Liana's staggering beauty could only be called regal, Jessie was pure soft sweetness. In all his thirty-six years, Beck had never felt such an overwhelming need to protect another human being. A thought that should have been terrifying was instead electrifying.

He gave her a quick tour of the apartment. "Are you hungry? We stocked the kitchen with just about everything we could think of."

"I'm fine. We stopped to eat on the way, but thank you."

"Okay then." Beck felt uncharacteristically awkward and tongue-tied. "I'll check on you in the morning."

"Do you have to go?" she asked and then seemed to instantly regret it. "I'm sorry. Of course you want to go. You must be anxious to get home."

"I don't mind hanging out for a bit."

"Really?" she asked with an audible sigh of relief. "They were careful to make sure we weren't followed, but I just worry he's going to find me."

"He won't. I swear to you, Jessie, no one gets in those gates who doesn't belong here." But as he said the words, he remembered the recent spate of vandalism on the North Point property and decided to double his security detail. No one was going to bother this woman—or Liana.

"I'll be okay," she said, attempting a confident smile that fell flat. "You can go."

He moved to the bar that Travis kept stocked for guests. "I don't know about you, but I could use a drink."

The look on her face when she realized he wasn't leaving tugged at his heart. "Is there any white wine?"

"Coming right up."

Liana awoke to the sound of the shower. Sunshine poured in through the full-length windows in Travis's bedroom. She stretched, and the soreness coming from various intimate places caused her cheeks to burn with shame as she remembered the wide variety of positions she had been in during the night. She'd lost track of the number of orgasms and could almost still feel him bent around her as he took her from behind.

Opening her eyes, she was startled to find Dash staring at her.

"You were watching, weren't you?" Liana asked the dog.

Dash studied her without blinking.

Burying her face in the pillow, Liana groaned. *How will I ever look at him again? I can't even look at his dog!* But as embarrassing as it was to remember it all, another part of her was thrilled because what she'd experienced with Travis was real passion—really *sweaty* passion. *At least now I won't have to live the rest of my life without ever knowing what that's like. I'll have these two weeks with him to remember.* The thought of having to rely only on memories filled her with sadness. *Oh, Liana, get real. You can't be in love with him after one night. One long, amazing night . . .*

When Travis emerged from the shower with a towel wrapped around his waist, her face was still buried in the pillow. He kissed his way up the bare slope of her back, causing her to shiver. "Why are you hiding in that pillow?"

Her cheeks burning, she didn't answer him.

"*Liana,*" he sang. "Show your face."

"Can't."

He laughed as he trailed a finger over her ribs. "I have ways of getting you out of there," he said as he tickled her.

She squealed and turned away from his tickling hand.

He brushed the hair back from her face. "Are you embarrassed, sweetheart?"

She bit her lip and nodded but still didn't look at him.

Travis bent his head to trail kisses over her neck. "There's nothing to be embarrassed about."

She winced. "If you say so."

He took her chin and forced her to meet his eyes. "You're a beautiful, sexy woman, Liana. Don't be ashamed of enjoying yourself in bed."

She lowered her eyes again when her cheeks burned.

"Liana," he said with a sigh as he kissed her blush. "Last night was the most incredible night, and I hate that I have to go to work, but I have a bunch of stuff going on today." He opened his hand and keys dangled from his finger.

"What've you got there?"

"Keys to my car and to this place. You've seen me use the key in the elevator, right?"

She nodded.

"Come and go as you please. Take the car. Go have lunch with your mother, and then bring her back with you to have dinner at the club tonight, okay?"

"Won't you need your car today?"

"I'm in meetings most of the day, and if I have to go anywhere, I can use one of the trucks. You do have a driver's license, don't you?"

She smiled. "I haven't driven in a while, but yes, I have a license. I don't want to take your car, though."

"It's insured."

She laughed and reached for his freshly shaven face. "Thank you," she said, kissing him softly.

"You aren't going to die of shame today, are you?"

"I might," she confessed.

"Don't." He nudged the sheet aside and drew her sore nipple gently into his mouth. "Because I want to do it all over again tonight."

She trembled as her body responded to his touch.

He pulled back with what seemed to be great reluctance. "I have to go," he said with another sigh. "Next week I'm taking some time off so we can stay in bed all day."

"You're going to kill me."

He reached for the box of condoms on the bedside table and shook it. The few that were left rattled inside. "I should've gotten the bigger box."

Liana went back into the pillow. "Stop," she said in a muffled voice.

"I had no idea you'd be so insatiable."

That got her out from her hiding place. *"Me?"*

He laughed and got up to dress in a dark olive summer suit.

As Liana watched him move around the room, she decided he was the sexiest man she'd ever known—and she'd known plenty of sexy men. But none of them possessed his unique combination of stunning good looks, sensitivity, and humor. Not to mention sexual prowess. *Yes, don't forget about that,* she thought with a little giggle.

"What are you laughing at?" he asked with a smile as he adjusted his tie and turned to her.

"Nothing."

He shocked her when he flopped down on top of her. "Tell me."

She was hit with a fit of the giggles, which he encouraged when he tickled her ribs again. "Travis! *Stop!*"

"Tell me what you were laughing at."

"Okay, okay," she said, trying to catch her breath. "I was making a mental list of all the things I like about you."

"This I need to hear."

As her hands sought out his back under his suit coat, she decided to indulge him. "You're very, very, *very* good looking, but I'm sure you know that."

"Yes, it's something I think about quite a lot."

With a smile, she said, "You're funny and fun and sensitive."

He groaned. "You had to throw that in there, didn't you?"

"It's true," she insisted.

He made a face at the compliment. "So which of my so-called attributes did you find humorous?"

She blushed again. "The sexual prowess part."

His grin was smug. "Prowess, huh? I like that one."

"I figured you would."

He rewarded her with a lingering kiss, and Liana was startled to realize he was aroused again.

"You'd better go," she said, running her fingers through his still-damp hair.

"I don't want to."

"You have meetings."

"I have the sexiest woman in the world in my bed. Suddenly, my meetings don't seem so important."

She gave him a little push. "Travis . . ."

With a rumbling groan, he rolled over and sat up. He looked back at her over his shoulder. "Don't retreat from me today, Liana."

The concern on his face moved her as she reached for his hand. "I won't."

He kissed her hand and then her lips. "Dinner at seven?"

"We'll be there."

"I'll think of you today," he said. "Will you think of me?"

"I think it's safe to assume you'll cross my mind."

He smiled. "Good."

CHAPTER 10

Travis whistled as he walked with Dash across the lawn to his office in the country club. The sun had chased away the rain, the bay sparkled, and the air was filled with the scent of jasmine. A perfect day after a perfect night. *How am I ever going to wait until tonight to see her again? How am I ever going to let her go in eleven short days?*

He told her he'd never married because he hadn't found anyone he could imagine spending that much time with. After one night with her he had little doubt he could spend forever with her and be totally content. But she'd made it clear she was leaving at the end of her two-week vacation, so it didn't do him any good to indulge in fantasies about something that could never happen.

"Trav!"

He stopped and turned to see Beck jogging to catch up with him.

"Morning," Beck said.

"Hey." Travis gave his friend a quick once over. "What's with the scruffy look today?"

"Never made it home last night." And right before Travis North's astounded eyes, Peter Beck blushed.

"You and Jessica Stone?"

"It's not what you think."

"Oh no?" Travis asked, enjoying Beck's embarrassment. "Then what is it?"

"She was kind of stirred up about the stalker and everything, so I stayed to keep her company, and we ended up falling asleep on the sofa."

"Is that so?"

"Totally platonic. I swear."

"If you say so. What's she like?"

"Adorable. It's hard to believe the sexy vixen in the pictures is really her. She wants to meet you to thank you for having her."

"I'll check on her later, and I'm sure Liana will, too."

"She'd like that."

"Any sign of reporters?"

"Afraid so," Beck said. "I got a call from the gate that there's about twenty of them camped outside."

"Shit," Travis hissed. "What about Liana's mother's house?"

"Ten more over there."

"Goddamn it!" Travis kicked at the gravel walkway with frustration. "All she wants is a little peace and quiet. Is that too much to ask?"

"Not if she stays on the property. We can keep them out of here, but once she leaves here, there's not much I can do."

"I just gave her my car keys. She's going to meet her mother for lunch."

"Why don't you have her mom come here instead?"

"She's not going to want to be locked up here like a prisoner." Frustrated, Travis ran a hand through his hair. "What are my other choices?"

"I could assign a couple of guys to tail her to make sure no one hassles her."

As he tried to decide what to do, Travis glanced up at The Tower.

"Trav?"

He thought about what Liana had said about crossing a line and letting them win. But his worries about her being pursued, bothered, taunted, or even possibly harmed in some way took precedence. "Do it."

Beck studied him for a moment. "Are you all right?"

"Yeah, sure. I'm fine."

"You and Liana McDermott." Beck shook his head with amusement. "Didn't see that one coming."

"Don't get all excited. It's temporary."

"Is that right?"

"She's leaving a week from Sunday to go back to work."

Beck rubbed at his chin as he nodded.

Travis sighed. "What? I can tell you're just dying to say something."

"I've known you a long time, and there's something different about you the last couple of days. It doesn't take a rocket scientist to wonder if maybe Liana McDermott is the reason."

"She's an amazing woman, Beck."

Beck chuckled at the understatement.

"I'm not just talking about how she looks. Once you get to know her, really know her, how she looks becomes almost secondary."

"Ah, yeah, okay," Beck said with a snicker.

"Seriously," Travis insisted. "Oh, never mind." He started to walk away, but Beck stopped him with a hand on his arm.

"Hey, I'm only razzing you, man. Just be careful."

"Of what?"

"I don't want to see you get hurt. If she means it when she says she's leaving, be careful."

Ready to change a subject that was getting far too close for comfort, Travis asked, "Did you find out who sold the picture to the rags?"

"We're all but certain it was the wedding photographer. I told him you wanted to see him at ten about a big commission."

"Good. Maybe you'd better be there, too—to keep me from kicking his ass."

Beck snorted. "I'd stand back and watch."

Liana decided to take a bath in Travis's big tub. The hot water eased away aches in places she'd never ached before. She rested her head against the tub, completely relaxed for the first time in longer than she could remember.

No one was waiting impatiently to do her hair and makeup, no wardrobe people were yelling at her to hurry up, no insufferable photographers were waiting to twist her into inhuman positions and then tell her to hold them for hours. Even the anxiety she'd felt only yesterday about when Travis would decide the time was right to make love to her was gone now. Only mindless relaxation remained, something she rarely experienced in her regular life.

She sighed and crossed her legs against the tingle that developed between them when she relived the night she'd spent with Travis. He'd been a passionate lover, but then, she had known he would be. Her cheeks burned when she remembered crying out from the almost painful pleasure he brought her. For all his big talk about one orgasm after another, he had definitely delivered. And even though it was embarrassing to think about it, she wished he hadn't left so they could do it again right now.

Soon enough, she thought, as she got out of the tub to get dressed in the same clothes she'd had on yesterday—minus the panties she couldn't find anywhere. She smiled when she realized he had hidden them from her. *This fling was the best idea I've ever had—or I should say, the best idea Enid's ever had.* Liana snickered when she thought of her cousin. *She'd be proud of me today.*

Half an hour later, she took the elevator to the parking garage. It stopped on the fifth floor, and when the doors opened Liana was surprised to find Jessica Stone waiting for the elevator. She had almost forgotten the other woman was coming to stay. "Hi, Jessie," Liana said, holding the door open for her.

"Hey, Liana. Thank you so much for arranging all this. I had no idea Artie was going to dump my troubles on you."

"It's no problem, and Travis is the one who arranged everything."

"I'd like to meet him to thank him, too."

"He'll be around later. He has meetings this morning."

"Is he an old friend of yours? I seem to remember you being from up this way."

"I'm from here," Liana said, her cheeks blazing with embarrassment when memories of her night with Travis resurfaced. "But I only recently met him."

"Oh."

"We're having a fling." The moment the words rushed out of her mouth Liana wished she could take them back.

Jessie stared at her, shocked. "*Oh.*"

"I've never done anything like this before. I don't want you to think—"

Jessie patted her arm. "You shouldn't worry about what anyone else thinks."

"No?"

"Of course not. You need to relax and enjoy your vacation."

"Yes, you're right." With a sly smile, Liana added, "I *am* enjoying it. What about you? Are you all right? Artie didn't say much about what's been going on."

"I've got this freak making my life hell," Jessie said in her cute Southern accent as they stepped off the elevator in the garage. "He's been bothering me for months, but lately it's gotten totally out of hand. I was about to have a breakdown, so Artie suggested I get out of town while the cops try to track him down. I feel bad that Artie sucked you into this. I didn't know he was going to ask you."

"I don't mind. This is the ideal place to hide out, but we might have some trouble with the press. There was a bunch of crap in the rags about me yesterday."

Jessie winced. "I heard. I'm sorry."

"I'd hate for them to figure out that you're here, too."

"They don't usually recognize me."

"Enjoy that while it lasts," Liana said with a sigh. "Well, I'm going to head to my mother's. Do you have everything you need?"

"I'm fine. Don't worry about me."

"You should try to relax while you're here. It's a great place to be stuck."

"It's beautiful. I'm going to go check out the beach."

Liana reached out to give the younger woman a quick hug. "I'll see you later." She walked across the garage, and with a look of trepidation for the gleaming burgundy Jaguar and a deep breath for courage, she opened the door. Driving slower than an old lady she left the garage and turned toward the main gate. "Oh, no," she groaned when she saw the gaggle of reporters and photographers gathered just outside the gate.

Reaching for the Red Sox cap she had left in the car the day before, she put it on and pulled it down over her eyes as she gunned the car through the gate and up the hill. A glance in the rearview mirror told her she had succeeded in escaping without drawing notice from the paparazzi. *They aren't expecting one of the world's top models to be driving herself,* Liana thought with a burst of giggles. How good it felt to win a round with the relentless media!

Liana turned up the radio and rolled down the window. Singing her way through Portsmouth, she reveled in the music, the warm summer breeze, and the powerful car. "I need to drive more often," she said. "I'd forgotten how much I like it."

She pulled onto McCorrie Lane and slowed to a crawl when she saw children playing in the street. Navigating the last bend before her mother's house, Liana gasped when she saw more reporters and photographers waiting for her. "Damn it!"

Maybe if I talk to them for a minute they'll leave me alone. She pulled into her mother's driveway, took off the hat, and ran a hand through her hair.

"Liana!" they yelled the moment she stepped out of the car.

Three men in North Point polo shirts attempted to keep them off her mother's lawn.

"Liana! What's going on with you and Travis North?"

"How did you meet North?"

"Is there any truth to rumors of an engagement?"

Where do they get this stuff? Liana made her way across the lawn to talk to them for a minute. Travis's three big men held them back as fast-action cameras clicked and flash bulbs burst.

"Did you know he gave up a chance to play in the NFL?"

"What do you have to say about the pictures on the Internet?"

That stopped her cold. "What pictures?"

"You and Travis North," one of them replied with a dirty grin.

Liana turned on her heel and went into the house while they renewed their efforts to get her to talk to them. Inside she went straight to her mother's bedroom. Liana had bought her mother a laptop and taught her how to use it so they could send each other e-mails when Liana was overseas. She opened the browser and called up one of the more salacious entertainment Web sites.

"Liana's New Lover Once Spurned the NFL," the headline said. "*Oh my God,*" she moaned as she watched time-progression photos of Travis taking her hands and leading her inside the night before. Since Travis's apartment was the highest place in town, the photos must have been taken from an airplane. Liana's mind raced as she watched the clip again.

I didn't even hear an airplane. I was too wrapped up in him to hear anything. The site included a link to coverage of Travis turning down the offer from the Arizona Cardinals. Liana clicked on the story and read it. The photo that accompanied it was of a much younger Travis. Another headline caught her eye: "North Supports Brother with Downs."

Liana's eyes filled when she opened the link to find a Special Olympics photo of Travis running alongside a boy who would have looked just like him except for the telltale Down's Syndrome features. Putting her head down on the desk, she was filled with dismay at the invasion of his privacy that she had caused.

Liana closed the browser and was startled to find numerous documents on the computer's desktop. Curious, she opened one of them. "Sociology 302, Agnes McDermott." Another said, "History 412." A third was labeled, "Creative Writing 400." She was so surprised by what she'd discovered that she didn't hear her mother come home.

"Honey?" Agnes said from the doorway.

Liana turned to her. "Were you going to tell me?"

"Tell you what, dear?" Agnes asked as she sat on the bed to take off her shoes.

"That you're going to college."

Agnes froze.

"*Why didn't you tell me, Mom?*" Liana cried, getting up from the desk. "Why would you keep something like that from me?"

Agnes grimaced. "I never meant to keep it from you. I wasn't sure if I was going to be able to do it, and I thought, why tell Liana if it's just going to be a class or two? Then one class led to another, and before I knew it I was halfway done. By then it felt like a sin of omission."

"I've been thinking you have Alzheimer's!"

Agnes stared at her, incredulous. "Alzheimer's? Why in the world would you think that?"

"Because! You've been so scatterbrained! We've been terribly worried about you—me, Aunt Edith, Enid, Uncle Charlie. And all this time you were in college!" Suddenly, Liana was so swamped with relief she began to laugh as she flopped down next to her mother on the bed.

"I knew you'd think it was ridiculous," Agnes said in a small voice.

"*What?*" Liana gasped. "Ridiculous? I'm so proud of you I could bust! So very, very proud."

"Really?"

Liana clutched her mother's hand. "Really. When do you graduate?"

"Next May with a degree in sociology. I'm sorry to have been scatterbrained, but it's taken all my energy to keep up with my classes."

"Is this why you left the wedding early?"

Agnes grinned sheepishly. "I had a mid-term the next day. That's where I was Monday morning when I said I had an errand to run. I was so mad when I had to take a summer class to graduate on time because I knew it would coincide with your visit."

Looping an arm around her mother's shoulders, Liana leaned her head against her mother's. "This is such a huge relief. I can't tell you how worried I've been."

"I'm sorry, honey. I should've told you, but the whole thing felt so silly at my age. Who goes to college at sixty?"

"It's *not* silly," Liana insisted. "It's amazing. Was it something you always wanted to do?"

"Not really. But after Dad died, I needed something to fill my time, so I started taking a class here and there. That's when I got the bug to go all the way."

"I'm so impressed," Liana said, suddenly remembering the reporters outside and what she had learned about Travis on the Internet.

"What's wrong, honey? Is it Travis?"

"No," Liana said. "Travis is amazing."

Agnes returned Liana's smile with one of her own. "Then it must be the reporters decorating my lawn."

"I'm so sick of them! They follow me everywhere I go. They even took pictures of Travis and me on his patio last night, and the photos are on the Internet today. They reported all kinds of personal things about him, too. I just feel so . . . violated. I can't even imagine how he's going to feel. I can't take it anymore!"

Agnes gathered her daughter into her arms. "I'm sorry you have to deal with that, but it comes with the life you've chosen, honey. You can't have one part of it and not the other."

"I know," Liana said, dejected. "They've never found me here before, and I just wanted two weeks off from it. Is that too much to ask?"

"Of course not, but since that's not going to happen, you have to work around it."

Liana raised her head off her mother's shoulder. "What do you mean?"

"Instead of going out and borrowing trouble, why don't we have lunch here and give each other manicures? What do you say?"

"As long as we get to spend some time together, I don't care what we do. You don't have to study do you?"

Agnes chuckled. "Later."

"Travis wants us to meet him at the club for dinner at seven. Can you do that?"

"Sure," Agnes said as she got up and slid into sandals.

"Mom? Can I ask you something else?"

"Of course."

"Do you have a boyfriend?"

Again Agnes froze.

Liana's eyes widened with surprise. *"You do!"*

"Liana—"

"I can't believe you've kept all this from me!"

"I didn't think you'd approve. Of the second thing, that is."

"Why would you feel like you needed my approval?"

"Because you're my daughter and the most important person in the world to me. What you think of me matters. You were so close to your dad and so devastated by his death. I didn't think you'd want to see me with someone else."

"I *want* you to be happy," Liana said with her hands on her mother's shoulders. "If going to college and dating makes you happy, I'd never stand in the way of that."

"I'm sorry, honey. I should've told you."

"Who is he? The man you're seeing?"

"His name is David," Agnes said shyly as she went into the kitchen to start lunch. "David Leary."

Liana followed her. "And how did you meet this David Leary?"

Agnes's cheeks turned red with embarrassment.

Liana laughed. "Now I know where I get my blush." She felt her own cheeks grow warm when she thought of how much Travis enjoyed making her blush.

"He was my freshman composition teacher."

"Mother!"

"We didn't go out until *after* the semester was over," Agnes clarified. She hesitated before she added, "There's one other thing you should probably know."

"What's that?"

"He's, um, younger than me."

"Define younger."

"He's fifty-five."

"That's only eight years, Mom, which is not exactly a scandal. But if he was your freshman composition teacher, then you've been going out with him for a while."

Agnes's cheeks lit up again. "Three years."

"And *no one* knows? Not Aunt Edith? Not Enid?"

Agnes shook her head. "I wouldn't have told them and not you, honey."

"But how did you keep this from everyone?"

"We go out of town when we go out. And he has a weekend place in Vermont. We spend a lot of time up there."

Incredulous, Liana asked, "When can I meet him?"

"Oh well . . . ah . . . I don't know."

"Invite him to dinner tonight," Liana said, stealing a pickle from the jar her mother opened.

"I can't do that! Travis didn't invite him."

"Travis won't care." She reached for the portable phone and handed it to her mother. "Here's what you say: Hello, David? It's me, Agnes. We're busted. So please come to dinner tonight with my daughter and me."

"And the very handsome Travis North," Agnes added.

Liana smiled. "Now you're getting into the spirit of things."

Shaking her head at Liana, Agnes dialed the phone. "Hi," she said when David answered. Her face turned beet red again. "We're busted."

Liana laughed, and the reporters on the lawn were forgotten.

CHAPTER 11

Jessie bent to pick up another shell. Growing up in rural Georgia, she had always dreamed of living at the beach. To consider herself "stuck" here was preposterous. She was in heaven! Beck told her the body of water fronting North Point was a bay, and the ocean was on the other side of the island. He'd promised to take her there to show her how to body surf. They had talked all night—not about anything important or special, but somehow he'd managed to make her feel both important *and* special. And safe. For the first time in longer than she could remember, she felt safe.

He told her about growing up with three younger sisters in Ohio, of playing football with Travis North at Ohio State, of working for a decade as an FBI agent before venturing into the private security business. While he was tall, blond, and built, she had been more attracted to his calm, quiet demeanor than his good looks. Without breaking a sweat or lifting a finger, he was the epitome of authority and competence. She needed as much as she could get of both right now.

With the hem of her T-shirt full of shells, she turned to start back to The Tower to wash them. Her heart skipped at the sight of Beck making his way toward her on the beach. As she watched his rangy stride eat up the sand, she recalled the odd jolt of recognition she'd experienced when she first saw him the night before.

"There you are," he said, seeming relieved. "I've been looking for you. After what you told me last night, I should've known to look here first."

"I'm sorry. I should've left a note or something."

"I don't want to smother you, but I promised to keep you safe." He handed her a cell phone. "Would you mind carrying this so you can come and go as you please but I can still find you?"

Relishing the idea of being found by him, she reached for the phone. "Sure."

"If you flip it open, you'll see the number there. Feel free to give it to anyone you want to have it." He paused, looking boyishly cute and yet every inch a man. "I thought you might like to meet Travis."

"I'd love to." Even more so after learning that Liana was having a fling with him. "Can I run up to drop off my shells and change first?"

"No problem," he said, falling into step with her.

"I expected to be tired after staying up all night."

"You're not?"

"Nope. I'm full of energy. What about you?"

"Must be that ten years I've got on you, but I don't have much get up and go today," he said with a wry grin.

"Sorry," she said, wincing.

"Don't be. I enjoyed every minute of it."

Smiling, she glanced over at him. "So did I."

"Do you think. . ."

"What?" she asked, suddenly breathless.

His face flushed with color that she found adorable. "Can I take you to dinner tonight?"

"I'd love that, but aren't you tired?"

He took her hand to help her up the short flight of stairs leading from the beach. "I have a feeling I'll get a second wind."

She smiled and didn't protest when he held on to her hand as they strolled across the parking lot to The Tower.

Liana took her time getting ready. While she was anxious to meet the man in her mother's life, she was almost desperate to see the man in *her* life again. The clock had never moved more slowly than it had today. She wore a form-fitting jersey dress with a plunging cowl neck and three-quarter sleeves in a color she knew was his favorite—a deep, dark burgundy.

Wait 'til he sees what's under this dress, she thought with a nervous giggle. Sliding on delicate black sling-backed heels, she ran her fingers through the thick dark hair that cascaded down her back. With one last glance in the mirror, Liana grabbed her purse, Travis's keys, and a bag she had packed so she could spend the night with him.

"Mom?" Liana said as she knocked on her mother's door.

The door opened.

"Oh, Mom, you're stunning," Liana said, approving of the black cocktail dress and high heels her mother had chosen.

"So are you," Agnes said with a light kiss to her daughter's cheek. "Travis will drool when he sees you."

"And David's going to faint when he sees you."

Agnes blushed. "Honestly, Liana."

Liana chuckled at her mother's embarrassment. "I'm going now. I'll see you there?"

Agnes snapped and unsnapped the clasp on her purse. "We'll be right along."

Liana put her hand over her mother's. "If you love him, I'll love him."

Agnes's eyes filled with tears. "Thank you," she said softly.

Liana kissed her mother goodbye. When she emerged from the house, the reporters sprang into action as she moved quickly toward the refuge of the car. She kicked off her shoes and drove the short distance barefooted.

Arriving at the club, she was rattled to notice a black car pull in just behind where she parked Travis's car in the spot reserved for "Mr. North." She darted under the burgundy awning and into the front door of the club before the two men in the car could follow her.

"Good evening, Ms. McDermott," a tuxedoed maitre d' said. "Right this way. Mr. North is waiting for you."

Liana felt the eyes of everyone in the room on her, but she had eyes only for the dark-haired man in a secluded booth in the corner of the large dining room.

He was on the phone but ended the call when he saw her coming. A pile of paper and a beer sat on the table in front of him. Pushing the pile aside, he stood up to greet her with a kiss to her cheek. "You're breathtaking," he whispered as he guided her into the booth ahead of him. He reached for her and with his back shielding them from the other diners, he clutched her hands and kissed her.

Liana wanted to weep from the relief of being with him again. When his tongue nudged at her lips she opened her mouth to allow him in. Her tongue met his in a burst of passion that quickly became urgent.

Travis tore his lips free of hers and gazed at her with an almost stunned expression on his face. "I missed you."

She smiled and ran her hand over his thigh.

He gasped when her forearm brushed his erection.

"So I see," she said, delighted by his reaction to her. "I missed you, too."

His jaw pulsed with tension. "I want to hustle you out of here and straight into bed," he whispered. "I think I saw a hint of something very interesting under this skin tight dress of yours, and since I can't wait for hours to see if it's true . . ." He reached for her leg and worked his hand up under her skirt, stopping short when he encountered the garter holding up her sheer thigh-high hose. "Oh, *Jesus*," he groaned.

"Later," she said, kissing his neck.

"Isn't your mom coming?" he asked after he had very reluctantly removed his hand from her leg and taken a long drink of his beer.

"It turns out you were right."

"About?"

"She *does* have a boyfriend."

Travis's smile lit up his face. "Really? Good for her."

"I hope it's okay that I asked him to join us."

"Of course it is." He brushed a finger over her bottom lip. "Why are you working that poor lip?"

"It's just that, well, I told her I was happy for her and encouraged her to bring him tonight."

"So then what's the problem, sweetheart?"

"I hope I'm ready to see her with someone else."

Travis brought her into his arms and held her tight against him. "I'll be right here with you."

She tipped her face up to kiss him. "That helps. Thank you. I also found out she doesn't have Alzheimer's."

"I told you that, too," he said with a satisfied grin.

"She's going to college! Can you believe it? She'll be done in May."

"That's amazing."

"I know. I couldn't believe it. What a relief it was to find that out."

"I'm sure it was."

She caressed his face. "I think I've decided."

He raised an amused eyebrow. "On?"

"Just a hint of stubble." She trailed her lips over his jaw. "I definitely prefer just a hint of stubble."

"I'll see what I can do about that," he said with a chuckle.

Remembering what she needed to ask him sobered her. "Did you see the junk on the Internet?"

"Maybe."

"Travis, I'm so sorry." She fought the lump that lodged in her throat. "What they wrote about you and your brother . . ."

He kissed her softly. "It's all right, sweetheart. I'm sorry I didn't tell you about Evan. I was going to."

"It's not all right! You shouldn't be forced into telling me personal things by the media. It's so outrageous."

"You'll be glad to know some good has come of all this."

Perplexed, she asked, "How?"

"The wedding photographer will be donating the hundred thousand dollars he got from the tabloid to the National Down's Syndrome Society—in the name of Evan North."

Liana gasped with amazement. "Really?"

"Uh huh," Travis said with a satisfied nod.

"And how did you manage that?"

"I reminded him of the confidentiality agreement everyone who works at North Point signs, threatened him with costly legal action, and let him know how many weddings will be held here in the next year. It didn't take him long to see the error of his ways." He reached for the pile of papers on the table and dug out a sleeve of negatives, which he handed to her. "All the photos of you—and us—from the wedding."

"Thank you."

"Thank *you*," he replied with another light kiss. "Because of you a very worthy cause is a little richer tonight."

"That feels good."

"Remember that feeling when you're thinking there's nothing else you can do but model."

Liana's heart contracted in her chest as she held his eyes for a long, intense moment. "I'll do that."

"I met your friend Jessie earlier."

"What'd you think of her?"

"She's gorgeous—but not as gorgeous as you, of course."

Liana smiled at his quick qualification.

"Beck seems quite taken with her and vice versa."

"She told me they sat up all night talking."

Travis's brow furrowed with concern. "He's been burned a couple of times, which has turned him into a bit of a love 'em and leave 'em type. She seems so fragile."

"I don't know her very well, but I have a feeling she's tougher than she looks."

"I had lunch with them. He could hardly take his eyes off her."

"Very interesting."

"Pardon me, Mr. North," the maitre d' said. "I'm sorry to interrupt, but the rest of your party has arrived. Shall I show them in?"

Travis gave Liana's hand a reassuring squeeze. "Yes, Stuart. Thank you."

They stood to greet Agnes and David, who was tall and distinguished looking with gray hair and bright blue eyes. He wore a dark suit and kept an arm around Agnes as they followed Stuart to the table.

Travis greeted Agnes with a kiss to her cheek. "It's nice to see you again, Agnes." He reached out to shake hands with David. "Travis North."

"David Leary. Nice to meet you."

"Likewise." Travis kept his arm around Liana. "I'm glad you were able to join us tonight."

"Honey, this is David. David, my daughter, Liana."

"It's a great pleasure to finally meet you, Liana." David held the hand she extended between both of his. "I've heard so much about you."

"I wish I could say the same," she said with an amused glance at her mother, who was suffering through the introductions.

"Well," Travis said, "I think we could all use a drink." He signaled the waiter and gestured for David and Agnes to be seated across from him and Liana.

"I know I could," Agnes said, and they all laughed.

They were enjoying a glass of port after dessert when Stuart returned to the table.

"I'm so sorry to disturb you, Mr. North, but you have an urgent phone call in the office."

"Will you please excuse me?" Travis asked.

"I hope everything's all right," Liana said.

"I'm sure it's nothing." He kissed her cheek. "I'll be right back."

Liana watched him cross the room and then shifted her eyes to find her mother and David watching her. "What?"

Agnes smiled. "You seem quite smitten, honey."

"Don't be ridiculous, Mother. We're just friends."

"Me thinks she doth protesteth too much," David said with an amused glance at Agnes.

"Me thinks she doesn't like you as much as she thought she did," Liana teased him.

David laughed. "He's an impressive young man."

"Yes." Liana trailed a finger over her wine glass. "He is that."

"You make such a striking couple," Agnes observed. "Your children would be gorgeous."

"*Mom!*"

Agnes chuckled and held up her hands to quiet her daughter. "Relax, honey. I'm just saying—"

"What?"

"He's perfect for you. That's all."

Amused, Liana said, "Don't hold back. Tell me how you really feel."

"All right. I will. You've become imprisoned by your career and the unwanted attention that comes with it. You've got reporters following you everywhere you go, and I think it's been a long time since you've enjoyed the work. That glamorous life doesn't suit you, honey. You don't fit into the crazy world you live in—you never have, and you never will."

When Liana began to object, her mother reached for her hand.

"You're too decent, too kind, too generous. It's time for you to settle down and have a family, and I can't think of a more ideal candidate for a husband than the man who's hardly taken his eyes off you all evening."

"Anything else?" Liana asked in a small voice.

"Yes, one more thing."

"I can't wait to hear this," Liana murmured.

"Since you're already in love with him, don't be a fool and pretend otherwise."

Before Liana could reply to that astounding statement, Travis returned to the table with a troubled look on his face. He slid in next to Liana.

"What is it?" she asked.

"Remember Niki, who you met the other night when we were trying to track down your mother?"

"She's the one who remembered Mom calling the cab," Liana said with a pointed look at her mother, who shrugged with chagrin.

"That's right. She's been in a pretty serious car accident."

"Oh, no, Travis! Is she all right?"

"She will be, but she broke her leg and a couple of ribs. She's in the hospital."

"That's terrible."

"She'll be out of commission for a couple of weeks," he said grimly. "I hate to think about work at a time like this, but she's overseeing weddings this weekend and next. I was so focused on Enid and Brady's wedding that I've had nothing to do with either of the next two."

"Can I help?" Liana asked.

He kissed the hand she had wrapped around his. "No, sweetheart. You're on vacation. Thank you, though."

"I want to," Liana insisted. "Surely there's something I can do to help. It'd be fun."

Travis studied her. "Do you really want to? It's a lot of work."

She nodded, surprised to realize just how much she wanted to help him if she could. That, coupled with her mother's observations, caused Liana's stomach to contract with nerves. *Am I in love with him?*

"Then I gratefully accept but only for a couple of hours a day. You need some down time while you're home."

Liana clapped her hands together. "When can I start?" She glanced over to find her mother and David looking smug and shot them a dirty look.

"Tomorrow," Travis said.

CHAPTER 12

After they said goodnight to her mother and David, Travis and Liana walked hand-in-hand along the boardwalk that lined the shore between the club and The Tower. The breeze off the water was warm and fragrant. A sliver of moon provided a slight glow to complement the soft lights on the boardwalk.

"Thank you for dinner," Liana said.

"It was my pleasure. David seems like a nice guy."

"Yes, he's lovely. He's exactly what I'd want for her."

"Now that the jig's up, he's probably going to want to marry her."

"I know."

"Is that okay with you?"

"Yes."

"Then why so sad?"

"I still miss my dad," Liana sighed. "We were always close, and even after seven years, it's still a shock to come home and realize he's not here anymore."

"He must've been very proud of you."

"He was, but I think he was also a little disappointed that I took the obvious and easy path by trading on my looks to make a living."

"What did he have in mind for you?"

"Nothing specific. I just always got the sense that he thought I could've done better."

"Well, maybe you'll find out what he meant one of these days."

"Maybe."

"In the meantime, there's nothing wrong with what you're doing now. It serves a purpose to the people you work for."

Liana smiled at him. "Actually, it's empty and shallow and vain. But I appreciate you trying to make it into something it's not."

They had reached a dark stretch on the boardwalk, and he pressed her back against the railing. "You look so incredibly beautiful tonight." He dropped soft kisses on her neck and jaw. "When I first saw you in the dining room, I almost stopped breathing. All I could think about was how lucky I was that you were coming to see me. And wearing my favorite color, too."

"I hoped you'd notice that."

His lips skimmed over hers, denying her the deeper kiss she craved. "I notice everything when it comes to you."

She reached up to hold him still. Using her lips, tongue, and teeth, she took possession of his mouth and was thrilled when a huge shiver of desire rippled through him. That she could have that effect on such a strong, handsome man was a powerful aphrodisiac.

"Liana," he whispered, holding her tight against him. "I want you so much I can't think of anything else."

Touched by his confession, she said, "You have me. For right now, for tonight, I'm yours, Travis."

"Let's go home."

They walked the short distance to The Tower. He kept her close to him in the elevator and when they arrived he walked her straight to his bedroom where he kissed her until she was weak. "Wait one second," he said.

She heard him moving around in the dark and startled when a match lit up the room. Liana watched him light two candles on his bedside table. "They weren't there this morning."

"I stole them from the club today so I could make love to you by candlelight."

"You're a romantic!" she said with delight.

He scoffed as he blew out the match and shed his suit coat. "That's worse than sensitive."

"All evidence points to a sensitive romantic." She giggled at the look of horror on his face as she tugged his tie free. "I like it."

"I like *you*." He reached for her and tightened his arms around her. "A whole lot."

She ran her fingers through his thick, dark hair. "I like you, too."

"Are you enjoying this little fling of ours?"

"More than I ever imagined I would," she said as she unbuttoned his shirt. "I'm so glad Enid picked you for me."

He laughed and dropped his pants. "What a bossy little brat she is."

"Hey! I love her."

"I love her, too." He unzipped Liana's dress. "After all, she's the one who put the idea of a sweaty fling in your head."

"Yes, she did."

His eyes smoldered when he unveiled the racy black bra, panties, and garter belt she had on under the dress. Staring at her, he swallowed hard. "And for that I shall be eternally grateful."

"Eternally?" she teased.

"Maybe."

"Travis . . ."

"Don't worry, sweetheart. I know it's a fling." He ran his hands over her, making her tremble with desire. "But damn, you're a total goddess in this get up. I don't even know where to begin. I want to touch you everywhere, and then taste you, and then nibble on a few very strategic places."

She released a nervous laugh as the intense look on his face made her stomach flutter.

He left a hot trail of kisses from her neck to her breasts to her belly.

Liana closed her eyes and let the pleasure take over. Her fingers found his hair and held on while he kissed the place where garter met stocking.

He released the garter and rolled the stocking down her leg with maddening patience before he moved on to the other leg. "I can honestly say," he whispered, dragging his tongue over the back of her knee, "that I've never seen anything sexier than you in black garters."

Trying to keep her knees from buckling and not wanting him to stop what he was doing, she didn't say anything. Besides, she couldn't have spoken just then if her life had depended on it.

"Are you the same girl who said you don't know anything about flirting and flinging?" he asked with his lips pressed to her inner thigh. In one swift move, he removed her panties and the garter belt. "It seems to me that a girl who owns such scandalous underwear knows something about both."

"I got to keep it after a catalog shoot," she said breathlessly. "Even though it was too warm for hose tonight, I thought you might enjoy the garters."

"You thought right, but I hate the idea of anyone else seeing you like this. I'm going to have to track down every copy of that catalog."

She didn't even notice that he had eased her down to the edge of the bed. A moment later, though, he had her full attention when he spread her legs and buried his face between them. She was so ready for him that it took just a few strokes of his tongue to send her spiraling into orgasm. She was still coming when he rolled on a condom and entered her with one swift thrust of his hips.

He released the front clasp of her bra and filled his hands with her breasts as he withdrew almost completely and then filled her again.

Liana gasped from the impact and clutched his backside to keep him inside her. For added insurance, she wrapped her long legs around him, which seemed to make him a little crazy.

He tugged her nipple into his mouth, and she came again with a deep moan of pleasure.

"*Liana*," he cried. "Oh, God, Liana . . ."

She held him tight against her with her arms and legs as he threw his head back and came with his eyes closed and his jaw clenched with tension.

He slumped down on top of her breathing heavily against her neck.

Liana brushed the hair off his damp forehead and kissed his face. *Mom's right. I love him. How could I not love him? But I was the one who insisted on the emotionless affair, so he can't know that I've broken all my own rules.* She closed her eyes against a rush of emotion and tightened her hold on him.

So, Travis thought as he rested on top of her, this is love. *This is what it feels like to find the missing piece and to realize you'll never be the same—that you'll never be whole again without her.* Never in his life had he experienced the complete loss of control that occurred when he was with her. Never. When she wrapped those endless legs around him . . . The memory made him tremble, and she held him closer.

"Am I crushing you?"

"No." She used her lips to deal with a stray strand of hair on his forehead.

The tender gesture filled his heart, and it was all he could do not to tell her he loved her. He had to remember that she didn't want that. She wanted a sweaty fling, and he'd promised her that with no emotion, no talk of tomorrow, nothing but right now. If he started talking about love, he would ruin their fling, and he'd lose her before he had the chance to show her what they could have together.

No, he would keep his feelings to himself and use the time they had left to make himself essential to her. That was his only hope. And if, at the end of their two weeks together, he hadn't done enough, well, then he'd spend the rest of his life missing her.

Beck walked around to the passenger side of his truck to open the door for Jessie. He had spent part of the afternoon cleaning his company truck while wishing he had a better vehicle to take her out in. But she hadn't seemed to mind. She was easy to please, which was both unexpected and charming. He had planned to take her to a fancy restaurant, but she'd asked if they could get take out and go to the beach instead. Knowing she loved the beach, he'd been happy to oblige and had to admit they'd had a lot more fun eating on the sand than they would have had in a stuffy restaurant.

"Next time we'll bring bathing suits," she said as he helped her out of the truck.

Her blond corkscrew curls brushed against his hand, and he wanted so badly to twirl one of them around his finger. At her mention of next time, his heart skipped a happy beat. "Definitely." He had been relieved to get her off the property and back in without rousing the interest of the reporters staked out at the gate, hoping for a glimpse of Liana and Travis.

Jessie tucked her hand in the crook of his arm. "Thank you for such a nice time tonight. I haven't had this much fun or been this relaxed in longer than I can remember."

"Me either," he said. "We've had some issues with vandals here on the property lately. I've been really stressed out about it."

"I'm sorry to hear that."

"I hate to let Travis down, you know?" He was surprised by how easy it was to confide in her—how easy everything seemed to be with her.

"I'm sure he doesn't see it that way. He knows you're doing everything you can."

He held the elevator door and stepped in after her. "Doesn't seem to be enough, though. Somehow they keep getting in, despite everything we're doing to stop them." He watched her swallow hard and wanted to shoot himself for being so stupid. "You don't need to be worried that he's going to find you here, Jessie. I'm sorry I mentioned the vandalism. I wasn't thinking."

"It's okay." She looked up at him with those bottomless blue eyes. "I just hate to add to your burden. You've got enough going on without having to baby-sit me, too."

He smiled. "Babysitting you is a real hardship, Ms. Stone."

Her eyes twinkled with mirth as she dug out the key to her apartment. Sounding just like Scarlet O'Hara herself, Jessie said, "Why you're just a regular charmer, Mr. Beck."

Taking the key from her, he opened the door. When he went to give it back to her, she surprised him by wrapping her hand around his.

"Can you come in for a bit?"

Struck dumb, he could only stare at her exquisite face. "I, ah, I should probably get home. We could both use some sleep." He had the best of intentions, really he did. She had come here seeking refuge from a man who was harassing her. The last thing Beck wanted to do was complicate her life any more than it already was. But when she looped her arms around his neck and leaned her lush body into his, he did what any man in that situation would have done—he dipped his head and fused his lips to hers.

Everything about that kiss rocked his world. From the way she pressed herself against him to the timid strokes of her tongue against his, from the mewling sounds that came from the back of her throat to her fingers spooling through his hair, Beck had never experienced anything quite like kissing Jessie Stone. The fragrance that reminded him of soft summer flowers drifted through his senses as he held her close to him and tried to rein in the overwhelming urge to plunder.

"Mmm," she sighed against his lips. "You're good at that."

He laughed. Damn, she was cute! And young—far too young for him, if he were being honest. The thought sobered him. He drew back from her. "I should get going."

"Oh." She released him and stepped back. "I'm sorry. I'm not usually so forward. I don't know what I was thinking."

"You weren't forward. I wanted that as much as you did—maybe even more."

"Then what's wrong?"

"I'm ten years older than you. You're here because you're trying to get away from a guy who's hassling you. This isn't what you need right now."

Her soft blue eyes hardened. "Aren't you presumptuous to be telling me what I need. Didn't you just meet me yesterday?"

Surprised to find a hell of a backbone under her genteel Southern exterior, he marveled at the transformation from magnolia to steel magnolia. "You're right. I'm sorry."

"Well, that's not fair," she huffed. "I was working up a good mad, and you just ruined it."

"You're a hell of a woman, Jessie Stone," he said with a chuckle as he reached out to caress her cheek. "And I'm still too old for you."

She reached for the hand that caressed her face and tugged him into the apartment, kicking the door closed behind them. Steering him to the sofa, she pushed him down and then sat on the coffee table to face him. "I've been on my own since I was fifteen."

"Why so young?"

She studied him and appeared to be deciding something. "I don't talk about this. Ever."

"You don't have to now."

"I know, but for some reason I want to."

Touched by her candor, he reached for her hand and laced his fingers through hers.

"My stepfather abused me."

Beck gasped. "Jessie. . ."

She paused for a long moment, as if she were gathering her thoughts. "He was so nice to me when he and my mother were dating. Brought me presents, took me places I'd never been, and treated me like a princess. He even called me that—princess."

Riveted by her softly spoken words and filled with anxiety over where this was leading, Beck watched her retreat into herself and her memories.

"I developed early," she said, a faint blush coloring her cheeks. "That summer, I noticed him watching me with this funny look on his face. I didn't know what it meant." Her voice trailed off. She continued in what was barely more than a whisper. "The bad stuff started when I was twelve. At first, I remember being shocked and confused and scared. Really, really scared."

Beck cleared the huge lump from his throat. "You couldn't tell your mother?"

She smiled, but it didn't reach eyes that had taken on a dull, flat hue. "She didn't believe me. She said I was jealous of her."

"Oh, honey. I'm so sorry."

Jessie shrugged, and the helpless gesture tugged at his already over-involved heart. "I've come to understand that she needed her marriage to work more than she needed to protect me."

He reached for her and brought her onto his lap. "She totally failed you."

Jessie rested her head on his shoulder. "I know, and that's why I couldn't fail myself. I was already doing some local modeling. I saved every dime I made. When I was fifteen, I took the bus to New York, and I've never looked back."

So for three years she put up with that monster's abuse, he thought. "I can't imagine being alone in that city at fifteen."

"It was scary, but not as scary as wondering what kind of mood my stepfather would be in when he got home at night. That was much scarier."

On the verge of vowing to make sure she would never be hurt by anyone ever again, Beck held her close to him.

"I got lucky with a few good modeling jobs early on, despite the fact that I looked even younger than I was. I'm told I still do."

"Except for in pictures. You look much older."

"I've decided that being young looking isn't such a bad thing in my business. Anyway, I made enough to lease a studio apartment, and I waited tables to fill in the gaps. Three years ago, I landed Artie as my agent and things really took off. I got Victoria's Secret and then *Sports Illustrated*. Everything's been kind of crazy since then, and not necessarily in a good way." Her face clouded, and he knew she was thinking of her stalker.

"Be careful what you wish for?"

"Exactly!" She seemed pleased he understood. "I've been lucky so far with the media. People don't recognize me away from work, so I don't have to deal with the insanity the way Liana does. I don't know how she can stand it."

"From what Travis says, she can't." He toyed with her fingers. "What about your mother and stepfather?"

"I haven't spoken to either of them since I left home. I've heard they're still together, but my mother has aged tremendously. She must know that if I was willing to walk away and never look back, that I wasn't lying to her."

"And yet she stays with him, knowing what he did to her daughter. It's disgusting."

"I'm sorry," she said. "You're upset. I shouldn't have told you this."

"Don't apologize to me, honey. You've got nothing to apologize for. I'd like to go find him and show him what happens to guys who pick on defenseless kids."

She smiled.

"What's so amusing?"

"You." With her hand on his face, she turned him toward her and kissed him. "Thank you for being mad on my behalf."

"Mad doesn't begin to describe what I am. Have you ever thought about reporting him? There's no statute of limitation on child abuse."

She shook her head. "I'd never want to revisit that chapter of my life."

"What if he didn't stop with you? What if there were others?" Beck could tell by her pained expression that she'd considered the possibility.

"I've spent a lot of years in therapy and worked really hard to distance myself from it. It's a big deal for me to even be able to talk about it. I don't think I could report it, even though I know I probably should."

"I understand. I'm not trying to make it harder on you. That's the last thing I want."

She nuzzled into his neck, rendering him paralyzed when her lips brushed against his skin. "You smell good," she whispered. "So good."

"Jessie—"

"Yes?"

He swallowed. "You're making it really hard for me to remember I'm trying to be a good guy and do the right thing by you."

Giggling, she squirmed against his erection.

He gasped.

"You weren't kidding."

He knew if he didn't get out of there in the next thirty seconds, he was going to do something he'd regret in the morning. "I should go." With his hands on her hips, he eased her up and off his lap and stood up.

"I've had trouble," she said, biting on her thumbnail as she looked up at him.

"With?"

"Men. Sex. I get to 'the moment' and can't bring myself to actually go through with it."

"So, you've never. . . With anyone else?"

She shook her head.

"Jessie," he said on a long exhale.

"I want it to be you." The words tumbled out fast, as if she was afraid she would chicken out if she didn't get it said quickly. "I want you to be the one to show me how it's supposed to be."

"But you don't even know me—"

"I know you, Peter." She rested her hands on his chest. "When I first saw you last night, do you know what I thought?"

Incapable of speech, he shook his head.

"There he is. He's the one. I've never felt anything quite so clearly."

Astounded that she had experienced the same powerful sensation of acute aware-ness, Beck placed his hands on her shoulders. "I'm honored, honey. You have no idea *how* honored I am."

She stepped back from him. "But you don't want me."

"Don't want you?" he asked, incredulous. "Are you serious? Any guy would *want* you."

"I don't want any guy. I want *you*."

He scrubbed his fingers through his short blond hair, realizing he was bungling what would no doubt go down as one of the most important moments of his life. Reaching for her, he wrapped his arms around her and propped his chin on the top of her head. "I have a suggestion."

"I'm listening."

He wondered if she purposely brushed her lips against his throat. "I propose we see each other for the next week. If you still feel the same way, I'll consider it."

"No."

"Why not?" he asked, startled by her vehemence.

She looked up at him. "We'll see each other for the next week, I'll still feel the same way, and you'll not consider anything. You'll act."

"Act?"

"*Act*," she said with a coy smile.

"Are you always this bossy?" he asked, amused and more intrigued by her with every passing moment.

"I've been running my own show for a long time, buddy. I know what I want, and I know how to get it."

"I'm a little bit afraid of you right now." *And a whole lot turned on,* he thought.

She tossed her head back and laughed.

As he watched her, he saw in her both a carefree girl and a woman wise beyond her years. That she had set her sights on him was nothing short of amazing.

"Will it bother you if I call you Peter? Since we plan to sleep together, I don't feel right calling you by your last name."

"Nobody calls me that, but you can if you want to. So we have a deal?"

She went up on tiptoes to kiss him. "You bet we do."

CHAPTER 13

Liana was sleeping in Travis's arms when a flash of lightning followed by a crack of thunder awakened her. Through the big windows, she watched the lightening streak across the sky and remembered hundreds of summer thunderstorms from her childhood. Back then she would run into her parents' bed, jump in between them, and pull the covers up over her head until the storm passed. Now all she could do was hope the storm would move quickly. She focused on breathing in and out to slow the pounding of her heart until a huge clap of thunder directly overhead caused her to cry out.

"What's wrong, sweetheart?" Travis asked in a sleepy voice.

"Nothing," Liana squeaked.

"Baby, your heart's pounding."

Another loud clap of thunder shook the room.

"Is it the storm?"

She nodded.

"Come here." He turned her into his chest and held her tight against him. "Better?"

"Yeah," she whispered. "I'm sorry I woke you."

He ran a soothing hand over her long hair. "Um, I think it might've been the huge crash of thunder that woke me. Have you always been afraid of it?"

She nodded again.

"Maybe it's time we change your memories of thunder and lightening," he said with that devastating grin of his as another bolt of lightening sent a blue glow flashing through the room.

"And how do we do that?"

He shifted her so she was on top of him and massaged her shoulders and then her back.

Liana sighed with relief as the tension and fear left her body.

With the next thunderclap, he kissed her tenderly. "How are we doing?" he whispered against her lips.

"Better."

"The next time you're afraid of a thunderstorm, maybe you'll think of being here with me and that'll take your mind off it."

"I can do that," she said, not wanting to think of being anywhere but with him. She tensed when another bolt of lightening streaked across the sky.

"It's okay, sweetheart," he whispered, his arms tightening around her. "You're safe with me, remember?"

So overwhelmed with love for him, she could only nod and then sigh with contentment when he pressed his lips to her forehead. Even though he was aroused he did nothing more than hold her close and whisper soft words of comfort as the storm began to subside. By the time the rumble of thunder was further away and the lightening less frequent, Liana wasn't afraid anymore.

"Thank you." She caressed his face and kissed him.

"For what?"

"For being sensitive and taking care of me."

He groaned. "You're not going to let that one go, are you?"

"Not with such strong evidence to support my argument."

"You should have been an attorney."

"You're going to be beat tomorrow."

"I don't care," he said.

"Well, *I* have to work tomorrow, so we need to go back to sleep."

"You don't *have* to work."

"We've already covered that. I want to."

Rolling onto his side, he took her with him. "The bride won't believe who her new wedding coordinator is." He kissed her lightly and tugged her closer. "If I were her, I'd be worried about being shown up by the staff."

Liana scoffed. "No one will be looking anywhere but at the bride."

"I know where I'll be looking, and it won't be at the bride. Thank you so much for pitching in."

"I'm looking forward to it. It really sounds like fun."

"We'll go see Niki in the hospital tomorrow, and she'll tell us what we need to do."

Liana yawned. "Okay, boss."

Travis laughed. "I think I'm going to enjoy this."

Liana smiled and the soft caress of his chest hair against her face was the last thing she felt before sleep took over.

The next morning, Liana was glad she had packed a skirt and top that would be appropriate to wear to work. *Work!* The idea of going to work in an office—Travis's office—gave Liana the giggles as she picked up her hairbrush.

Travis snuck up behind her and startled her when he kissed her neck. "Are you thinking about my sexual prowess again?"

She laughed. "Not this time."

He took the brush from her and ran it gently through her silky hair.

Liana tipped her head back to encourage him. In the mirror she watched him and was unnerved by the raw desire she saw on his face.

"What were you laughing about?" he asked, continuing the long, slow strokes through her hair.

"Going to work with you—in an office. Another thing I haven't done before."

"I'm never going to be able to concentrate with you around."

She turned to him. Today he wore a burgundy North Point polo shirt with khaki shorts. "I expect to be treated like any other employee," she said with mock sternness.

"Sure, sweetheart." He reached out to touch the hair he had brushed. "Whatever you want."

Liana waited for him to kiss her, but he didn't.

"Are you ready to go?"

"Yes," Liana said, puzzled by his sudden withdrawal. "Is everything all right?"

"Why wouldn't it be?" He took her hand to lead her out of the bathroom. "The paparazzi will probably follow us to the hospital, but I think we should just ignore them."

"The pictures will be everywhere," she warned him.

"I don't care if you don't."

His tone was so businesslike, almost cold, that Liana felt a trickle of fear work its way down her spine. He was retreating from her. After the tender way he had cared for her during the storm, the loss hurt. "Travis?" She worked hard to keep the disappointment out of her voice.

He slid his wallet into his back pocket, picked up his keys, and turned to her.

She closed the small distance between them and put her hands on his shoulders. His dark eyes were unreadable as she went up on tiptoes to kiss him. His lips were rigid with resistance until her tongue glided over his bottom lip. With his hands on her waist, he dragged her to him and tilted his head to kiss her with what felt like desperate need.

"Liana," he whispered against her lips.

"What is it?" she asked, her hands on his face.

When words seemed to fail him, he reached for her hands and held on tight.

"Travis, is something wrong?"

The quick, charming smile she'd become accustomed to returned as suddenly as it had left. "No," he said with a final kiss. "Nothing's wrong. Let's go see Niki and figure out what we've got to do in the next two days."

Liana wasn't convinced, but she went with him anyway.

In the car, Travis focused on evading the media that followed them when they left North Point on the way to Newport Hospital. Concentrating on driving was better than thinking about what had almost happened in the bathroom. Brushing her hair had been so intimate, almost even more so than making love, that he'd been swamped with want—not the physical kind but the emotional kind.

He wanted her to love him. All at once he wanted her love so badly he ached more than he ever had when he had only wanted her physically. He'd almost told her he loved her. The effort not to had been painful and apparently obvious to her, for she'd tuned right into his dismay. That she read him so well and so easily was both frightening and exhilarating.

During the storm, he had been touched by her courage as she tried to combat her fear. He hated imagining her in some luxurious hotel room suffering through a thunderstorm alone. He wanted to always be there to make her feel safe and loved.

What was I doing a week ago today before I knew her? I have no idea. What will I be doing two weeks from today when she's gone? I can't imagine . . .

Liana reached for his hand and laced her fingers through his. "What's going on over there?"

He smiled and squeezed her hand. "Just thinking about the wedding this weekend. We're meeting with the bride and groom at two to go over everything one last time. I'm sure Niki has it all under control, but there are probably a few last-minute things to tend to."

"I'm sure we can handle it."

He glanced over at her, knowing he could handle anything with her by his side. "I have no doubt."

When they arrived at the hospital, Liana suggested he drop her off at the door and then come in after her so the photographers couldn't get a shot of them together. But Travis refused to sneak around like they had something to hide. He parked the car and took her by the hand to walk through the crowd of photographers.

Liana fought the urge to cringe as she imagined the headlines. Reporters called out questions to them, but they pushed their way through without answering.

"Is it me or are there more of them than there were yesterday?" Liana asked once they were inside.

"A lot more. I should've brought a couple of guys with us."

Liana cast a glance over her shoulder. "There were two men following me yesterday. I forgot about that until right now."

Travis cleared his throat. "They might've been the guys I assigned to keep an eye on you in case the press got unruly."

"Travis! I told you I didn't want that!"

"I know, sweetheart. But I was worried that once they realized they had a story here it might get crazy." He gestured to the crush of reporters outside the main door of the hospital. "Looks like I was right. Forgive me?"

"For wanting to keep me safe? I think I can forgive that." As they walked to the elevator, she said, "I've never understood what they find so interesting about me. I'm just a model. I don't act or sing or dance. I'm actually pretty boring when it comes right down to it."

"Boring?" Travis laughed. "You're the most fascinating person I've ever known, and they're probably interested in you because you've never given them anything to chew on—or at least you hadn't until now—so they're left to speculate on that glamorous life of yours."

"Did you know who I was when you saw me at Enid's wedding?"

Travis flashed her an embarrassed grin. "I knew I had seen you somewhere before, but one of the twenty-something waiters had to connect the dots for me."

Liana laughed. "Why do I believe that?"

"It's never been about your public image to me, Liana."

She slipped her hand through the crook in his elbow. "I know."

Niki was in pain but relieved to see them since she'd been worried about the upcoming weddings. She gave them a long list of final details that needed to be addressed and filled them in on where to find everything in her office.

"Don't worry about anything, Niki." Travis squeezed her hand. "Just focus on getting better."

"I had no idea," Liana said when they were in the hallway.

"About?"

"How many details there'd be."

"Weddings are pretty involved, although thankfully for us, most are not as involved as Enid's was." He rolled his eyes. "You want to talk details?"

Liana laughed. "I can only imagine."

"You're sure you're up for this?"

Her eyes sparkled with excitement. "I can't wait."

In the lobby they were dismayed to find the press corps had grown during their hour-long visit with Niki.

"Why don't we find a side door and sneak out," he said.

She took his hand. "No."

"No?"

She shook her head. "Maybe if we give them a little something, they'll get their story and leave."

Travis raised a skeptical eyebrow. "You think so?"

"Not really."

He laughed and followed her into the maelstrom.

Travis was right. The bride, Justine, and her fiancé, Tom, were star struck when they found out who would be taking over their final wedding preparations. Liana had read their file and sat with the couple to go over every detail, from the arrival of the bridal party to the departure of the last guest. She asked a hundred questions and took tons of notes. By the time their meeting concluded, Justine and Tom had almost forgotten who she was.

Almost.

When Liana looked up from her notes to glance at Travis across the table her heart skipped an erratic beat. The expression on his face reminded her an awful lot of the way Brady had looked at Enid at their wedding. *Is it possible? Could he love me? No, Liana, don't be foolish. He's grateful. That's all it is.*

She cleared her throat and forced her wandering mind back to the task at hand. "Um, Travis, do you have any final questions for Justine and Tom? Did I forget anything?"

His eyes danced with amusement. "It seems you have everything covered."

Liana gathered the papers into a neat pile. "We're going to make sure everything runs smoothly. You just enjoy your day and try not to worry."

Justine and Tom exchanged glances.

"Do you think," she said tentatively, "that we could have your autograph?"

Liana smiled. "Of course."

Justine reached into her purse and produced a copy of their wedding invitation. She slid it across the table.

Liana turned it over and wrote several lines before she signed her name and returned it to Justine.

"Thank you so much," Justine said.

"My pleasure. We'll see you Saturday. Call the office if you need to speak with either of us before the wedding."

Travis and Liana walked them out, and when they were gone he turned to her.

Liana rolled her lip between her teeth as a flurry of details and questions floated around in her mind.

Travis poked lightly at her abused lip. "Why don't you give that poor lip a break and tell me what's on your mind?"

"I just can't believe how much goes into a wedding. I've never once considered what happens behind the scenes. You figure there's food, drinks, flowers, music, cake. What's hard about that?"

Travis laughed and put his arm around her to lead her to his office. "It gets complicated when the tablecloths have to be an exact shade of apricot and the crab has to come from Alaska and the fresh flowers for the cake are delivered separately from the table arrangements and the band needs fresh-squeezed orange juice backstage." He closed the office door and gathered her into his arms. "I'd understand if you wanted to back out."

"Don't be ridiculous."

She rested against him and swayed to a Sinatra song that played on the club's sound system. "I do have just one question," she said after several quiet minutes.

"And I have just one answer, but first I need this." His kiss was deep and searching, his fingers spooling through her hair. "You can't get so busy that you forget about our fling, do you hear me?"

"Yes, boss."

He smiled and kissed her again. "Okay," he said between kisses. "I think I'm ready for your question."

Liana caressed the light dusting of stubble he had left on his jaw just for her. "What do we do first?"

Travis laughed and hugged her to him.

CHAPTER 14

Jessie took her coffee to the patio that overlooked the sparkling blue bay. Everything was so beautiful here—from the water to the beach to the flowers and landscaping at North Point. Fascinated, she watched a lone sailboat make its way across the span of water and disappear around the tip of one of the islands.

From the moment she arrived, she had been swamped with the sensation that she could spend the rest of her life right here and never want for anything. Having been uprooted from her home at such a young age, she hadn't felt at home anywhere since—that is until she came here.

She knew she should be ashamed of the way she had thrown herself at Peter, but somehow she couldn't quite seem to get there. He wanted her just as badly as she wanted him. If she'd had any doubt about that, she never would have asked him to be "the one." She had a feeling that with him it would be different—everything would be different.

God, I really hope so, she thought with a sigh. *I don't know how much longer I can go on the way I am.* As she imagined Peter naked and ready, her whole body hummed with pent-up desire. And curiosity. Crossing her legs tight in an attempt to curb the throbbing, she longed to get in on the secret every other woman seemed to already know. She had no trouble prancing down the runway in scraps of lace that screamed S-E-X, but was unable to actually experience the act itself.

Since this whole business with the stalker began, she'd retreated even further into herself until desire and frustration reached epic levels. *Poor Peter,* she thought with a giggle. *He has no idea what he's signed on for.*

The doorbell rang, and she got up to answer it, despite the fact that she wore only the thigh-length nightshirt she'd slept in. Checking the peephole, she was hit with a flush of delight when she saw who was there.

Her heart raced as she opened the door to find Peter holding a bunch of wildflowers. "Morning," he said, running his eyes over her with appreciation. Today with his trademark khaki shorts he wore a white polo shirt with the burgundy North Point logo embroidered on the left side. The white shirt offset his deep tan, and she noticed upon quick inspection that he hadn't bothered to shave that morning. The light dusting of gold whiskers only made him sexier—if that was possible.

She took the flowers he offered. "They're beautiful." Waving him in, she went to the kitchen to find a vase. "Thank you."

"I picked them myself."

"That's very sweet." She filled a vase with water and arranged the fragrant flowers to her liking. Turning, she was startled to find him standing right behind her.

As if she were weightless, he lifted her onto the counter. Wrapping her legs around his waist, he pulled her in tight against his instant erection.

Breathless with anticipation, Jessie clutched his broad shoulders, dying to know what he had planned for her.

He dipped his head and captured her earlobe between his teeth. "I couldn't sleep last night," he said, his voice husky with desire. "All I could think about was you and wanting you."

"It was your big idea to wait a week," she reminded him.

His lips hovered over hers. "Tell me again why I thought that was such a great idea?"

She licked her bottom lip and watched his blue eyes turn to flame. "I can't remember."

Nudging at her mouth, he replaced her tongue with his. "Sweet Jessie. I could just devour you."

"Don't let me stop you."

Pressing his erection into the V of her legs, he crushed his mouth to hers. The assault of lips, tongue, and teeth had her body throbbing with need. His tongue mated with hers in a sexy, sinful dance that made her nipples hard and her panties damp.

He turned his attention to her neck, and when he closed his teeth over the sensitive tendon that joined neck to shoulder, she cried out.

"Sorry," he mumbled, drawing back from her.

She tightened her hold on him. "Didn't hurt," she said, panting. "Do it again."

He ran his hands right up under her shirt and cupped her bare breasts as he clamped down once again on the tendon.

Jessie had never before felt the need to come quite as acutely as she did just then. "Peter. . . I need. . . *Please.*"

He ran his thumbs back and forth over her painfully hard nipples. And then he scooped her up and carried her into the living room. As they landed on the sofa his mouth took furious possession of hers.

Jessie sank her fingers into his hair and anchored him to her.

With a fierce growl, he parted her legs and shifted to bring his erection up tight against her.

Her shirt flew up and over her head, leaving her naked except for the two scraps of silk that made up her panties.

Before she had time to prepare herself, he cupped her breasts and bent to suck hard on one nipple and then the other.

Jessie raised her hips to seek him.

As he laved at her breasts, his big hand cupped her bottom. He gripped the back of her panties and tugged. They ripped apart like they were made of paper, and he tossed them aside.

Jessie burned from the inside out. She had gotten this far with other men, but none of them had made her *want* the way she wanted this one. Bringing him back up to her, she pressed her face into the curve of his neck and breathed in the fresh, clean, masculine scent of him.

His hand coasted down the front of her, stopping to pay respect to her breasts before continuing its downward journey.

Jessie squirmed and worked her legs apart to give him access to where she wanted him more than she'd ever wanted anyone else. She felt hot all over and on the verge of something big and powerful. "Please. . ."

His fingers slipped into the heat between her legs. "Oh, God," he moaned, his face pressed to her neck. "Jessie. *God.*" Using his leg to spread hers, he slid a finger into her.

Unable to stop herself, she pushed hard against his invading finger.

He added a second finger and rubbed his thumb over the place that throbbed for him.

Jessie's world imploded. The sensations rocketed through her, from fingertips to toes and everywhere in between. He stayed with her through the whole thing, and then coaxed her up again into a second, more powerful release. Her cheeks were wet with tears by the time he finally withdrew his hand. He had reduced her to a trembling, shaking shell of her former self. Whatever he had done, he had changed her forever.

"You're so beautiful," he whispered. "The most beautiful woman I've ever known. I want to bury myself inside you more than I want the next breath."

"Yes," she said. "*Yes.*"

"I want to lick you." He returned his hand to her over-stimulated sex. "Right here."

Raising her hips against his questing hand, she moaned. No one had ever said such things to her, and the vision of his face buried between her legs was almost more than she could bear.

A ragged deep breath rattled through his big frame, and he rested his head on her shoulder. "This isn't why I came over. I wasn't even going to kiss you."

Laughing, she said, "And yet somehow I ended up naked on the sofa while you're still fully dressed." She tugged his shirt out of his shorts and raked her fingernails over his back. "That doesn't seem fair."

He trembled from her touch. "I need to get back to work."

"Okay," she said but didn't let him go. Instead she sent her hand straight into the back of his shorts. When he raised himself up to protest, she took advantage of the opportunity to slide her hand around to the front.

His gasp turned to a groan as she gripped his throbbing length and stroked him. "Jessie. . . *Jesus.*"

She smiled at his reaction to the light drag of her fingernail. "I want to give you the same thing you gave me," she whispered, awestruck by the size, the weight, the width. Imagining him buried to the hilt in her, she quivered.

"Later." He tried to remove her hand, but she held on tighter.

"Now." With her free hand she released his belt and unzipped him. "Sit up."

"Jessie, wait. Honey. . ."

She pushed on his shoulders to arrange him the way she wanted him and pulled his shorts down to his thighs. Naked and full of her own power, she hovered over him and took a moment to appreciate his long, thick penis. Wrapping her hand around him, she began to stroke.

His eyes closed, and he let his head fall back in surrender.

Since he wasn't looking, it was all she could do not to straddle him and take him deep inside her. But they had a deal, so instead she ran her finger through the pearly fluid that had gathered at the tip. When she replaced her finger with her tongue, he almost levitated off the sofa. Lowering herself to hold him in place, she took him into her mouth.

His sharp intake of breath encouraged her and fired her with a kind of passion she couldn't remember ever experiencing. Giving, it seemed, was every bit as exciting as receiving.

Jessie moved her lips slowly up and down, sweeping her tongue over him as she went. She had only done this once before and had no idea if she was doing it right.

But then his fingers slid into her hair, and she felt his hands tremble. Apparently, she was doing something right. "Is that good?" she whispered.

"*So* good. So amazing. But you should stop before we make a mess."

"I'm not stopping *until* we make a mess."

"Christ," he muttered, pulling up his shirt to remove it from the line of fire.

She took him as deep as she could, sliding him into her throat and lashing him with her tongue.

He raised his hips, up and down, making love to her mouth.

Sliding her free hand down, she cupped his sac and squeezed lightly.

Crying out, he surged once more and sent a warm stream of semen flooding into her throat.

Jessie struggled to swallow it all, but some of the fluid escaped out the corners of her mouth. She wiped it away with her hand and then collapsed against his chest.

Still breathing hard, his hand curled around her head in a protective, appreciative gesture. "Have you ever done that before, honey?"

"Not the whole thing."

"I've never had better."

Ridiculously pleased, she glanced up at him. "Really?"

"Swear to God. Nothing has ever been that good."

She nudged his shirt up and flicked her tongue over his nipple. "Are you *sure* we have to wait a whole week to get to the good stuff?"

He groaned, and his cell phone rang in his shorts pocket.

Jessie retrieved it and handed it to him.

"This is Beck." As he listened, she watched his relaxed face tighten with tension. "I'll be there in a minute." He closed the phone and returned his attention to her. "I have to go. We've got unruly reporters at the gate—way more than yesterday."

Jessie started to get up, but he stopped her. With his hands cupping her face, he studied her for a long moment. "I think I'll bring you flowers tomorrow, too."

She giggled and reached for her nightshirt, her body thrumming with aftershocks and the need for more. Knowing she wouldn't be satisfied until she had all of him, she tugged on her shirt and watched him adjust his own clothes. "Can I make you dinner tonight?"

"I'd love that."

"Thanks for the flowers. And the orgasms."

He laughed. "Entirely my pleasure." Pressing his lips to hers, he added, "Many more where those came from."

"I can't wait."

His heart still beating fast like it did whenever he was near Jessie, Beck took the elevator to the garage to find Travis emerging from his car.

"Hey," Travis said. "What've you been up to?"

"Nothing. Why?"

Travis looked him up and down. "Your face is kind of red."

Beck shrugged. For whatever reason, he wasn't ready to tell his friend about what was happening with Jessie.

"How's Jessie?"

"Fine. Why?"

"Jeez," Travis said, laughing. "What's with you?"

"Nothing."

Travis propped his hands on his hips. "What gives, Beck?"

Since he couldn't very well tell his friend and boss that he'd just been on the receiving end of the most incredible blowjob from the woman he was supposed to be keeping an eye on, he decided to wing it. "We've got press everywhere."

"I know. It just took me ten minutes to get through the gate."

"Sorry. I've got four men out there, but I can't spare any more off the patrols with the vandalism."

"If you need to call in extra help, do it. I don't want Liana—or Jessie—bothered while they're here."

Beck wondered if what he had just done with Jessie counted as *bothering*. "I don't either."

Travis took another long look at him. "You're sure everything's okay?"

"Couldn't be better." That much was true.

"All right then. I'll see you later."

Beck started for the gate. "See ya."

He spent the rest of the day managing the crowd at the gate, meeting with his staff to ensure the regular patrols of the property were continuing undeterred despite the media onslaught, and trying not to think about Jessie every minute. By six o'clock, he was tight with tension that he blamed on the Southern belle residing temporarily on the fifth floor of The Tower.

Holding his head in his hands, he wondered if there was some way he could get out of dinner. He needed to take a step back to try and find his lost sanity.

"Beck?" Liana said from the doorway.

Startled, he looked up at her. "Oh, hey. How's it going?"

"Are you all right?"

"Sure. What's up?"

Her long dark hair had been corralled into a ponytail that somehow made her look even more glamorous than usual. He had a feeling she could don a brown paper bag and make a fashion statement. No question that she was breathtakingly beautiful, and whereas he might have been wowed by her two days ago. . . Now, well, she wasn't Jessie.

"I wondered if I could talk to you about the situation with the press and the wedding this weekend?"

"Of course." He waved her in and gestured for her to have a seat. Forcing himself to focus on his job, he walked Liana through the plans he made earlier with his staff to ensure a smooth arrival for the wedding guests.

"I'm really sorry to be causing you extra work, especially with the other trouble you've been having."

"It's no problem. You have a right to your privacy, and Travis wants you to enjoy being here."

"I love being here," she said softly.

He wondered if she also loved the man who owned the place.

"How's Jessie doing?" she asked. "I've been meaning to call to check on her but things have been so crazy with the wedding and everything."

His mind went totally blank. He couldn't think of a thing to say.

"Beck?"

"She's fine."

Liana sat back in her chair and chewed on her pen cap as she studied him with a knowing look in her eyes. "You like her."

"Sure I do. What's not to like?"

"You *like* her like her."

"I hardly know her," Beck protested, reminding himself that Liana was sleeping with his boss—the same boss who'd asked him to take care of Jessie.

"I don't know her that well myself, but she seems like a real sweetheart."

"Uh huh." Beck checked his watch. "Well, I need to get going. Let me know if you need any more help with the security for the wedding."

"I'll do that."

On his way out, Beck walked her to Travis's office. "Liana?"

She turned to face him.

"If I did—like her like her—would that be bad?"

Her face softened into a smile. "Of course not."

"It's just that she came here looking for a place to hide out because a guy was hassling her. I don't want to take advantage of her."

"Does she like you, too?"

"Ah, yeah, she seems to," he said with a laugh, still finding it hard to believe.

Liana rested her hand on his arm. "You might be exactly what she needs."

"You think?"

"I do."

"She's a lot younger than me."

"From everything I know about her, she's competent and mature and well-regarded in the business. In our world, you grow up fast or you don't go the distance."

"So liking her doesn't make me a dirty old letch?"

Liana laughed. "Hardly."

Travis came into the clubhouse through the front door. When he saw Beck having an animated conversation with Liana, he came to a stop. "Are you moving in on my best girl?"

"She's all yours," Beck said with a wink for Liana. "You guys have a nice evening."

"You, too," she called after him.

"What was that all about?" Travis asked Liana.

"It seems your friend Beck has a thing for my friend Jessie, and vice versa."

Travis glanced at the door. "He never said a word about that to me when I saw him earlier. But I could tell something was on his mind."

Liana steered him into his office, stashed her files on his desk, and slipped her arms around him. "He didn't exactly give it up easily to me."

"Still, he told you."

She kissed the pout off his lips. "I think he's embarrassed."

Travis's eyebrows knitted with confusion. "Why?"

"Because he's quite a bit older than her, because you asked him to help her, because he doesn't want to let you down."

Travis shook his head. "I hate when he acts like I'm doing him a favor by letting him work here. He's the backbone of this whole place, but because I hired him after he burned out of the FBI, he's got this whole gratitude thing going on that pisses me off. Like we hadn't been friends for years before he ever came here."

"He feels like he owes you."

"But he doesn't!"

"You should talk to him." As she dropped soft kisses on the stubble he'd left on his jaw for her, she felt the tension drain from his shoulders.

"Not tonight. The only one I want to talk to tonight is you."

"Fine by me." She hooked her arm through his. "What's for dinner?"

CHAPTER 15

Beck crossed the parking lot to The Tower. In the lobby, he eyed the house phone. He picked it up and put it back down just as quickly. Pacing the beautifully decorated lobby, he went through all the reasons that pursuing this fascination with Jessie was a bad idea and kept coming back to the same thing—she had come here for peace and quiet, not to get wrapped up with him.

Besides, it couldn't go anywhere. In a week or two, she'd go back to her life, and he'd get on with his. What was the point? And who needed the heartache? Not him. That's for sure. He'd already had enough of that to last him a lifetime. Determined to get control of the madness that had temporarily overtaken him, Beck picked up the phone to dial her extension.

She answered as if she had run for the phone, and his gut contracted with regret.

"Hey," he said. "Something's come up. I can't make it tonight."

"Oh."

Feeling like a total shit, he closed his eyes and worked at keeping his tone gruff. "I'm sorry."

"So am I," she said in a small voice. "I cooked."

"Listen, Jessie—"

"Nothing good ever follows those words."

His whole body thrummed with tension.

"Are you trying to tell me it's over between us?"

"Yes."

"*Why?*"

"Because it'll never work. You know that as well as I do."

"Since you're not even man enough to talk to me about this in person, I suppose you're right."

"Jessie—"

"Save it, Peter. You disappoint me. I thought you were different."

Now *that* made him mad. He was trying to do what was best for *her*. "I'm coming up."

"Don't bother. I'm not interested."

"I'm coming." He slammed down the phone and stalked to the elevator. Being a good guy was never as great as it was cracked up to be. That was for sure. On the fifth floor, he pounded on her door. "Open up, Jessie."

"Go away before I call security."

"I *am* security. Now open up."

"I'll call Travis and tell him you're harassing me."

"No, you won't." In a softer tone, he added, "Open the door. Please." With his forehead resting on the door, he waited for several long moments while beating himself up for being so stupid. The moment she told him she wasn't interested, he realized she was the only thing he really wanted. He had no idea how he'd managed to convince himself that walking away from her was in any way the right thing to do.

"I'm sorry," he said. "Jessie. I'm sorry."

The door opened so suddenly he fell into the apartment and landed hard on his back. With the wind knocked out of him, he looked up at her in a filmy, floral dress that was sexy as hell. Her cascade of blond curls fell untamed, framing her exquisite face, which was currently convulsed with laughter.

He tried and failed to draw a breath. Clutching his chest, he sat up and forced air into his lungs.

"I'd give the execution a five out of six," she said, one hand propped on her hip in a saucy pose. "You really stuck the landing."

"I'm glad you're amused," he said when he could speak again. Rising gingerly to his knees, he took a few more breaths for good measure and discovered that something smelled really good. "What'd you make?"

"Tenderloin, my grandmother's au gratin potatoes, asparagus, and my famous tossed salad. Too bad you broke up with me over the phone." Leaning far enough forward to give him a dazzling view of her cleavage, she added, "I bet you would've enjoyed it."

Beck swallowed hard. "I'm trying to do what's best for you."

"And what would that be?"

"It's not me. You know that, Jessie."

Big blue eyes flashed with anger. "What I *know* is I felt something different for you the first instant I saw you. How can you take that away from me before I've had a chance to find out what it means?" Her tough exterior began to crumble. "How can you do that to me?"

He pushed himself up to his feet. "I don't want you to regret anything."

"I'd rather regret than continue to wonder."

Not sure if he still had the right, he reached out to her and breathed a sigh of relief when she let him bring her into his embrace. "My intentions were good."

"Maybe so but your delivery stinks."

"I know. I'm sorry." He tipped up her chin and kissed her softly. "Am I forgiven?"

Looking up at him with bottomless blue eyes, she said, "Do you really care about forgiveness or are you just hungry?"

He smiled. "I really care, and that scares the hell out of me."

"Me, too."

He held her for a long time, filled with relief even as it sunk in that he'd probably missed his last chance to escape.

Late on Friday afternoon, Liana sat with Travis at the club's bar to go over everything one last time. She nursed a glass of wine as she went through her checklist point by point.

"You're so organized," Travis said, impressed.

"Everyone here has been incredibly nice and helpful. Did you ask them to hold my hand?"

He shrugged. "I asked them to do their jobs, but I also had every confidence you could do yours."

She smiled. "Well, you have some very fine people working for you." An entertainment show on the TV over the bar caught her eye when she saw herself and Travis walking into the hospital the day before. "There we are."

He looked up in time to see a montage of headlines from the day's tabloids:

"Travis and Liana Engaged?"

"Liana Giving Up Modeling for Travis?"

"Travis Scores a Touchdown with Liana"

"Has Liana Found Her True North?"

The last headline, "Travis Puts Liana to Work," included a photo taken from a boat as she supervised workers in the tent.

Liana swallowed hard when she noticed the tick of tension pulsing in Travis's cheek. "I'm sorry, Travis. I know it's so invasive."

"I don't like the reference to scoring," he said quietly. "Not one bit."

She reached for his hand. "They think they're being clever referring to football. That's all."

His eyes, riveted to the television, widened all at once.

"What?" she asked.

"Jesus," he whispered. "They're chasing down my high school football coach."

Liana winced watching the older man wave his hand to say "no comment" as he pushed through a crowd of reporters. "I'm sorry," she said.

Travis recovered and forced a smile. "You have nothing to be sorry about. At least it's not my kindergarten teacher."

"I'm glad you can joke about it."

"Hey," he said with a finger to her chin. "It's no big deal, all right?"

"It's horrible."

"It's gossip. That's all it is."

"What your employees must think—"

"I don't care what they think. I pay them well for their discretion."

"I didn't intend for our fling to turn your whole life upside down."

"It hasn't," he insisted. "Well, not in the way you mean, anyway."

Intrigued, she studied him. "How then?"

He took her hand and brought it to his lips, keeping his eyes fixed on hers. "All I can think about—morning, noon, and night—is how long I have to wait until I can get you back in my bed."

A bolt of heat shot straight through her.

Travis smiled at her flustered reaction and skimmed a finger over her blush. "I've missed that the last few days. I'm glad to know I can still make it happen."

Liana finished her wine in one big gulp. "Let's get out of here."

Travis got up and held out his hand to her. They went to his office to drop off the wedding file and pick up Dash before they headed to The Tower. The dog ran on ahead of them, and Liana laughed when Dash unearthed a rabbit and gave chase toward the beach.

Travis groaned. "Great. She'll be gone for half an hour."

Liana looped her arm around his waist. "You've waited this long. Another half hour won't kill you."

"It might," he said. "It very well might."

She laughed at the look of dismay that crossed his handsome face. "How about a walk on the beach until we find her?"

"The press has taken to the high seas," he reminded her, gesturing to the boats anchored just off the shore of North Point. Photographers with huge zoom lenses sat waiting for a glimpse of them.

"That's okay. It'll be dark soon anyway. They won't get much."

"You've gotten ballsy this week," he said with pride.

"In more ways than one," she said with a giggle that made him groan with desire. She rendered him silent when she shifted their joined hands so she could trail a fingertip over his palm.

"Dash knows the way home," he said in a choked voice.

"Can she operate an elevator, too?" Liana teased, tugging him toward the beach. "What kind of daddy are you to let your little girl run off on her own?"

He whistled for Dash and swore when he got no response. "Come on," he said begrudgingly. "Let's go find the disobedient brat."

Beck took a rare half-day on Friday to go to the beach with Jessie. He'd done his best to teach her how to body surf, but they'd spent more time making out than surfing. By the time they returned to The Tower at sunset, his nerves were beginning to fray. He wanted her so badly he ached.

"You were quiet on the way home." She handed him a beer and sat down next to him on the patio. "Everything all right?"

He reached for her hand. "Today was fun."

"It was. I loved the waves."

"I loved the bikini—and so did every other guy on the beach."

She winced. "I'm sorry if that bothers you. I don't even notice it anymore."

"That's not what bothers me."

"Then what?"

"The thought of some guy out there being fixated on you, scaring you, following you. That *really* bothers me. You can't hide out here forever. Eventually, you'll have to go back to your life."

"I know," she said with a sigh.

"I'd like to contact the New York police. I know some people. I could pull some strings. I want to help you, Jessie. Will you let me?"

"You have so much to deal with here—the vandals and the press. I don't want to be a distraction."

He brought their joined hands to his lips. "Too late."

She rested her head back on the lounge, turning to study him. "You've very sweet to want to help."

"I *need* to help."

"All right. But your first priority is your own work."

"I think I can keep my own priorities straight, thank you very much." He gave her hand a tug to encourage her to join him on his lounge.

Wearing a short sundress over her bathing suit, she stretched out next to him and dragged a finger over the stubble on his jaw. "I like to look at you."

He snorted. "*You* like to look at *me?*"

"Got a problem with that?"

"I got the better end of the whole looking thing. I get to look at you."

She burrowed her face into his neck. "How many more days?"

The caress of her breath on his fevered skin made him hard as a rock. "I've lost track. Surely, it has to have been a week by now, right?"

"Feels like a month."

He cupped her face and brought his open mouth down on hers. In a matter of seconds he shifted on top of her, she wrapped her legs around his hips, and his tongue explored every inch of her mouth. "I know I said we should wait, honey." He sounded as breathless as he felt. "But I can't wait anymore. I want you so much I feel like I'll die if I can't have you."

"Yes," she said. "Now."

He looked down at her. "Are you sure?"

She nodded.

Raising himself up and off the lounge he reached for her hand. He brought her into his arms and held her for a long time.

When he finally released her to lead her inside, he hoped he was doing the right thing. He reminded himself that this was her first time, and he needed to be careful with her. This wasn't about him. This would be all about her.

"Peter?"

"Hmm?"

"What's that?"

"What's what?"

"There." She pointed.

On the south end of the property, flames shot from the roof of one of the houses under construction. "Oh no, oh *shit*," he whispered as he released her hand. "Stay here. I'll be back as soon as I can." He ran for the elevator.

After they located Dash, Travis and Liana spent an hour on the beach with her. Travis threw the stick at least a hundred times and they marveled at her ability to find it even in the encroaching darkness. The paparazzi had gone wild the moment Travis and Liana stepped onto the beach, but the photographers could only take so many shots of two people playing with a dog before even they got bored.

Liana was thrilled when Dash brought the stick back to her.

Travis gazed at her with amazement as she tossed it.

"What?"

"She won't fetch for anyone but me. Not even Beck. It drives him crazy."

Delighted, Liana smiled. "Really?"

"Really."

Dash returned with the stick and dropped it at Liana's feet.

"Don't forget who feeds you, you ingrate," Travis growled at the dog.

She ignored him and barked at Liana to get back to the game.

Liana sent the stick flying and cried out in surprise when Travis tossed her over his shoulder and spun her around. "I'm going to puke," she shrieked between gales of laughter. "Put me down!"

"Wouldn't the photographers love to get a shot of the very fancy Liana McDermott with her rear end in the air. Over here, boys."

"Travis! All the blood's rushing to my head!"

He ran a hand over her bottom. "Mine, too."

"Oh, that's so disgusting," she said between new fits of laughter. "Put me down. I'll give you your dog back. I promise."

He let her slide down the front of him and held her there. In the inky darkness he could barely make out her features but could see her looking up at him with eyes full of what looked an awful lot like love. Did he dare to hope?

Dash's sharp bark interrupted the moment.

Travis bent to get the stick and sent it sailing down the beach one last time. While Dash took off in hot pursuit, Travis leaned in to kiss Liana softly. He wasn't sure which one of them moaned first, but by the time Dash returned their arms were tight around each other.

The dog whimpered and rolled in the sand while she waited for them.

Dazzled, Travis was shocked to realize that were it not for the prying eyes of the media he would have eased her down onto the beach and taken her right then and there. That loss of control was new to him, and it made his heart and mind race. But he showed her none of that when he put his arm around her and whistled for Dash to come with them.

They were bending to pick up their shoes where they left them by the steps when they heard Beck frantically calling their names, just as Travis's cell phone rang.

Travis raced up the stairs ahead of Liana and Dash. "What's wrong?" he asked his frazzled security director.

"Fire," Beck said, out of breath. He pointed to the south end of the property.

Travis looked to where Beck pointed and saw the plume of smoke and dancing flames.

"Fire department's on the way," Beck said.

Liana caught up to them and gasped when she saw fire licking the sky in the distance.

"Go on up to my place, Liana," Travis said without taking his eyes off the fire. "I'll be there as soon as I can."

"I want to come with you," she said, gripping his arm.

He took her hand. "No."

"Please, Travis."

Travis tore his eyes off the fire long enough to glance at her and see the concern in her eyes. "All right."

As they ran toward Beck's truck, Dash rocketed past them heading in the direction of the fire.

"*Dash!*" Travis yelled. "Dash, stop!"

The dog ran off into the darkness like Travis hadn't spoken.

"*Goddamn it!*" Travis said.

"She wouldn't go near the fire," Liana assured him as Beck sped down the dirt road that led to the construction site. "She's too smart for that."

While he drove, Beck conversed with members of his staff on the radio.

They arrived at the fully engulfed house just ahead of the fire department.

"There wouldn't be anyone in there at this hour on a Friday night, would there?" Travis asked.

"We're trying to confirm that with the contractor," Beck replied.

They froze when they heard Dash's bark coming from the direction of the burning house.

Travis lunged toward the house, but Beck held him back.

Dash's barking became more frantic.

The fire captain directed men and hoses before he rushed over to talk to Travis and Beck. "Is there a dog in there?"

"We hope not," Beck replied with a grim set to his mouth.

"There must be someone in the house if she's barking like that." Travis struggled to swallow the overwhelming fear that lodged in his throat.

The captain hollered into a walkie-talkie to alert his men that there might be someone in the house.

Travis, Liana, and Beck stood back and watched two firemen enter the house while the others pointed hoses at the fire.

The barking had stopped, and Travis was staring at the fire when Liana's hand closed tightly around his.

"She's going to be okay," Liana whispered.

The fire radios crackled with the news that the firemen had found someone inside. Paramedics came flying out of the ambulance carrying equipment and a stretcher.

A few seemingly endless minutes later, two firemen carried a body out of the house.

"He's alive," one of the firemen called to the paramedics. "But just barely."

As the paramedics went to work on the injured man, Travis let go of Liana's hand and pulled his arm free of Beck's grasp.

"Did you see a dog in there?" Travis yelled to one of the firefighters who had been inside the house. "A yellow lab?"

"No." He wiped the sweat from his face. "We heard a dog barking, but we couldn't find it."

The paramedics loaded the injured man into the ambulance and took off with the siren blaring and emergency lights flashing.

"Dash! Dash!" Travis called. Bolting toward the house, he heard Liana scream for him to come back. He kept moving until his feet were pulled out from under him. He landed hard on the ground under Beck just as the second floor of the house crashed down onto the first.

"*What the hell do you think you're doing?*" Beck roared.

"Dash is in there! I've got to get her!"

"You're not getting yourself killed for a dog."

"*It's Dash,*" Travis wailed, fighting Beck's iron grip.

"I know, but you can't go in there, Travis. You can't."

Travis had tears rolling down his face when he let Beck pull him up and lead him back to where Liana waited for them, her own face awash in tears.

She held out her arms to Travis.

He fell into her embrace. "We've got to get her."

"Maybe she didn't go into the house." Liana held him close. "Maybe she was barking from outside."

"Then where is she?"

"She could be scared, Trav," Beck said.

Travis began calling for her and yelled until he was hoarse from the acrid smoke and the strain on his voice. Long after the firefighters had the fire under control, he still called for her.

The fire captain walked over to them with a grim expression on his face. "Arson," he said, holding up a singed gas can.

"We've been having problems with vandals," Beck said. "Nothing like this, but the police are aware of it."

"I'm calling in the state fire marshal," the captain said. "Until we complete our investigation, this is a crime scene. No one goes in there. Am I clear?" He directed the question to Travis, in particular.

"You'll have our full cooperation," Beck assured him.

"Mr. North?"

Travis nodded.

The fire captain walked away, and Beck turned to Travis. "I'll get my whole team down here to look for her. We're going to find her."

Travis couldn't look away from the burnt ruination of the house or stop the flood of tears that cascaded down his face.

"Why don't you go home, Trav?"

Travis shook his head. "No," he said in the hoarse whisper that remained of his voice. "Not until we find her."

Beck put his hands on Travis's shoulders. "She might be hiding because she's scared of the way you sound. You need to go back to your place and wait. I'll call you the minute we find her."

Travis gestured to what was left of the house. "What if she's in there?"

"Then we'll get her when the fire marshal arrives. Go home, Travis." He handed his keys to Liana and steered Travis toward the truck. After he had gotten Travis into the passenger seat and closed the door, Beck squeezed Liana's shoulder. "Take care of him. I'll find Dash."

Liana nodded. "Okay."

CHAPTER 16

Travis stared straight ahead as Liana drove them to The Tower.

She glanced over at him, and her heart broke at the shattered expression on his face.

In the garage she parked in Travis's spot and went around to open the passenger door.

"Liana!" Jessie cried, emerging from the darkness with a flashlight. "Is everyone all right?"

"We hope so. The firefighters pulled a man from the house and took him to the hospital." Lowering her voice, she added, "And we can't find Travis's dog, Dash."

"Oh no. What can I do?"

"Keep your eyes out for Dash. She's a yellow lab."

"I will. Is Beck on his way back, too?"

Liana shook her head. "He stayed to look for Dash. I need to get Travis upstairs."

"Of course. Let me know if y'all need anything. I'm so sorry about this."

"Thanks." Liana leaned into the car. When he didn't move, she touched his shoulder. "Travis? Honey, come on. Let's go upstairs." She took his hand and gently tugged at it to encourage him out of the car and into the elevator.

When the elevator doors opened into his apartment, he went straight to the sofa.

Liana followed him, sat on the coffee table in front of him, and took his hands. "Beck will find her," she assured him.

"What if she's dead?" His battered voice was little more than a whisper. "What'll I do without her? She's my . . ."

"What, baby?"

"My family," he said as new tears flooded his eyes.

Liana moved onto his lap and wrapped her arms around him. She wanted to tell him she would be his family if Dash was gone but couldn't seem to get the words out.

He buried his face in her shoulder. "I can't believe she ran into a burning house."

"She probably saved that man's life," Liana reminded him. "And you did, too. You knew something was wrong because of the way she was barking."

"I need to check on him," Travis rasped.

"I'm sure Beck will, and he'll let you know what he hears. Besides, you can barely talk. Do you have any honey or lemon?"

He shook his head. "Call the club. Someone will bring over whatever you want."

"I want it for you." She kissed his forehead and got up.

Liana called the club and asked them to send over hot tea with honey and lemon. Then she went into the kitchen, wet a paper towel, and brought it with her when she returned to the sofa. Turning him toward her, she wiped smudges of dirt and dried tears from his face.

He rested his forehead against hers. "I'm glad you're here."

"I'll be here for as long as you need me," she assured him.

Twirling a lock of her long hair around his finger, he sighed. "You can't stay that long."

The raw longing she heard in his injured voice tugged at her heart.

The intercom buzzed, and she got up to answer it. A minute later, a waiter from the club arrived with the cup of tea.

"I heard about Dash, Mr. North," the young man said after he had given the tea to Liana. "I'm really sorry."

"Thanks, Sam," Travis said.

"Well, you all take care," Sam said as he left in the elevator. "Let us know if you need anything else."

Liana took the tea over to Travis. "Here," she said. "This'll help your throat."

Travis took a sip. "Thanks."

"He seems like a nice kid," Liana said, struggling to think of some way to take Travis's mind off Dash.

"He's the one who gave me the four-one-one on you," Travis said with a small smile. "I asked him to come back next summer to work in the office since he's going to business school."

"That's quite an opportunity for him. He'll learn a lot from you."

Travis shrugged and lifted his arm to invite her to sit closer to him.

She looped her arm around his waist, rested her head on his chest, and listened to the steady rhythm of his heart. "How's your throat?"

"A little better."

"Maybe I can be a nurse if modeling doesn't work out."

"Or a wedding coordinator."

"Yeah, right."

"I mean it." His voice sounded only slightly better than it had earlier, and she could tell he was making an effort to keep his mind off Dash. "We're going to have weddings every weekend of the year, sometimes two a week. Big ones outside in the summer and smaller ones in the clubhouse during the off-season. There's no way Niki can handle all of them, and I've got other things I need to be focused on now that our first big one is behind us. We've been talking about hiring a second coordinator. The job's yours if you want it."

Astounded, Liana looked up at him. "You're serious."

"Of course I am. I never joke about business."

"But surely you'd prefer to have someone more experienced, someone who knows what they're doing."

"I'd prefer to have you," he said, kissing her forehead. "You have style and class and star power that certainly won't hurt North Point. And after watching you in action the last couple of days, I have no doubt you can do it."

"You really think so?"

"I know so. You've told me you can't imagine a life without modeling. I'm just offering a suggestion of something you might like to do."

She returned her head to his chest.

"It's nothing that has to be decided now. Think about it."

He was offering her the chance to stay with him, to help him nurture his dream at North Point. Liana had to admit the idea appealed to her. She'd enjoyed the last two days even more than she had expected to. But he hadn't said anything about what it would mean for them as a couple if she were to stay, and that would make all the difference in what she decided to do. One of the tabloid headlines had been running through her mind all night: "Has Liana Found Her True North?" Very possibly, but she'd never be able to stay with him if he didn't love her the way she loved him.

His cell phone rang, and Liana sat up so he could get it out of his pocket.

"Yeah," he said into the phone, which he put on speaker so Liana could hear, too.

"Hey," Beck said. "We're still looking. The good news is there's no sign of her inside the house. It's still pretty hot in there, but the fire marshal's team took a quick look, and they don't see her."

Travis sighed with relief. "She could still be hurt, though, or even worse."

"Possibly, but not finding her in the house is definitely good news."

"Agreed," Travis said.

"We're going to call off the search for tonight. There's no moon, so it's dark as hell out here. I'll have some guys out at dawn."

"Okay," Travis said. "Thanks for trying."

"I want to find her, too."

"I know you do. Did you hear anything about the guy they took out of the house?"

"He's a cabinetmaker who was working late. He's in fair condition at Newport Hospital with second-degree burns and smoke inhalation, but they expect him to make a full recovery."

"That's a relief," Travis said.

"There may be one other bit of good news," Beck said.

"What's that?"

"The photographers who've been stalking you and Liana? One of them got some film in the area of the house right before the fire. He may've captured something the cops can use to nail the bastards who've been screwing with us. He turned his memory card over to the cops a few minutes ago."

"Wouldn't that be something?" Travis asked.

"Definitely. Well, try to get some sleep. I know you're worried, but we're going to find her. One way or the other we *will* find her."

"Thanks, Beck. I'll talk to you in the morning." He closed the phone and glanced at Liana. "Can you believe that?"

"How awesome would it be if one of our stalker photographers led us to the vandals? That would make all the aggravation worth it."

He kissed the end of her nose. "And we'd have you and your celebrity to thank for it."

"I hope he got something the cops can use."

"God, all I can smell is smoke."

She took his hands, pulled him up from the sofa, and led him into his bedroom. Turning to him, she lifted his dirty North Point polo shirt over his head and let it drop to the floor.

"I like Liana the nurse," he said with a sad smile as he unbuttoned her blouse.

Liana watched his face as they undressed each other. The frenzy of passion from earlier was gone. In its place was something infinitely more tender.

He gathered the pile of smoke-infested clothes and brought them with him to the bathroom where he tossed them into the washing machine with a healthy dose of detergent while Liana turned on the shower.

She let the warm water wash away the smoke and the strain of the last few hours.

Travis stepped in behind her, wrapped his arms around her, and rested his head on her shoulder.

She turned to him. "How are you doing?"

"Hanging in there."

"Your voice seems to be recovering."

"My throat hurts."

Liana held him close for a long time before she reached for a bottle of shampoo and washed his hair.

After she was done, he took the bottle from her. "My turn."

Liana relaxed against him as he worked the shampoo through her hair.

When he turned her to rinse the shampoo, he bent his head and captured her mouth in a long, lingering kiss.

Liana wound her arms around his neck, and with his hands on her hips he brought her close to him.

As he eased her back and lifted her, she gasped from the chill of the tile wall. Tearing her lips free of his, she held him back. "Travis, no. Not without protection."

He pressed his lips to her neck. "Just for a second."

"No." She pushed him away. "*No.*"

He seemed stunned by what he'd wanted to do. "I'm sorry, sweetheart. I wasn't thinking."

"It's all right," she said, even as her heart pounded with unfulfilled desire. She ducked under the water to rinse off the last of the shampoo.

Travis got out ahead of her and waited with a towel when she stepped out. He wrapped it around her and hugged her. "I'm sorry."

"Don't worry about it." She wrapped her hair in a second towel. "Your mind is elsewhere tonight."

"That's no excuse for being careless with you." He kissed her bare shoulder, and his eyes met hers in the mirror. "Would it really be so awful?"

"What?"

"If you got pregnant."

Liana's eyes widened. "*Yes!* It *would* be awful."

"Oh, yeah, I forgot your body is your meal ticket."

A surge of anger cut through Liana, and she turned to face him. "That's *not* it."

"Is it the idea of having *my* baby that's so repulsive to you?"

"There's a right way to bring a baby into the world, and this isn't it," she shot back, incredulous. She pushed by him, went into the closet where her bag was, and pulled on a pair of shorts and a loose-fitting T-shirt. When she came out, Travis waited for her, still wearing a towel and still appearing to be making a supreme effort to remain calm.

"Do you care to explain that?" he asked.

"We're halfway through a two-week fling. We said no emotion, no strings. Where do you see a baby fitting into that?"

"What did you think would happen if you got pregnant during this non-emotional affair of ours? Condoms have been known to break, you know."

His fierce expression unnerved Liana, who suddenly found it hard to look at him. He solved that problem for her when he raised her chin and forced her to make eye contact.

"What did you think I would do if you got pregnant?"

"I never considered it."

He laughed but there was a harsh edge to it. Liana wasn't sure if that was because of the subject matter or his injured throat.

"Like hell you didn't. You knew you'd be able to count on me no matter what or you never would've gone to bed with me in the first place."

Liana couldn't think of a thing to say to that. *How well he knows me . . .*

"Well, I guess that leads us back to vanity."

"You're being a jerk."

His smile was almost a sneer. "Did I hit a nerve?"

Her eyes filled. "*No!* Not at all! Whether you choose to believe it or not, it's *not* about vanity. It's about morals. Remember them? Just because I was willing to have a fling with you doesn't mean I'm interested in having a baby out of wedlock. *If I ever have a baby, Travis, I'll be married to a man I love and who loves me—not a man I'm having a two-week fling with. Does that clear things up for you?*"

His face was a study in sadness. "Yeah. I get it." He went into the closet and dressed in old jeans and a shirt.

"Where are you going?" she asked when he reemerged carrying a flashlight.

"To look for Dash on the beach."

When she was alone, Liana braced her arms on the countertop and too several deep breaths to calm her racing heart. I should've told him. *I should've said that nothing would make me happier than to have his baby—a handsome, dark-haired boy with his daddy's devastating grin and those dark, searching eyes. Maybe I would've told him if he hadn't seemed so intent on provoking me.* She raised her head and looked into the mirror. "I love you, Travis," she whispered, wishing she could bring herself to say it to him. "I love you so much."

Travis stalked off the elevator into the garage and used the flashlight to check under the cars for Dash. "Why did you have to do that?" *Just because you don't have the balls to tell her how you feel doesn't mean you should back her into a corner like a freaking lunatic. And what makes you think a woman like Liana McDermott would want to be saddled with your kid?*

He ached when he imagined a little princess with her mother's shiny dark hair and bright violet eyes. *Why didn't you just tell her that you want to be the guy who loves her and marries her and gives her babies—and anything else she wants or needs? Why didn't you just say it? Because you know that's not what she wants. She made that clear again just now. She's in it for the sex, and she has been from the beginning. Yeah, well, I've delivered on that, haven't I? But if that's all it is to her then why did she take such loving care of me after the fire?*

She'd gotten him tea. Even his own mother had never made him feel so cared for. Not like Liana had. If that wasn't love then maybe he didn't know love. But *damn!* It had felt like love to him, and he'd liked it. A lot.

CHAPTER 17

Creeping along in the truck, Beck took one last trip around the perimeter of the property, shining his flashlight into the bushes and calling for Dash until he was almost as hoarse as Travis. Beck felt utterly defeated. He hadn't kept the vandals off the property, a man had been gravely injured, a million-dollar home reduced to rubble, and Travis's beloved dog was missing.

When Travis first proposed the security chief job, Beck saw it as a bullshit post at a posh resort. He'd scoffed at the freefall his career had taken, from FBI special agent to babysitter of the rich and pampered. But once he saw what Travis was doing here, he wanted to be part of it. Apparently, though, he couldn't even do a bullshit job right.

Unable to think of anywhere else to look for Dash, he pulled into his parking space at the clubhouse and got out of the truck.

"Peter!"

At the sound of Jessie's voice, he turned to her, remembering for the first time in hours what they had been on the verge of doing when she spotted the flames.

"Are you all right?" she asked, breathless from her jog across the parking lot.

"Yeah," he croaked.

"Oh you sound awful!" She tucked the flashlight under her arm and reached out to him.

He took a step back. "I'm filthy."

"I don't care about that! I was so worried. It'd be just like you to run into a fire if someone needed you."

"I had to tackle Travis to keep him out of there. We think Dash. . ."

"I know," she said, caressing his face. "I heard. Is there anything I can do?"

He shook his head.

"Why are you blaming yourself for what someone else did?"

"Because! If I'd been here instead of frolicking at the beach with you this might not have happened." He expected that to anger her, to force her to step back from him, but instead she looped her arms around his neck and held on tighter.

"You're not allowed to take any time off?"

"That's not the point," he said, trying to shake her loose, but she wouldn't budge.

"Come with me. Take a shower at my place, have something to eat."

"I have stuff I need to do."

"There's nothing more you can do tonight, and you know it." Her hands slid down over his arms to capture his hands. Walking backward, she led him to The Tower. He stopped her so he could grab a bag from the cab of his truck.

They were quiet as they rode the elevator to her apartment. Once there, she steered him in the direction of the bathroom and got out a towel for him.

"Take your time," she said, reaching up to brush some dirt from his face.

"Thanks."

In the shower, Beck hung his head under the spray, wishing it could wash away the shame and disgust that had plagued him since the vandals began targeting North Point. When he thought about the man they'd found in the house, that someone could have been *killed* on his watch . . . Beck shuddered and forced the thought from his mind.

Tomorrow they would start all over. They'd rework the patrol schedules, shake things up, and find the bastards who were doing this. One way or another, he *would* find them and make them pay for causing Travis a minute of unease. That was the part that bothered Beck the most—seeing Travis so upset. He had poured his heart and soul into this place, not to mention millions of dollars. And to see him weeping over his lost dog. . .

Beck dried off and pulled on the shorts and T-shirt he kept in the truck for emergencies. Was this an emergency? It sure felt that way. Jessie was waiting for him, but after what he said to her he wouldn't blame her if she wanted nothing more to do with him. That thought made him sadder than all the others put together as he prepared himself to face her.

While she was alone in Travis's apartment, Liana called her mother.

"Hi, honey," Agnes said.

"Did I wake you?"

"I wish. I'm studying."

Liana chuckled. "That still sounds funny coming from you."

"I'm glad you're amused."

Liana told her mother about the fire and how Dash was missing.

"Oh, honey, his beautiful dog!" Agnes cried. "He loves her so much."

"I know," Liana sighed. "He's heartbroken. He's out looking for her now."

"Please tell him I'll say a prayer for Dash tonight."

"He'll appreciate that. Were you out with David earlier?"

"Just for a quick dinner, and then I sent him home so I could study."

"I'll bet he can't wait until you're done. I wouldn't be surprised if he asked you to marry him now that you're out of the closet."

"He asked me quite some time ago, actually."

"Well, now you can say yes."

"Can I?"

"Of course you can. I told you I want you to be happy, Mom. If David makes you happy then marry him."

"Thank you, honey. Your support means everything to me."

"I like knowing you have someone taking care of you when I can't."

"And I like having you right across town and in the same time zone as me."

"Speaking of across town, Travis offered me a job coordinating weddings at North Point."

"Did he now? What did you say?"

"Nothing yet. He asked me to think about it, but I don't know."

"What don't you know?"

"If I'm ready to give up modeling, if I could handle planning a bunch of weddings all at once, if I could handle being with him every day."

"I'd think that would be the easy part."

"He didn't say anything about us when he mentioned the job. It was strictly a business discussion."

Agnes laughed. "Get real, Liana. He wants to keep you in his life, or he never would've offered you the job. He's competing against the pull of your glamorous world with the only thing he's got—his business and the life he's building there."

"I don't think it has anything to do with us as a couple."

"I *saw* the way he looks at you, Liana. Maybe you're so used to men looking at you that you can't see the difference in how *he* looks at you."

Liana thought about the way he'd looked at her during the meeting with Justine and Tom. She had wondered then if what she saw in his eyes was love. Could that be what her mother had seen, too? "If he loves me why doesn't he just say so?"

"Because he thinks you don't want it, honey. You told him you're going back to work next Sunday, right?"

"Yes."

"Then he's got to protect himself from getting hurt. If he tells you he loves you and you still leave, what's he going to do?"

"I don't know," Liana said in a small voice.

"If you want him to love you, Liana, then make room in your life for him."

"I don't know if I'm ready to do that."

"Until you figure it out, don't expect him to throw himself at your feet and beg. He's not that kind of man. If he was you wouldn't be interested in him, and you certainly wouldn't love him."

"When did you get so smart? Is it all that college?"

Agnes laughed. "It's called life, honey. It's what you pick up along the way. Why don't you just tell him how you feel?"

"I can't," Liana said with a sigh. "Not when I was the one who insisted on no strings."

"Rules were made to be broken. Think about it."

"I like knowing you're right up the street, too, Mom."

"Good luck with the wedding tomorrow. I'll keep my fingers crossed for you."

"Keep them crossed for Justine, the bride. She's got an inexperienced wedding coordinator overseeing the biggest day of her life."

"You'll be great," Agnes assured her. "Travis wouldn't let you do it if he didn't think you could handle it."

"Thanks for the vote of confidence. Let's do something on Sunday, okay?"

"It's a date."

Liana hung up and hugged the phone to her chest. She pulled her feet up under her and rested her head against the back of the sofa. *If you want him to love you then make room for him.* Her mother's words of wisdom echoed through her mind while she waited for Travis to come back. She hurt for him as she imagined him out in the dark searching for his beloved dog.

He had been gone for more than an hour when Liana heard the elevator chime to announce his return. She held her breath, hoping he would have Dash with him.

But the doors opened, and Travis walked into the apartment by himself, his head hung with despair.

Liana got up and went to him. "No sign of her?"

He fell into her embrace. "I'm sorry. I don't know why I said those things to you."

She kissed his cheek, his forehead, his lips. "You're worried about Dash. I understand."

"I shouldn't have taken it out on you."

Cradling his face in her hands, she kissed away his apology. "You were right about something."

"I was?"

"Uh huh," she said as she kissed him again. "I knew you'd be there for me if we got more than we bargained for out of our fling."

"I would be," he insisted.

"I know, Travis," She buried her fingers in his hair. "I know that."

He held her tight for a long, quiet moment.

"How would you feel about helping me out with another new experience?" she asked with a coy smile.

"What's that?"

She tugged on the button to his jeans. "Make-up sex."

"Oh," he said with one of those grins she loved even if his eyes were still sad. "That's the best kind."

"So I've heard."

He scooped her up and carried her to bed.

An hour later, Liana lay facing him. "Travis?"

He didn't open his eyes when he said, "Hmm?"

"Can we fight again tomorrow?"

He laughed, reached for her hand, and held it to his chest. "I'm sure we'll have words during the wedding."

"I hope so," Liana said with a yawn.

"So I guess this means you like make-up sex."

"*Oh yeah.* I've definitely been missing out."

"Thanks for taking care of me tonight and for putting up with me."

"You're pretty tough to put up with." She tugged her hand free of his so she could caress his tired face. "My mother wanted me to tell you she's going to say a prayer for Dash tonight."

"That's good. Make sure you thank her for me."

"I will."

"You're too far away over there."

Liana moved into his arms and sighed with contentment as a light bay breeze drifted in though the open bedroom windows. She rubbed his back and his breathing grew heavy with sleep. Liana fought to stay awake, wanting to watch him sleep and enjoy being held by him. Soon enough she would be sleeping alone again, and she'd be left with only memories of moments such as this.

Even in sleep he was so handsome she couldn't resist skimming her hand lightly over his face. *If I were going to make room for anyone it would be you. I just don't know if I'm ready. If only we had more time and everything didn't feel so urgent. I'm so busy trying to decide what to do about you I'm afraid I'll stop enjoying you. I can't let that happen. I need to live in the present and stop worrying about the future. After all, the future will take care of itself. At least I hope so.* She smoothed the hair off his forehead and touched her lips to his.

He awakened with a start, his eyes holding hers with an intensity that stopped her heart.

"I'm sorry," she whispered. "I didn't mean to wake you."

With his hand buried in her hair he brought her mouth to his, devouring her as he rolled her under him and took her to the place she could only go with him.

CHAPTER 18

When Jessie heard the bathroom door open, she got up to go to him. With any other man, she would have told him to get lost after the way he'd lashed out at her. But she knew he was distraught over the vandalism and needed to vent. For some reason, she was pleased he had chosen to take it out on her. People only did that to those they were most comfortable with.

"I made you a sandwich." She led him into the kitchen and nudged him down into a chair. Placing a heaping turkey sandwich and a beer in front of him, she reached for her glass of wine and sat with him while he ate.

"Thanks," he said.

"No problem."

He swallowed a bite of sandwich and took a long drink of his beer. "I'm sorry for what I said."

"I'm sorry if I've distracted you from your work."

"You haven't." His face lifted into a small smile. "Well, you have, but I'm not complaining. It wasn't fair for me to talk to you that way."

She reached for his hand and linked her fingers with his. "You were upset, I was handy. It's okay."

"It's not okay."

As he looked at her with those piercing blue eyes, a strange sensation came over her. *Oh God, I love him.*

"Jessie? What's wrong?"

She cleared her throat and took a sip of her wine. "Nothing."

"You just got this crazy look on your face, like you were freaked out by something."

Smiling, she marveled at how he saw right through her. "I'm just very grateful that you weren't hurt in that fire."

He finished the sandwich and pushed the plate to the side. "I'm sorry you were worried."

"Will you talk to me about how you're feeling? You're all but vibrating with tension and frustration."

Abruptly, he released her hand and got up to put his plate in the sink. He stood there for a long moment before he turned back to her.

What she saw on his face broke the heart she had recently given to him.

"Can we go outside? I need some air."

"Sure we can." She followed him to the patio where the night sky was peppered with stars, and the moon cast a silvery glow on the bay. "It's so beautiful here."

"Isn't it? When Travis first told me what he wanted to do, I thought he was nuts. He'd made a fortune in the stock market and could've lived large for the rest of his life. Instead, he wanted to build something lasting."

"That's admirable."

Beck nodded. "He had a real vision, and I have to give him credit. Against tremendous odds, he's made it happen."

"And you hate that someone's messing with it."

"Hell yes I hate it! It pisses me off."

"And you hate that you can't stop it."

"Yes," he said softly.

"It's not your fault, Peter. You've done everything you can and then some."

"But it's not enough. Someone was nearly killed here tonight. Do you know what that would've done to Travis?"

"How about what it's doing to you?"

"That doesn't matter."

She stepped closer to him and slid her arms around his waist. "It matters to me."

He shook his head. "I'm not worth it, Jessie."

"I don't agree." She resisted his efforts to break free of her embrace. "You can fight me and you can push me away, but I'll keep coming back."

"Why?" he asked, baffled.

She wasn't sure he was ready to hear the real reason, and she wasn't certain she was ready to say it. "Because you *are* worth it."

"I don't deserve you."

"*Why* would you say that?" she asked, alarmed to see him so defeated when he was usually upbeat and confident.

"I've got a miserable track record." He paused and looked down at the floor, his shoulders stooping. "I've been engaged. Twice."

"What happened?"

"They both found someone they liked better."

Jessie's eyes burned, and her heart ached. "And you're worried that if you take a chance on me, on what's happening between us, I'll do the same thing?"

He shrugged. "Look at you. All you'd have to do is snap your fingers—"

"After everything I've told you, everything I've *shared* with you, do you think I'd snap my fingers at someone else? I've told you things I've never told another living soul."

"Why me? That's what I don't get. Why me?"

She reached up to run her fingers through his thick blond hair. "Because I recognized you. That first moment I saw you I knew you, and I'll never want anyone but you."

"*How can you know that?* You've only known me a few days!"

"I know it. I know it all the way down to my soul." Moving her hands to the back of his head, she drew him down to her and poured all her love into a kiss. "I'll never leave you for someone else. I swear to you."

"I'm supposed to be taking care of you. How'd you end up taking care of me?"

"There's no reason we can't take care of each other."

His strong arms tightened around her and lifted her. "I love you, Jessie. I hardly know you, but I love you so damned much."

"And I love you. Just as much." Jessie gripped his shoulders, surprised by how easily the words came with the right person in the right moment. "Take me to bed, Peter."

He didn't ask any questions this time. Rather he tightened his hold on her and walked them into the bedroom. Easing her down to her feet, he brushed his lips over hers.

"Will you do something for me?" she asked.

"Anything at all."

"Will you not treat me like I'm fragile? Will you treat me like you would any other woman?"

"You're not any other woman. You're *the* woman."

"You know what I mean."

"I don't want to hurt you."

"You'll hurt me if you coddle me. Make me *your* woman."

"You already are, Jessie," he whispered as his lips took fierce possession of hers. His tongue swirled through her mouth, darting and plunging. He tugged at her tank top. "Take it off."

Holding his gaze, she reached for the hem and pulled the shirt up and over her head.

His eyes darkened at the sight of her bare breasts. He reached for her flimsy pajama pants at the same instant she tugged on his shirt.

They laughed.

"Hurry," she said as clothes landed in a heap on the floor.

When they were naked, he rolled on a condom and then took a step back from her.

"What?"

"I just want to look."

A nervous giggle rippled through her.

He sighed. "Amazing."

"You're not too bad yourself. How 'bout you bring that over here? I've been waiting an awfully long time for this."

"I'm having performance anxiety," he muttered as he drew her down next to him on the bed.

"Don't." Jessie could honestly say she had never experienced anything quite like the sensation of being pressed against his hard, muscular body. His chest hair tickled her breasts as his leg worked its way between hers. Nuzzling her nose into his neck, she took a deep breath of sexy man. "Peter?"

His hand traced a lazy trail up and down her back. "Hmm?"

"Will you do whatever you did the other day to make me. . . You know. . ."

"Come?" he whispered in her ear, sending a sizzle of tension straight through her.

Her face heated with embarrassment. "Yes."

He massaged her shoulder. "You're so rigid, baby. Try to relax. Nothing's going to happen unless you want it to."

"I'm afraid I'll chicken out," she confessed, looking up at him. "Don't let me, okay? No matter what I say or do, don't stop."

"I'm not going to force you, Jessie."

"You won't be forcing me. Promise me."

"How about you just relax and let nature take its course?" He urged her onto her back.

Jessie struggled to calm her racing heart and trembling body.

"Close your eyes," he whispered. "Just relax and remember I love you more than I've ever loved anyone." He cupped her breast and ran first his thumb and then his tongue over her pebbled nipple.

The movement of his tongue sent hot darts of desire straight to her core. He sucked her nipple into his mouth, and she cried out. As he moved to give her other breast the same treatment, Jessie couldn't stay still—or quiet. She squirmed under him, raising her hips, the need building like a tidal wave. Since she had done as he asked and kept her eyes closed, she wasn't prepared for his tongue to dip into her belly button.

"What. . . What're you doing?"

"Shh. Relax, honey. Trust me?"

"I do. You know I do."

"Then let me make you feel so good." He continued to kiss his way down until he was poised between her legs. "Spread your legs a little more."

Jessie bit her lip to keep from dissolving into tears. Everything he had done so far had been wonderful, but the nagging bead of fear that had ruined this in the past lodged in her chest. Determined not to let it happen again and reminding herself that this time was all about love, she gingerly moved her feet further apart on the bed.

Using his broad shoulders, he coaxed her knees until she was spread open before him.

Her face burned with shame and greedy desire that was all new to her.

"So beautiful," he whispered against her inner thigh. Before she had time to panic over what he intended to do, he slid his big hands under her, cupped her buttocks, and raised her to meet his questing tongue.

"Oh *God*," she groaned. The position alone was almost enough to undo her, but with the added strokes of his firm tongue, he had her dangling on the edge in no time at all. Closing her eyes tight against the mortification, she listened to him feast on her wetness. The aroma of sex mingled with the scented candles she had lit earlier.

"Come for me, Jessie," he said, rolling her throbbing clitoris between his lips. He flicked his tongue over her. "Now."

On his command, the orgasm pounded through her with such force it knocked the wind right out of her. She gasped for air as the sensations rocketed from her over-sensitized breasts to the soles of her feet and everywhere in between. Still in the throes of the powerful release, she gasped in surprise when he slid into her.

Her eyes flew open to find him gazing down at her with love and wonder and infinite tenderness. If she hadn't already loved him, she would have fallen for him right then.

Once he was fully sheathed in her, he held still for a long, breathless moment. "Okay?"

Biting her lip, she nodded.

Propped up on trembling arms, his jaw pulsed with tension. To Jessie, he had never been more handsome—or more fiercely sexy. "God, baby, you're so tight." Without moving his hips, he bent to kiss her.

Jessie tasted her own essence on his lips and tongue. Wrapping her arms around his neck, she held him in place and tightened her internal muscles to hug his throbbing penis.

Uttering a jagged gasp, he said, "Jessie. . . I need to move."

She raised her hips to encourage him.

His thrusts were slow and measured.

Jessie could feel him holding back and appreciated his effort to ensure this first time was good for her.

A bead of sweat formed on his forehead, and she reached up to brush it away.

"Are you okay, honey?" he asked, his voice tight with tension and concern.

"Yes," she whispered. "Feels so good." Nothing about this was in any way related to what had happened in the past. Filled with joy that she had finally managed to experience this with a man she loved and respected, Jessie climbed toward another climax.

His open mouth came down hard on hers, his tongue mimicked the action of his hips, and when he cupped her bottom to hold her tight against him, Jessie came.

He pumped hard into her a few more times, milking her orgasm, before he let himself go. Breathing hard and sweating, he buried his face in the curve of her neck to whisper sweet words of love and comfort that she couldn't quite hear.

It didn't matter, though. He didn't have to say anything. He'd already told her everything she needed to know and had given her the priceless gift of a first time she'd never, ever forget.

Liana thought she was dreaming when she woke just before dawn to the sound of a dog barking. She lay still for several minutes and listened to the distant barking. Then she reached for Travis.

"Travis," she said, shaking him.

"Mmmm."

"Travis! Wake up."

"What's wrong?"

"I think I hear Dash."

His eyes opened as he lay still to listen. "It's her!" He flew out of bed, grabbed jeans from the pile on the floor, and jumped into them.

Liana stayed in bed and listened to him leave in the elevator. After he was gone, she got up and went to his closet to borrow his robe. She was dying to go out on the patio to try to see them but was afraid there might be paparazzi lurking. The last thing she wanted was to give them a free shot of her in a bathrobe. So while she waited she paced back and forth in the living room. Her heart raced with excitement when the elevator chimed a few minutes later.

Travis carried Dash into the apartment.

Liana clapped with joy. "Dash!" Tears sprang to her eyes as she hugged the dog and Travis at the same time.

Dash licked her face.

Liana smiled at the enthusiastic greeting. "Oh, you had us so worried! Where were you, sweet girl?" She glanced up and caught Travis gazing at her again just as he had in the meeting the other day—as if she was the answer to his every prayer. "What?" she asked softly.

He shook his head.

Not sure whether he was unable or unwilling to tell her what he felt, Liana returned her attention to the dog. "Is she all right?"

"She's filthy and stinks of smoke, but I can't see any obvious injuries. I'll take her to the vet this morning just to be sure. Until then," he said, kissing the top of the dog's head, "it's to the tub with you."

Dash whined and buried her face in Liana's armpit.

Liana laughed and coaxed the dog out of hiding. "I can't *believe* the way she always understands what you're saying." She followed Travis into the bathroom and helped him prepare the tub.

"You might want to take shelter in the bedroom. This usually gets ugly."

Liana bent to kiss Travis's cheek. "I'm so glad you found her."

"*You* found her," he corrected, reaching up for a better kiss. "Why don't you try to go back to sleep for a while? We've got a long day ahead of us."

"I'll try."

"Will you call Beck's cell to tell him we found Dash? The number is in my phone."

"I'll take care of it." She left him to bathe the dog, made the call to an elated Beck, and got back in bed. While she had good intentions of going back to sleep, she snickered at Travis's muttered swears as he did battle with the disobedient dog. When he emerged from the bathroom a few minutes later soaked from head to toe, Liana laughed so hard she cried.

"You think it's funny?" he asked with a scowl.

The face he made as he approached the bed only made her laugh harder. "Travis . . ." Realizing all at once what he intended to do, she attempted to escape, but he grabbed her ankle, pulled her back toward him, and plopped down on top of her.

She squealed from the blast of wetness he brought with him and dissolved into a new wave of hysterical laughter.

He pinned her hands on either side of her head and shook like a dog, spraying cold water all over her.

"*Travis!*"

Even his lips were cold as they skimmed over her neck. Liana shuddered from both the chill and the heat of his touch.

Dash came charging out of the bathroom and rolled around on the carpet before she stood up and with a mighty shake sent a fountain of water flying through the air.

Travis laughed. "It was time to change the sheets anyway." He dipped his head to kiss Liana.

"Probably." She opened her lips to welcome his invasion. When she finally pulled back from him, she said, "Let go of my hands. I want to touch you."

"No." He raised her arms over her head and curled her fingers around the wooden slats of the headboard. "Leave them there." His eyes narrowed with desire as he tugged at the belt of the robe. He unveiled her like a child opening his last gift on Christmas morning and wanting to make it last as long as possible.

Liana's knuckles were white, her lips dry, and her heart racing as he worshiped each new discovery. His hair, still damp from bathing the dog, trailed over her belly and she gasped from the sensation. "Travis."

He glanced up at her with eyes heavy with desire. "What do you want?"

"You," she said, breathless. "I want you."

He nudged her legs apart, but didn't touch her there. Instead he left soft, wet kisses on her calf, her knee, her inner thigh.

Liana groaned and lifted her hips off the bed in invitation.

He laughed. "What a difference a few days makes."

"Shut up," she said, panting, "and just do it, will you?"

"Gladly." He skimmed two fingers over her, causing her to cry out. "Are you sure this is what you *really* want?" he teased, as he pushed his fingers into her.

Liana whimpered and broke out in a sweat. He drove her mad with his fingers and tongue until she came with a shriek not once but twice. She was like a rag doll by the time he reached for the last of the condoms.

With his hands framing her face, he slid into her. Brushing his lips over hers, he moved slowly.

Drowning in him, she looked up to find him watching her and wanted so badly to tell him she loved him. Instead, she wrapped her legs around him and used everything she had to show him.

CHAPTER 19

Awakened by the call from Liana, Beck propped his head on his hand to watch Jessie sleep. Sprawled face down on the bed hugging the pillow, her blond curls formed a wild halo. Between bouts of passionate lovemaking, she had slept in his arms throughout the unforgettable night. He twirled a curl around his finger and brought it to his nose to breathe in the scent of flowers and sunshine that was all Jessie.

He marveled at the way she had stormed into his life and turned his well-ordered existence upside down. If only he could see past the next week to how they would manage to make a life together. Imagining her getting into a limo to return to New York, he saw himself going with her. He'd give up his job, his home, his entire life if that's what it took.

And to think, he hadn't even known her a week ago. The thought made him laugh softly as he pressed his lips to her shoulder.

She stirred, and one bottomless blue eye fluttered open. "Hey."

"Hey, yourself."

"I was just having the most amazing dream."

He shifted to cover her body with his. "Yeah?"

"Mmm." She raised her bottom to press against his erection.

Blinded by lust, Beck couldn't believe he already wanted her again. "What happened in this dream of yours?"

"I saw you and me and three little blond kids running around. You were wearing faded jeans and an unbuttoned red plaid flannel shirt. I watched you with the kids, and all I wanted was to kiss the bit of chest I could see under your shirt. There was a Christmas tree and a fire in the fireplace. I could smell the pine and the smoke and maybe a turkey roasting in the oven. It was so vivid. I wanted to reach out and touch it."

Choked with love and emotions he had never experienced quite so acutely, Beck slid his hands under her to cup her breasts. He watched a lone tear trickle down her cheek and kissed it away.

"I want it so bad," she whispered. "It's the only thing I've ever really wanted—a home of my own that's safe and full of people who love me."

"I'll give you that, Jessie. I want to give you everything."

She squiggled under him, seeking him.

"Wait, honey. I need to get a condom."

"No condom. Just you."

"We can't."

She reached back to stop him from leaving her. "We can. The timing's not right anyway."

He slid into her from behind. Knowing the position was new to her, he moved carefully, reveling in her heat and the rare sensation of sex without a condom. "You'll be sore, honey."

"I don't care." She pushed back at him frantically. "Don't go slow."

Biting his lip to keep from coming too soon, Beck raised her to her hands and knees, spread her legs further apart, and gave her what she wanted.

Travis and Liana spent the day overseeing final wedding details. He left for an hour to take Dash to the vet, who found nothing at all wrong with the dog. At five o'clock, an hour before the wedding was due to begin, Liana stood in the middle of the deserted tent and gave the setting one last visual inspection.

Travis watched her as she chewed on her lip, her brows knit with concentration. *My sweet, amazing girl. Your father was right—there's so much more to you than your exquisite face. And now that I know just how much, what am I ever going to do without you? Was it really not even a week ago that I had to ask Sam who the lovely creature in the hideous dress was?*

He stepped into the tent to rescue her from the obsessive attention to detail. Massaging her shoulders, he kissed the back of her neck under her heavy ponytail. "Everything looks perfect, sweetheart."

She turned to him. "Are you sure it's right? Did you check?"

"Not that I needed to, but yes, I checked. You did a terrific job." He toyed with the wireless headset that lay around her neck. "You're a natural. Everyone here says so."

She laughed off the compliment. "They have to say that. They know I'm your girlfriend." Her eyes clouded. "Or, well, your something . . ."

"My girlfriend." He kissed her softly. "At the very least, my girlfriend."

The sparkle of excitement in her eyes delighted him. "Yeah?"

He nodded. "Want to go steady?" he asked with a small smile.

"Another thing I've never done."

Travis drew her into his arms, touched by her on so many levels. Once again the words he wanted to say to her burned the tip of his tongue. "Liana . . ."

Resting her head on his chest, she said, "Hmm?" When he didn't answer, she looked up at him. "What is it, Travis?"

He shook his head. "Nothing." He kissed her forehead and then the tip of her nose. "Let's go get changed."

Travis showered, shaved, and took his tuxedo into the bedroom to give Liana full run of the bathroom.

Dash lay on her bed in the corner and watched him with tired eyes.

When he was dressed, Travis squatted down to scratch Dash behind the ears. The dog sighed with pleasure.

"How you doing, girl?" He spoke softly, and Dash seemed to hang on his every word. "I sure am glad you're back. You knew you had to come home so I wouldn't be alone when Liana left, didn't you? We'll be all right, though, won't we? We were all right before she showed up, and we'll be all right after she goes."

"Travis?"

Still in a squat he twisted around. Dumbstruck by the sight of her in a simple black gown he could only stare.

She smoothed her hands over the long skirt. "Is this all right?"

Travis stood up and crossed the room to her. "When did you find the time to go shopping?"

She smiled. "It pays to know people in the fashion world. My friend Marco sent it by overnight mail yesterday. I work at his shows, so he has my measurements. I didn't want anything too fancy, but since the wedding was formal . . ." Her voice trailed off. "It's all wrong, isn't it?"

"No, sweetheart," he said, his voice thick with emotion as he ran his hands over her bare shoulders. He could see she had made an effort to downplay her appearance, but had succeeded only in making herself even more beautiful than usual. "It's perfect."

"I was worried about what you said. Maybe having a minor celebrity at their wedding will annoy Justine and Tom. I don't want to do anything to take the attention away from them, so it might be best if I wasn't there. You could take care of anything that comes up."

"First of all, if the number of reporters sitting outside my gate is any indication, you're a *major* celebrity. And second, Tom and Justine don't mind if you're there. In fact, they think it's very exciting."

"How do you know?"

"I asked them before I put you in charge of their wedding."

Amazed, she said, "You did?"

He nodded and kissed her nose. "So did your friend *Marco* send shoes to go with that dress?"

Liana's face lit up with a delighted smile. "Are you jealous?"

"Don't be ridiculous," Travis said with a sniff. "Jealous of a man who makes dresses for a living? Whatever."

Liana laughed. "You *are!*"

He tapped on his watch. "Shoes, Liana . . ."

She looped her arms around his neck. "Did I mention Marco is a full-blooded Italian with that jet-black hair and that fabulous olive-toned skin that all Sicilian men have? Mmmm . . ."

"You're just trying to piss me off so you can have more make-up sex," Travis said.

She tossed her head back and laughed.

He took advantage of the opportunity to sink his teeth lightly but possessively into her neck.

Liana gasped.

"You need to break the news to your Italian stallion that you're going steady," Travis said, trailing his tongue over her collarbone.

"Marco and his lover will be thrilled to hear that. They've been after me for years to get a boyfriend. They say everyone should have one."

With his arms tight around her, Travis lifted her off her feet. "You're an evil bitch," he said with an amused scowl.

She framed his face with her hands and kissed him with complete abandon. "And you're very sexy when you're jealous," she whispered. "Especially in Armani."

"Let me guess," he said, raising an eyebrow as he set her back down. "Another friend?"

Since she couldn't deny it, she nodded and slid her hands over his lapels. "He'd want you to model for him if he could see the way you wear him."

Travis cringed. "Not in this lifetime, sweetheart."

"You could make a fortune," she insisted.

"I'd rather live out of the back of a Pinto."

Travis saw the flash of hurt that crossed her face and was sorry he had been flippant.

"Do you really think it's so terrible?" she asked.

"For me it would be. That's all I'm saying. For you, it's something you've been very successful at, and you should be proud of that."

"I am," she said with a defiant lift of her chin. "I know it's not exactly a noble profession, but I've always believed if you're going to do something you should be the best at it."

Travis died a little inside as she defended her work, reminding him that she'd be going back to it far too soon. "And you are. The very best. Now, get your shoes, and let's go before we're late."

Liana started to say something, but seemed to think better of it. She turned and went back into the bathroom where she had left her shoes.

Hand in hand, they walked the short distance between The Tower and the club with Dash trotting along at their heels. Photographers with huge long-range lenses went wild at the North Point gate and in boats that dotted the shoreline.

"You'd think they'd be tired of us by now," Liana said.

"We seem to get more interesting to them with every passing day."

"I can't wait to see the headlines our formal attire will generate."

Travis stopped walking all of a sudden and pulled her into his arms.

"What are you doing?" she asked in a scandalized whisper.

"Making their day," he replied the moment before his lips captured hers in a passionate kiss.

Liana's face was scarlet by the time he finally let her go. "You shouldn't have done that," she said as she brushed a hand over her mouth.

Surprised to see she was genuinely annoyed, Travis asked, "Why?"

She gave him a look that said he should know why and went into the club ahead of him.

Inside, they were hit right away with several last-minute issues, and Travis never had a chance to pursue it further.

Hours later, he stood at the side of the tent—in almost the same spot as when he first saw her—and watched Liana oversee the cutting of the cake.

Beck walked up to him. "Everything going all right?"

"Seems to be. Liana's got it all under control. Is Dash behaving?"

"She's been sleeping in the office all night."

"She's done in from her big adventure."

"No doubt."

"You talked to the photographer?"

Beck nodded. "I made it very clear we'd slap him with a lawsuit if any pictures of you or Liana end up in the press."

"Thanks. How's Jessie doing?"

"She's great. Fabulous, in fact."

Travis studied his friend, noted the smug, satisfied look on his face, and would bet big money that he'd recently gotten laid. "Anything you want to tell me?"

"I love her."

Taken aback, Travis stared at him.

"Don't act so surprised. Like you aren't in the same boat."

"Yeah, well. . ."

"Can't deny it, can you?"

Travis knew it was pointless to even try. "No."

They stood together in silence and watched Liana interact with the bride and groom.

"She's got a real way with people," Beck observed. "Look at her. She's almost made them forget who she is."

Pleased his friend was able to see beyond Liana's glossy veneer, Travis nodded. "I offered her a job coordinating weddings for us."

Beck raised an eyebrow in surprise. "Really?"

Travis shrugged but never took his eyes off Liana. "I thought she might enjoy it. She hasn't come right out and said no, but she's leaving next weekend to go back to her real life. That's probably for the best."

"Is that so?"

"It's where she belongs."

"Let me ask you this: When you offered her the job did you tell her you love her?"

Travis winced. "Didn't mention that."

"Why not?"

A knot of tension settled in Travis's chest as he watched Liana share a laugh with the bride. "I figured I'd start with the job, and if I was able to convince her to stay we'd figure out the rest later."

"And of course you know that was ass backward."

"Um, no, not until you graciously pointed it out to me," Travis said, dripping with sarcasm. "Thanks for that. Did you tell Jessie yet?"

"Yep. Last night. When you know you're looking at 'the one,' it's not hard at all to say the words."

Travis glanced over at Liana again. "Yeah. I guess."

"Tell her, Trav."

He shrugged. "I don't want make her feel obligated to me. Whatever she decides, she has to do it on her own."

"She can't decide anything if she doesn't know how you feel."

Travis had to concede that Beck had a point. "I'll think about it. What are you going to do about Jessie?"

"I haven't the foggiest idea."

Travis laughed. "Let me know when you figure it out, will ya?"

"You'll be the second to know."

Travis navigated his way through the tent to where Liana consulted with the wait staff captain, took the headset off her, tossed it to the surprised waiter, and reached for her hand.

Liana, who had stopped talking in mid-sentence, tugged at the grip he had on her hand. "What are you *doing?* I was working."

"You're done," Travis said as he took her into his arms on the dance floor.

"Says who?"

"The boss."

"Oh, you're being so insufferable!"

He kissed her cheek. "You did a wonderful job, sweetheart. The whole thing was smooth as silk." He was aware of the exact instant her head of steam dissipated.

She turned her eyes up to meet his. "Really?"

Touched once again by her vulnerability, he said, "Really." He pulled her tight against him and swayed to the music.

"Travis."

"What?" he asked against her ear, sending a tremble through her.

"Thank you for letting me do this, for showing me there are other things I can do."

"I should be thanking *you*. You really bailed me out this week."

"It was fun. This whole week has been the most fun I've had in far too long."

"For me, too. I've been all work and no play for years. Speaking of play, what do you say we get out of here for a couple of days this week?"

"And go where?"

"New Hampshire. Beck has a place on Squam Lake. We can sneak away, leave the paparazzi behind, and hide out for a couple of days. What do you think?"

"I'd love that, but I promised my mother I'd spend some time with her tomorrow."

"That's fine. We can leave Monday morning. How about we take her and David out on the boat tomorrow?"

"I'll ask her. She adores you, so I'm sure she'd love to spend the day with you."

"Adores me, huh?" Travis said with a smug grin.

"You're being insufferable again."

"And what does her daughter think of me?" Travis asked, gazing down at her as he held his breath in anticipation of her reply.

Liana reached up to caress his face. "Her daughter thinks you're a very special man." With a smile, she added, "A *sensitive*, romantic, special man."

It wasn't what he wanted, but it was a start.

CHAPTER 20

The brisk westerly wind the next day helped Travis dodge most but not all the photographers who followed them in boats.

Liana kept twisting around to see how close they were.

"Relax, honey." Agnes patted her daughter's knee. "Just ignore them. They can only ruin our day if we let them."

"You're right, Mom. I'm sorry. Can I get you another Diet Coke?"

"No, thank you."

Travis had brought the dinghy so they could row into the beach after they anchored the sailboat off Prudence Island. On his second trip to the beach, Travis swore when Dash jumped out of the boat and beat him to the shore.

Watching from the beach, Liana and Agnes laughed as he glowered at the dog.

They enjoyed the lunch Travis had brought, even though they were being photographed the entire time. After they had eaten, Agnes wandered down to the water. When her wide-brimmed straw hat blew off her head, Travis gave chase. He finally caught up to it and returned it to her.

"Thank you, Travis."

"No problem." He glanced back at the blanket, saw Liana absorbed in conversation with David, and decided to walk along the water's edge with Agnes.

"This has been a lovely day," Agnes said. "I haven't been sailing in years."

"I'm glad you're enjoying it. I hope you'll come again, even after Liana leaves."

Agnes glanced up at him. "Are you so sure she's going to leave?"

He shrugged. "There's nothing for her here."

"Oh, Travis. How can you say that? I think she'd give it all up if only you'd ask her to."

"I don't want her to do it for me. It has to be her decision, or one day she might resent me for it."

"Maybe if she knew what would be waiting for her she might seriously consider it."

"Maybe, but I still say she has to figure out what she wants to do with her life before she can figure out what she wants to do about me."

"I was thirty-five when I had her," Agnes shared. "I had given up on having children, and then I was pregnant. It was the most exciting time." Shading her eyes from the sun, she looked up at him. "I remember how it felt when she came into my life. I can't imagine what you're feeling is all that different."

"Probably not," Travis conceded.

"You're just what she needs, Travis."

Travis laughed, surprised by the compliment. "Why do you say that?"

"Because you're secure enough in your own skin to be the man who brings Liana McDermott to the dance. And you know how to have fun. You've shown her this week there's more to life than work—something no one else has been able to do since she left home."

Touched, Travis smiled. "David's a lucky man. I like him. He's easy to be around."

"Yes, he is. In fact, I believe he's over there asking my daughter for my hand in marriage." Agnes cringed. "He's old-fashioned that way."

"That's very sweet," Travis said, amused by the blush that was so much like her daughter's. "I'd like to have your wedding at North Point. It'd be my gift to you."

Agnes gasped. "Travis! I could never! That's too much!"

He stopped walking and looked down at her. "I've spent the last few years building that place and nurturing it and watching it grow. What good is all that work if I can't occasionally do something I want to there?"

"I just . . . I don't know what to say."

"Say yes."

She went up on tiptoes to kiss his cheek. "You're a lovely young man, and I hope my daughter realizes how lucky she is to have met you."

"Thank you," he said, humbled. "So is that a yes?"

"I'll say yes to having the wedding at North Point. We can fight about the details later."

Travis laughed. "She's your daughter, all right."

"I'll take that as a compliment."

He offered her his arm to walk her back. "As well you should."

On the blanket, David took a drink from his bottle of beer and glanced over at Liana. "So, Liana, has your mother mentioned that I asked her to marry me?"

"Yes, she did."

"And how do you feel about that?"

Liana reached over to put her hand on his arm, anxious to put the poor man out of his misery. "I want my mother to be happy. And you make her happy. It'll give me a lot of peace of mind to know she has you when I can't be here."

"Thank you for that," he said with visible relief. "She's given me quite a run for my money."

Liana laughed. "I have no doubt."

David shook his head with amusement. "She's worth it, though. Now that you finally know about us, we're going to be married before the end of the year. She doesn't need to be done with school to get married. I don't want to give her all that time to change her mind."

"That's probably the best plan."

"She'll want you here for the wedding."

"And I will be."

He looked over to where Travis and Agnes were having an animated conversation. "She was under the impression you might be sticking around for a while."

Liana glanced wistfully at Travis. "I have contracts. Legal obligations. I can't just walk away without regard for the people I employ. They're counting on me."

"What about what you want?"

She shrugged.

"I know it's not really my place . . ."

"You're going to be my stepfather before too much longer. I want you to feel that you can speak freely to me."

He smiled. "I'm doing my best to think of you as Agnes's daughter and not the world-famous Liana McDermott."

"I appreciate that."

"You're not at all what I expected, Liana. In fact, you're a pleasant surprise. And what I was going to say is there's no contract you can't get out of, no legal obligation that can't be dissolved if you want something else. Don't let that stop you from doing what it takes to be happy. Take it from me—true love comes along once in a lifetime, twice if you're lucky like I've been."

"How do you know if it's true love?"

"When he or she is all you think about, and every ounce of your energy goes toward getting through whatever you have to so you can get back to him or her again."

Liana looked over at Travis, who had her mother on his arm as they walked along the shore together. By David's definition, what she felt for Travis certainly qualified. She returned her attention to David. "I'm going to enjoy having you in my family." She embarrassed him when she kissed his cheek. "I'm glad my mother finally told me about you."

He laughed. "So am I. You have no idea how glad I am."

Travis and Agnes rejoined them on the blanket.

"So, honey, Liana has given us her blessing." David reached for the backpack he had brought with him to the beach. He withdrew a jeweler's box and opened it to unveil a diamond ring. "Now you can take this without any reservations."

Liana sighed and leaned back against Travis.

He looped an arm around her shoulders.

Agnes battled tears as David slid the ring onto her finger and kissed her.

"No getting out of it now," David said, wiping away her tears.

Agnes swatted him. "I can't believe you brought the ring with you to the beach!"

"I've had it with me every time I've seen you since I first asked you, just in case you changed your mind. I told you I wasn't going to give up."

"Congratulations, Mom." Liana brushed at tears of her own. "It's a gorgeous ring."

Agnes reached out to hug her daughter. "Thank you, honey."

"Well," Travis said. "Looks like we have another wedding to plan."

Beck was in his office setting up the patrol schedule for the next forty-eight hours when his personal cell phone rang.

"Peter Beck."

"Mike Tripp here. What a blast from the past to get your message, man! It's been what? Five, six years?"

Smiling, Beck sat back in his chair. "I've been meaning to call, but you know how it is. Time gets away."

"I've been busier than a one-legged man in an ass-kicking contest myself," Tripp said in his thick Brooklyn accent. When Beck worked for the FBI in New York City, he often crossed paths with the NYPD lieutenant who had since made captain. After they had caught up for a few minutes, Tripp said, "So listen, I checked into your friend Jessica Stone's situation. The guy who's been hassling her? Bad dude, man. Level three sex offender on parole."

Beck's smile faded, and his chest tightened with tension. "Why can't you arrest him as a violator?"

"He keeps slipping through our fingers. We almost had him yesterday, but we lost him."

Beck sat up straight as an arrow of fear shot through him. "What do you mean you lost him?"

"He disappeared into a crowd, and we haven't been able to locate him. We're looking though. As long as your friend is out of the city, she should be safe. He knows he'll be violating his parole if he steps one foot off Manhattan Island."

"Can you fax me a picture of this guy?" Beck asked, giving him the number.

He stood watch over the fax machine as the mug shot came though. Thomas Spector was an average-looking white guy with beady eyes and a round, doughy face. Otherwise, there was nothing remarkable about him except for his rap sheet, which Tripp had included as page two of the fax.

Beck swallowed a sudden surge of panic as he scanned the sheet. "Is it possible to get daily reports until you locate him?"

"No problem. What's the deal with you and this model, Beck?"

"She's my. . ." My world, he wanted to say but didn't. "We're involved."

Tripp let out a low whistle. "Lucky dog."

Beck got up, locked his office, and headed for The Tower at a quick clip. "Yes, I am, and until you find Spector, she'll be right here with me." He'd tie her to the bed if he had to, but she wasn't going anywhere.

"We'll find him—hopefully off island so we can throw his ass back in jail where it belongs."

Beck jogged across the parking lot, desperate to get to her. "That'd work for me. Keep me posted."

"I will."

In The Tower lobby, Beck pressed the up arrow to the elevator repeatedly. After an interminable wait, the elevator arrived and delivered him to the fifth floor. He knocked on her door, his heart beating hard with anxiety and dread and love—more love than he'd known it was possible to feel. "Jessie?" He pounded on the door. Without a second thought, he used his passkey to open the door. "Jessie?"

Running through the apartment, he discovered she wasn't there.

He called the cell phone he had given her and got the automated voicemail message. Reaching for the walkie-talkie on his belt, he barked out orders to his staff to find her—immediately.

On the patio, he scanned the beach and boardwalk, but both were empty. His heart pounded with fear. *Where the hell is she?*

He took the elevator back down and was running to the clubhouse when he received word from one of his employees that Jessie was in the gym.

Weak with relief, Beck stopped, bent in half, and rested his hands on his knees as he fought to get himself under control. He had never been more afraid in his life. After several deep, calming breaths, he stood upright to find one of his men watching him.

"Everything okay?"

Beck nodded. "Thanks for the help. Go on back to work."

With a brisk nod, the other man headed for the main gate.

Beck went into the clubhouse and made a beeline for the gym.

Alone in the small exercise room, Jessie was gathering up her belongings when he walked in. Her face was flushed from exertion, and Beck longed for a robe to throw over the tiny leotard she wore. He didn't want anyone else to see her luscious body.

"I heard you were looking for me. Is everything all right?"

He crossed the room and scooped her up.

"*Peter!* I'm all sweaty."

"Don't care."

"Put me down! I stink!"

"Just give me a minute, Jessie. One minute."

She stopped fighting him and sank into his embrace. "Will you tell me what's wrong? Your face is red, and you look all flustered. What's going on?"

"Couldn't find you. You weren't at your place or on the beach. You didn't answer your phone. I couldn't find you." It was all he could do not to weep at the sweet relief of having her back in his arms. "Scared me."

"I'm right here." She ran her fingers through his hair and dropped soft kisses on his jaw. "I'm here."

Putting her down all of a sudden, he took her hand and half led, half dragged her into his office. He shut and locked the door.

She took a step back from him. "What're you doing?"

"This." He pinned her to the closed door and ravaged her mouth. Hooking his fingers under the straps to her leotard, he pulled the garment straight down to her knees.

As her breasts sprang free, Jessie gasped and tried to cover herself. "Not *here*," she said urgently. "You've lost your mind!"

"Right here," he insisted, dropping his shorts and lifting her. He impaled her on his erection before she could utter another word of protest.

Her pretty pink lips formed a surprised "Oh" as her blue eyes burned with desire. "This is crazy," she said on a long exhale. "*You're* crazy."

"About you." Gripping her bottom, he moved her up and down over his rigid length, her breasts dragging against his chest.

Her head fell back in surrender, and Beck took advantage of the opportunity to sink his teeth into her long, elegant neck while breathing in her earthy, feminine aroma. What she considered stink was sweet aphrodisiac to him. "I love you, Jessica," he whispered. "I love you, love you, love you."

With her fist buried in his hair and her other arm hooked tight around his neck, she rode him with abandon.

He pressed her against the wall and pounded into her until her breathing suddenly changed and her tight channel clutched his cock in a series of spasms that took his breath away. Muffling her cries with his lips, he surged into her, the climax seeming to come straight from his toes.

A full minute of silence and throbbing aftershocks later, Jessie let out a nervous laugh. "I'll have to get lost more often."

"Please don't. You scared the hell out of me."

"I'm so sorry. I had my iPod on. That's why I didn't hear the phone."

Emotionally and physically spent, Beck sagged against her, supporting them both on shaking legs. "S'okay."

"Did something happen?"

He suspected she already knew her stalker was a paroled sex offender, but she didn't know the police had lost track of him. If Beck had his way, she'd never know that. "Nothing happened. I just couldn't find you. Didn't like it."

She tightened her arms around him. "I'm right here, and I'm not going anywhere without you."

Beck closed his eyes to indulge in another personal first—a silent prayer of thanks.

CHAPTER 21

Travis left for the grocery store at seven o'clock, hoping to get out and back before the media gathered at their post outside the gate for another day of watching "Triana," which was the silly code name they had given them. Only two photographers manned the gate, both of whom snapped photos of him leaving. Travis wondered how they could stand the boredom of waiting hours for people to do something interesting.

At the store, he stocked up on what they would need to hibernate in New Hampshire for a few days. He took the groceries to the checkout counter and glanced with trepidation at the tabloids, still finding it hard to believe he saw his own face looking back at him. Reaching for one of them, he winced at the huge front-page photo of him kissing Liana before Tom and Justine's wedding. "Oh, she's going to *love* that," he muttered, tossing the paper onto the conveyer belt. "Nice move, North."

He returned from the store and stashed the cold food in a cooler with ice and put it with the other grocery bags in the back of one of the North Point SUVs.

Beck pulled into the garage in his truck. "Are you guys ready?"

"Let me go get Liana. She's moving slowly this morning. We'll be right down." He took the elevator to his condo and went into the bedroom. "Ready, sweetheart?"

"Uh huh," Liana said with a big yawn as she zipped her bag.

"You brought some jeans and a sweater, right? It gets chilly up there at night, even in the summertime."

"Uh huh."

He hugged her. "Sorry we had to get up so early. I wanted to get out of here before the reporters showed up."

"No problem," she said, another huge yawn rattling through her.

"You can sleep in the car," he said with a kiss to her forehead. He picked up their bags and whistled for Dash. They took the elevator to the garage, and Beck held the passenger door for the dog while Travis stowed their bags in the back of the SUV.

Travis opened the back door for Liana. "After you."

She got in, and he followed.

"Why don't you lay down, and then I'll lay next to you," Travis suggested.

When they were settled, Beck tossed a blanket over them.

The moment they were in the dark under the blanket, Liana was hit with a fit of the giggles. "This is so ridiculous."

The absurdity of it also struck Travis, and they were both laughing by the time Beck started the car.

"You guys better cut it out or I'll be laughing, too, and then all of this will have been for nothing when the reporters realize I've got other people with me."

Travis fumbled around until he found her face with his hand and held her still so he could silence her giggles with a deep kiss.

"Oh, *jeez*," Beck groaned when he heard them kissing. "I think I preferred the laughing."

Travis laughed against her lips, but when he began to pull back from her, Liana wound her arm around his neck and held him in place.

"We're through the gate with no one noticing," Beck said. When he was greeted with silence, he said to no one in particular, "Thanks, Beck. That's good news. We're glad to hear we made a clean getaway." Greeted by more silence, he sighed and mumbled, "I feel like I'm back in high school or something."

Beck drove them off the island to a prearranged spot along Route 24 where another North Point employee waited for him in a second car. "All right, you two, time to come up for air." He got out of the car and knocked on the back window. "You're on your own."

"Thanks, Beck," Travis called. To Liana, he said, "Are you going to let me go?"

"Not yet." She pushed her hands into the back pockets of his jeans and anchored him to her.

"What are you up to?" Travis's amusement turned to desire when she skimmed her tongue over his ear. "Liana . . ."

"Want to know what else I've never done?" she whispered.

"I'm almost afraid to ask."

She tilted her hips provocatively. "In a car . . ."

Travis swallowed hard. "If you're going to have sex in a car, sweetheart, you're better off doing it in the dark and not on a major highway."

"It's dark where I am," she argued.

"If we ever got caught—"

"I thought you liked taking risks," she said, sliding her hand into the front of his jeans.

He gasped when she stroked him.

"Come on," she pleaded. "You wouldn't deny me, would you?"

Knowing he could deny her nothing, he shook his head. "No."

"Do you have a condom?"

"Wallet," he managed to say as she unzipped him.

She tugged his wallet out of his pocket and handed it to him.

He pushed the blanket aside to get enough light to retrieve the condom.

She took it from him. "Let me."

Travis fell back on the seat and gritted his teeth when she rolled on the condom.

She wiggled against him in the tight space as she removed her shorts and panties. "This is so exciting," she whispered, her violet eyes sparkling in the early morning light.

He was filled with love for her as he brushed the hair off her forehead and tipped his head to find her lips. Shifting so he was between her legs, he kissed her deeply as he entered her.

She arched into his thrusts and pulled her legs back to give him better access.

"Liana," he groaned. "You're making me crazy."

She laughed and clutched his back in encouragement. "Be crazy, Travis," she whispered. "Let go of all that control you're so proud of."

Her words fired his passion, and he could feel the sweat pooling on his back as he pounded into her. For the first time in his life he cried out when he came, at the same instant she did. "Oh my God," he said when he had recovered the ability to speak. "You've put some sort of spell on me, haven't you?"

She giggled. "It must be the same spell you've put on me."

He drew back to look at her. "I love you, Liana." The words tumbled out before he could stop them.

She gasped.

"I know I wasn't supposed to, but I do."

Under him, she struggled to sit up.

Travis used a tissue to get rid of the condom and pulled his clothes back on while Liana did the same.

When they were dressed, Travis glanced over at her and found her face set in an unreadable expression. "Would you say something? Please?"

She looked up at him with violet eyes shining with tears. "I love you, too."

Travis thought he would die from the relief of hearing those words from her. He reached for her. "Really?"

She nodded against his chest.

"For how long?"

"Almost from the beginning. What about you?"

"Since I saw you in that pink monstrosity at Enid's wedding, and you were so worried about your mother."

She sighed. "What are we going to do?"

He kissed the top of her head and hugged her tightly for a long moment. "Right now we're going to kick Dash out of the front seat so we can go to New Hampshire. We'll figure out the rest later." Tilting her chin up he kissed her. "I love you. I've been dying to say that to you for days, and I can't tell you how good it feels to be able to say it now."

Nibbling on her lip, she looked up at him. "I'm scared."

"Of what, sweetheart?"

"Of hurting you, of disappointing you, of so many things."

"How about we do this for now—let's just take today and tomorrow to enjoy being in love without any worries about what happens next. Can we do that?"

"Yes," she said with a firm nod. "Yes, we can."

Running through his to-do list on the way back to North Point, Beck made a mental note to talk to his staff about a couple of things he wanted to try to catch the vandals. He also needed to check in with the local police to see if they had gotten anything off the film they'd confiscated after the fire. They needed a break, and hopefully they'd get one before anything else happened.

Navigating the long access road that led to North Point, he couldn't believe what he saw outside the gates. The media mob had easily tripled since the day before. "Jesus," he muttered. He couldn't imagine making a living by hoping for a glimpse of a celebrity.

Approaching the mob, he slowed to a crawl and laid on his horn to get them out of the street. "Freaking idiots." Glancing to his right, he gasped as he made eye contact with the beady-eyed, dough-faced man from the mug shot Tripp had faxed to him. Beck slammed the truck into park, leaped from the car, and pushed his way into the crowd.

Unfortunately, they pushed right back.

"What the hell are you doing?" one of them cried. "Get your hands off me!"

"Get out of the way!" Beck shouted, pushing his way past the outraged photographer.

The rest of them closed ranks around their colleague and refused to let Beck through.

Scanning the nearby thicket of trees and brush, he reached for his cell phone and dialed 911. "This is Peter Beck, chief of security at North Point," he said as loud as he could. "I just saw a level-three sex offender wanted in New York City among the press gathered outside our gates."

Suddenly the mob wasn't so resistant, and he was given access to the back of the crowd. By then, though, Spector had managed to meld into the mix. Despite a frantic effort, Beck couldn't find him amid the hundreds of photographers and reporters. Sweating profusely, he searched every car in the long line of vehicles parked along the road.

When the police arrived a short time later, he filed a formal report and showed them a photo of the man he was looking for. As he was finishing up with them, he took note of a buzz circulating through the growing crowd.

"Is Jessica Stone staying at North Point, too?" one of them asked.

Beck turned toward the voice. Making an enormous effort to keep his face blank, he said, "No, she isn't."

"We have reliable information that she's staying here," another said.

"She's not."

"And you would know?"

"I know everything that goes on here."

The local cop used a bullhorn to let the reporters know they were expected to stay out of the road and away from the North Point gate. "Anyone who creates an obstruction or nuisance will be arrested," the cop added.

Beck shook his hand. "We appreciate the help."

"No problem. Never seen anything quite like this in these parts."

"No kidding."

Beck got back in his truck and dialed Mike Tripp on his cell phone. "I saw him," Beck said without preamble. "Spector. He's here at North Point where we're hiding Jessica. I lost him in a mob of photographers and media, but I saw him. I know it was him."

"I'll issue a warrant and get with your local folks. I may come up there myself if it comes to that."

"How in the hell would he know she's here?" Beck asked, his heart racing as he parked at The Tower.

"No idea, but I'd love to get my hands on whoever told him."

"So would I," Beck said from the elevator. "I'll check in with you later."

He let himself into Jessie's apartment and went right to the bedroom where she was curled into a ball in the middle of the bed. Propping his hands on the doorframe, he hung his head with relief and exhaustion. His mind raced with plans and scenarios and ideas. He needed to get her out of here, but he couldn't leave North Point. Not with the vandals still on the loose and Travis away. And how would he have a minute's peace if he couldn't see to Jessie's safety himself?

"Hey, you're back," she said, yawning. "Come here."

Beck went to the bed and stretched out next to her.

"Did Travis and Liana make a clean escape?"

"Uh huh."

"You were gone a long time." She snuggled up to him. "And you're hot and bothered." Her lips coasted over his jaw. "I'm the only one who's allowed to get you that way. So who is she, and how can I kill her?"

He forced a smile and stared up at the ceiling, trying to decide how much he should tell her.

"Peter? What is it? You're rigid with tension."

"We need to talk."

She went still in his arms. "I thought we resolved all that."

"Not about us."

Her body relaxed against him.

He rolled over so he was on top of her. "I'll never leave you, Jessie. So don't ever, ever, *ever* worry about that, okay?"

She ran her fingers through his hair and brought him down for a kiss. "Okay."

"I don't want you to panic or freak out or anything. . ."

"Is that why you're lying on top of me?" she asked with a saucy smile.

"One reason." He took a deep breath and leaned his forehead against hers. "Baby, I saw Spector outside the gate."

She gasped. "No. That's not possible."

"It was him. I know it was, but he got away before I could grab him."

"He can't be here," she said, a hysterical edge creeping into her voice.

"Listen to me." He kissed her. "Are you listening?"

Big blue eyes flooded with tears as she nodded.

"He's not getting in here. Every one of my staff has his photo. I swear to God he won't get to you."

Her body trembled beneath his. "I'm scared."

Beck slid his arms under her and held her tight against him. "There's nothing to be afraid of. I promise you. I won't let you out of my sight. No one will ever hurt you. Not ever again."

"I should leave. I should go somewhere else. I'll fly to Tahiti or something."

"That's an option," he said, swallowing his own panic. He couldn't very well force her to stay at North Point knowing her stalker was outside the gate, but how could he let her walk away from him, even temporarily, when she was in danger? "If you want that, I'll arrange it."

"Only if you come with me."

"I can't, honey. Not now, and especially not with Travis out of state."

"Then I'm not going, either."

"I hoped you'd say that." He watched a different look come over her face, a gutsy courageous look that warmed his heart.

"I'll stay here, and we'll get through it together."

He pressed his lips to hers. "That's my girl."

CHAPTER 22

Travis and Liana were quiet on the three-hour ride to Beck's cabin in Holderness, New Hampshire, both of them struggling to process the change in direction their emotionless fling had taken. Through Boston and into New Hampshire, the radio provided the only soundtrack to the scenery.

From the driver's seat, Travis stole occasional glimpses at her as he tried to stay quiet and give her the time she needed to get used to the idea that he loved her. *That poor lip,* he thought, wishing he could stop the car and take her into his arms. *Soon enough we'll be at the cabin, and I can hold her for two days. She loves me, too. That's all that matters. We'll figure something out as long as we both feel the same thing. Before she leaves on Sunday I'll ask her to marry me. I can't let her go—even temporarily—without telling her I want us to have a life together. I know she has commitments and obligations, but I can wait until she's free. As long as I know she loves me, I can wait.*

He reached for Liana's hand and laced his fingers through hers.

She looked over at him and smiled, but her eyes were sad.

Determined not to let anything take away from the giddy joy he felt at the moment, he chose not to question the sadness. He would do everything he could over the next few days to show her that love was not something to be feared or regretted—and it certainly shouldn't make her sad.

"Have you spent any time up here before?" Travis asked when the silence in the car began to get long as they headed toward the White Mountains.

"My parents and Enid's parents used to bring us up to ski every winter."

"Were you two always close?"

She nodded. "We were both only children, so we were like sisters only better. We could go to our own homes at the end of the day and weren't on top of each other all the time the way sisters are."

"And brothers," he added.

"You would know about that. How many do you have?"

"Four brothers, two sisters, seven nephews, and three nieces."

Liana shook her head. "I can't imagine having such a big family. Are you close to any of them?"

"Just Evan, really," he said, looking almost pained. "The others not so much. Our lives have gone in different directions since I left home. None of them went to college, and they kind of hold it against me that I did."

"That doesn't seem fair."

He shrugged. "What they fail to get is I had something none of them have ever had—ambition. Even without the athletic scholarship I would've found a way to go to college. That's the difference between me and them—they'd rather bitch about not going than do whatever it took to get there."

Liana twisted around in her seat so she could see him better.

"I'll tell you what," he said with a bitter grimace. "None of them have any trouble asking me for money—often."

"Do you give it to them?"

"Most of the time, but I've started saying no a lot more than I used to."

"I'm sorry, Travis."

"It is what it is. You can pick your friends, but you can't pick your family," he joked. "Luckily, I have Evan. I'd take ten of him over one of the others."

Liana smiled. "What's the age difference between you?"

"I was eleven when he was born, and I adored him from day one. While everyone else was caught up in what was wrong with him, all I saw was the cutest baby ever." He glanced over at her. "Remember when I told you I set my parents up before I spent any money at North Point?"

She nodded.

"I kind of blackmailed them into making me Evan's legal guardian before I gave them the money. I didn't like the way they were treating him, so once I was his guardian I got him placed in a good group home and helped him find a job he loves."

"Where does he live?"

"In Newport."

"Really? I didn't realize you had him so close to you."

Travis nodded. "He spends a couple of weekends a month with me, and we talk most days on the phone."

"Do you think I could meet him?"

"I'd love for you to meet him."

She leaned over and kissed his cheek.

"What was that for?"

"For being a good guy."

"I guess that's better than sensitive."

"That, too."

He groaned. "We're almost to Holderness," he said, anxious to change the subject.

Liana glanced out at the lake region scenery. "It's so pretty, isn't it?"

"Yes," he said, looking at her and not the scenery. "It sure is."

"You seem to know exactly where you're going."

"Beck and I come up here to go fishing all the time."

"Can't you do that at home?"

"I find it hard to relax when I'm within a hundred miles of North Point," he confessed. "Plus the skiing is better here than in Rhode Island."

"That's true. How did you meet Beck?"

"We played football together at Ohio State. He was my favorite receiver. His grandfather built the cabin and left it to Beck when he died."

The SUV bounced along the unpaved road that led to the cabin. Travis parked the car and walked around to open the back door for Dash and the passenger door for Liana.

She got out and took a deep breath of the pine-scented fresh air. "Oh, this is beautiful," she said, taking in the view of the lake in front of the log cabin.

"Go check it out. I'll unload the car and come find you."

"I'll help."

"I've got it." He lifted the cooler out of the car. "Go ahead. Keep half an eye on Dash."

"All right."

Liana wandered toward the path that led through the trees to the lake where Dash already splashed about. She sat on a log and watched the dog play. For the hundredth time in the last few hours she thought about Travis professing his love for her. *What am I going to do? All I think about is him. All I want is to be with him.*

Dropping her head into her hands, she thought about the months of work she had ahead of her. On Sunday she'd be on her way back to Milan for two days to redo portions of the *Vogue* job that, fortunately, they had been unable to reschedule during her vacation. Then she had three weeks in Spain to shoot the first part of the next *Sports Illustrated* swimsuit issue. After that came the fall fashion shows in Paris, Milan, and New York, followed by two weeks or more in the Bahamas to finish *Sports Illustrated*. Then there was a catalog job, a couple of charity events around the holidays, and whatever else Artie had committed her to since she'd been on vacation.

Just the idea of all that work brought Liana to tears. *How am I going to get through that when I only want to be with him?*

That's when Travis found her. He dropped to his knees in the sand in front of her and put his arms around her. "Baby, what's wrong?"

Liana clung to him.

Dash whimpered and lay down in the sand, her head on Liana's foot.

Travis held Liana close to him for a long time.

"I'm sorry," she whispered.

He wiped the dampness from her face. "Don't be sorry, sweetheart. Just tell me what I can do for you."

"Nothing." She caressed the face that had become dearer to her than any other. "I'm the only one who can do what needs to be done."

"I don't like the sound of that."

"Would you believe me if I told you it has nothing to do with you?"

He kissed her hands. "Would you believe *me* if I told *you* that after this morning everything about you has something to do with me? I want to make you happy, Liana. That's all I want."

She combed her fingers through his thick dark hair as she studied him. "You do make me happy."

He stood and tugged her up off the log. "Come see the cabin."

"Is that a line?" she asked with a weak grin, hoping to salvage their day after her mini-meltdown.

With his arm around her shoulders he smiled and escorted her up the path to the house.

Liana took in the rustic furnishings, the huge fireplace, and the knotty pine walls and floors. "Oh, what a great place!"

"I'm glad you like it." He went into the kitchen to unload the rest of the groceries. "I thought it would be a good place to hide out for a couple of days."

She came up behind him and wrapped her arms around him. "It's perfect. Thank you for bringing me here."

He squeezed her hands. "I just want you to relax and enjoy yourself, all right?"

"Mmm." She rested her face against his back. "I can do that."

He pulled a box of cereal from the bag, and the tabloid newspaper dropped to the floor.

Liana bent to retrieve it. "Oh," she exhaled when she saw the photo of them in formal attire kissing.

Travis turned to her and reached for the paper. "Give me that, Liana. You don't need to be looking at that. I don't know why I bought it."

She waved him off and took the paper into the living room where she sat down to read the article that accompanied the photo. "Listen to this: 'Travis and Liana celebrated their recent engagement with a formal dinner at Travis's exclusive North Point Country Club. They plan a New Year's Eve wedding at North Point, where they met just a week ago. The whirlwind romance has taken one of the world's most beautiful women off the market and has broken the hearts of men everywhere.'"

"They just make shit up," Travis said, incredulous. "Except for the world's most beautiful woman part, of course. I'd sue them if I thought it would make any difference."

"It's not worth the bother."

"Let's put that where it belongs." He joined her on the sofa, eased the paper out of her hands, and tossed it into the fireplace to be burned later. Turning to her, he brought her closer to him and tipped his head to kiss her softly. "What do you feel like doing this afternoon? We could swim, take the canoe out on the lake, go fishing. What sounds good to you?"

"Whatever you want to do is fine with me."

He hooked an arm around her neck and kissed her with more passion this time. "Or, we could spend the afternoon in bed . . ."

"That's an option?" she asked with a teasing smile.

"Sweetheart, that's *always* an option."

Kissing his neck, his jaw, his face, and then his lips, she said, "Why don't we take a little 'nap' and then go fishing?"

He pretended to think it over. "Is sleeping required during this nap of yours?"

"Strictly prohibited."

"How about pajamas?"

"Also prohibited."

He moved so fast she had no time to react when he scooped her off the sofa, tossed her over his shoulder, and carried her to the larger of the cabin's two bedrooms.

She laughed as he deposited her on the bed.

He made slow love to her and told her over and over again that he loved her while telling himself it didn't matter that she didn't say it back.

Travis built a bonfire on the beach to cook the rainbow trout they had caught on their fishing expedition in the canoe. After dinner Liana took a flashlight and walked back to the cabin to get the marshmallows they had forgotten to bring to the beach.

On her way through the living room, she bent to retrieve the tabloid from the fireplace grate, tore off the front cover, and returned the rest of the paper to the fireplace. She studied the picture for a long moment, remembering how annoyed she'd been by Travis's audacity in front of the press. Now it was hard to take issue with the beautiful picture they made with the sun and the bay behind them as they shared an intimate moment with the world. She folded the page and went to tuck it into her suitcase, knowing that soon pictures and memories would be all that remained of their blissful idyll.

She rejoined Travis at the beach and handed him the marshmallows.

"You were gone a long time. Did you have trouble finding them?"

"No, they were right where you said they'd be."

"Everything okay?"

She crouched down next to him, rested her arms on his shoulders, and kissed his cheek. "Everything's perfect—the lake, the trout, the cabin, you."

"In that order?" He lifted an eyebrow in amusement. In the firelight he was even more handsome than usual.

"No, not in that order."

He put his arm around her and brought her down next to him on the blanket they had spread on the sand. The fire provided some welcome warmth against the cool breeze blowing in off the lake.

Travis gave Dash the first two marshmallows.

Liana laughed as the dog attacked the sticky gob. "She is so spoiled."

He shrugged but didn't deny it as he presented Liana with a golden marshmallow.

She slid it off the skewer and popped it into her mouth. "Oh, that's good."

Travis reached for her hand and used his lips to clean up her sticky fingers before he reloaded the skewer.

"It's so peaceful here."

"It really is, but of course anywhere is peaceful when a hundred reporters aren't chasing you."

"That's true. I'm sorry it's turned into such a circus at home."

"I told you before you don't have to be sorry." He pulled the skewer out of the fire and Liana fed one of the marshmallows to him. Tossing the skewer into the sand he pulled her to him and kissed her with a mouthful of warm marshmallow.

"Mmm," she said. "That's yummy."

"Yes, you are." He urged her down to the sand beside the bonfire and kissed her again.

"Guess what else I've never done?" she whispered when they finally resurfaced.

He trailed his tongue over her bottom lip. "What's that?"

She trembled with desire from what he was doing to her lip and from the warm skin she had discovered under his Ohio State sweatshirt. "Sex on the beach—and not the drink."

He chuckled. "It's kind of chilly for that tonight, sweetheart."

Liana reached for the blanket and rolled them over so she was on top of him and the blanket wrapped around them.

"Well, when you put it like that. . ."

She laughed and bent to kiss him.

CHAPTER 23

Beck lay awake next to Jessie, listening to the soft cadence of her breathing. After spending just a few nights with her, he couldn't imagine ever sleeping alone again. His mind raced, and he didn't realize he was grinding his teeth until they began to ache. He sat up, took a deep breath, and released it.

Moving to the window, he surveyed the North Point property, wondering if Spector was out there somewhere watching them. Had he figured out where Jessie was staying? Beck stared into the darkness until his eyes began to water from the effort. Turning back to the bed, he reached for his shorts and pulled them on. He was tugging on his T-shirt when Jessie turned over looking for him.

"Peter?"

"I'm here, baby."

She pushed unruly curls off her face. "What're you doing?"

"I need to go downstairs for a few minutes." He flipped on a nightlight for her. "I'll be right back."

"Don't go."

He sat on the bed and rested his hand on her satiny smooth shoulder. "I'll only be gone a minute."

"You're looking for him. Spector."

"No, I just—"

"Don't lie to me, Peter. Please don't."

He replaced the hand on her shoulder with his lips. "I want to take a quick look around. I promise I'll be right back."

"I've been thinking…"

"About?"

"Well, I wondered if maybe we could bait him somehow. Let him see me and then maybe—"

"No. Not happening."

"*Why?*" she cried. "I can't stand waiting for him to make his next move. It's making me crazy. At least this way I'd know when it was going to happen. I could plan for it and control it. With your help, that is."

"It's out of the question, Jessie.

"It's my life."

"And your life means everything to me, so don't ask me to dangle you in front of a psychopath. Do you know what this guy has done to other women? Do you have *any* idea?"

"No," she said in a small voice that tugged at his heart. "I told the cops I didn't want to know."

"Well, if you did, you wouldn't be so willing to be used as bait. Believe me."

Crossing her arms over her breasts, she sat up in bed. "If you're going, hurry up so you can come back."

"I don't have to go. I was just feeling edgy and needed to do something."

"I hate that feeling. That's why I want to put an end to it. Can you understand that?"

"Of course I can, but endangering yourself isn't the way to do it. Let's give the cops a chance to hunt him down. Every police department on the island is looking for him, and New York is sending a couple of guys, too. We'll find him, honey." He dropped his shorts, removed the shirt, and crawled into bed with her.

She cradled his head against her chest and ran her fingers through his hair. "What are we going to do about everything else?"

"What do you mean?"

"You know—you, me, us."

"Oh, that."

"Yes," she said with a chuckle. "That."

"Well, I sort of hoped you might marry me."

Jessie gasped.

"What?" He tilted his face up so he could see her. "You don't want to?"

"I want to. I really, really want to."

Beck slipped an arm around her neck and brought her down for a passionate kiss. "That doesn't count as my official proposal. I can do better."

"I don't want better. That was perfect."

"No wine? No roses? No bended knee and diamond ring? What will people say?"

"They'll say Jessica Stone landed herself one *hot* husband."

He hooted with laughter. "Sure they will." Linking his fingers with hers, he brought her hand to his lips. "I love you, Jessica Stone. Will you marry me?"

"Yes, Peter Beck. I'll marry you."

"What about your modeling career?"

Her saucy smile stopped his heart. "If you knock me up, no one will want me."

"I will." In a swift move, he turned them and spread her out under him. "I'll always want you."

She looked up at him, her expression a mixture of surprise and desire.

"One knock up, coming right up."

Laughing, she hooked her legs around his hips to urge him on.

Liana awoke in a panic on Wednesday morning when she realized they had just four days left before she had to go back to work.

She turned onto her side to watch Travis sleep. He hadn't shaved since they arrived at the lake and had the start of a beard after three days. Liana wanted to bottle him up and bring him with her so she would never have to be without him again. But he had his business and his life in Portsmouth, and she would have to think about her own work again before much longer.

Resting her head on his chest, she put her arm around him, wanting to be as close to him as possible, to savor every minute she had left with him.

"Travis," she whispered, dropping soft kisses on his chest. "Time to wake up. We have to go home."

He tightened his arms around her but didn't open his eyes. "Don't wanna."

"We have a wedding to get ready for," she reminded him.

"Don't care."

She propped herself up on an elbow. "Yes, you do."

"Can't we stay here forever?"

"I wish we could."

His eyes finally opened. "Do you, Liana? Do you really wish we could?"

"Yes."

He ran his fingers through her hair. "Are you ever going to say it again, or was it a one-time thing?"

Her heart racing, she studied him. "It wasn't a one-time thing." She caressed his face, giving special attention to the stubble on his jaw. "We need to get going. We have to meet with Ben and Lucy at noon."

"Yeah." He turned away from her, got out of bed, and shut the door behind him when he went into the bathroom.

Sighing, Liana fell back against the pillow. She wanted to give him what he needed but was afraid she wasn't ready yet to give him everything. Until she was it didn't seem fair to be talking about love all the time. He knew how she felt, and for now that would have to be good enough.

After more than two days of waiting for a glimpse of Triana, the press corps went wild when they spotted them returning to North Point just before noon.

"Jesus Christ," Travis muttered. "There're three times as many as when we left."

His security detail was no match for the crush of reporters and photographers who surrounded the SUV, blocking their way onto the property.

Liana reached for the door handle.

Travis lunged across her to grab her arm. *"What are you doing?"*

"I was just going to ask them to move so we can get by. They're usually very polite to me."

"Liana, look at them. They've been broiling in the hot sun for two days thinking we were somewhere on the property. Do they look happy to be finding out we weren't even here?"

"What are we going to do? We can't sit here all day."

"I'm sure Beck has called the police by now."

Liana bit her thumbnail. "This is awful for your business."

"On the contrary. The club's receipts were through the roof last week, most likely because the members were hoping to catch a glimpse of you." He began to inch the car forward, forcing the photographers to get out of the way.

She worked on her bottom lip as they approached the North Point gate where several of Travis's security staff attempted to clear a path for them.

Dash barked at the reporters through the window.

A few minutes later they cleared the gate and were able to enter the property.

"Wow." Travis shook his head as he pulled into his parking space at the club and looked over at her. "This is a whole new ballgame, Liana. I hope you realize that. They're like a pack of rabid dogs. Until you leave on Sunday, you have to stay on the property. That's the only way we can keep you safe. And I want you to get serious about security when you go back to work. They're not going to drop this story just because you're not here anymore. It's going to be like this from now on."

"I'm afraid you're right."

"You can't be without security. Not even for one day."

"I know." She got out of the car and went into the club to prepare for their meeting.

Travis watched her go, filled with frustration and fear and love. He punched the steering wheel before he got out to follow her.

The next two days passed in a blur as Liana saw to what seemed like a thousand details in preparation for Ben and Lucy's wedding. She spent a great deal of time on the phone reassuring the jittery bride that everything was going to be perfect.

Beck did them a favor and drove Travis's brother Evan to North Point for a visit on Thursday evening, and Liana fell instantly in love with the sweet young man. Seeing Travis interact with his brother only made her love him more. On Friday morning, her Aunt Edith called to invite Liana to a welcome home dinner for Brady and Enid that night.

"I'd love to come, Aunt Edith. What time are they due in?"

"Uncle Charlie's already left for Boston to meet their noon flight," Edith said. "I know she'd love to see you once more before you have to go back to work."

"I'd like that, too."

"So you've made quite the stir around here since you've been home," Edith said. "The entertainment shows and the tabloids are all about you and that adorable Travis North. And did you see the cover of *People* magazine this week?"

"It's been quite a nuisance actually."

"I'm sure it has," Edith said with a laugh. "Do bring him with you tonight, honey."

"I'll ask him. So how about Mom getting engaged? Were you shocked?"

"Floored! Just absolutely floored—and so relieved to find out she wasn't losing it."

"I know! Have you met David yet?"

"We will tonight. I can't wait."

"You'll love him," Liana assured her aunt. "He's perfect for her. Did she tell you I've been helping out with a couple of weddings here at North Point?"

"She did. That sounds like fun."

"It has been, but I have a meeting with the staff in fifteen minutes, so I have to run. I'll see you tonight?"

"We're looking forward to it."

As Liana ended the call, Travis walked into the office carrying his golf clubs, which he propped in the corner. He had spent the morning entertaining representatives from the Newport County Convention and Visitor's Bureau.

"How was it?" she asked, noticing with disapproval that he was sunburned.

"Pretty good. I let them win hoping they might be persuaded to beef up their out-of-state promotion of North Point."

"Sounds like a good strategy. No sunscreen again, huh?"

"Didn't need it," he said with a grin at the face she made at him as he leaned across his desk for a kiss. "Who was on the phone?"

Liana relayed her aunt's invitation to dinner.

Travis ran a hand over the stubble on his jaw. "Why don't we just have them all here?"

"Because they invited us there."

"But Liana, the media . . ."

"The media is *not* going to run my life."

"I'm afraid you're not taking this seriously enough, sweetheart."

She got up, grabbed the files she needed for her meeting, and walked around the desk. "Guess what, Travis? I'm a full-grown adult, and I've handled my life pretty well up to this point. I don't need you or anyone else telling me what to do."

"Excuse me for being worried about your safety. By all means, do whatever you want."

"Thank you. I will."

"Great."

"You're welcome to come with me to my aunt and uncle's tonight," she said on her way out the door. "If you don't wish to, let me know, and I'll have my mother and David pick me up."

"I'll go," he grumbled.

"Great," she said, mimicking his tone.

Jessie found Liana working alone in Travis's office and knocked on the door.

"Oh hey," Liana said. "Come in."

"I'm sorry to disturb your work."

"I could use a break. How's everything going?"

With a glance over her shoulder at the door, Jessie slid into a chair in front of the desk. "He's driving me crazy," she whispered. "He won't let me out of his sight."

"He's worried. We all are."

"And I appreciate that. Y'all have been so nice to me, but I can't stand the tension. I feel like I'm going to snap. And Peter. . . Between the vandals and the stalker, he's not sleeping or eating. He's a wreck."

"I wish there was something we could do," Liana said, nibbling on her pen cap as she thought it over.

"There is something. . . I've been thinking about it, but I'd need your help."

"Whatever I can do, Jessie. I'm happy to help."

Jessie got up to shut the door. "Here's my idea."

CHAPTER 24

Armed with a stack of photocopies that she held behind her back, Jessie told Beck she was taking a walk with Liana.

"A walk to where?" he asked, his eyebrows narrowing with suspicion.

Jessie swallowed. "Just on the boardwalk."

"Give me a minute, and I'll go with you."

"No," she said emphatically—more emphatically than she'd intended. "I need some girl time, Peter."

He sat back in his chair, and she could tell by the set of his shoulders that he was resisting the urge to insist on accompanying her. "Are you going to talk about me?"

Jessie smiled. "Maybe."

"Keep it clean and hurry back. I'll be worried."

"I'll be fine. Why don't you go over to my place and take a nap? You look ragged."

"I don't need a nap," he said, appearing offended by the suggestion. "Go have your girl time, but stay within sight of the club, do you hear me?"

"Yes, dear." She blew him a kiss and skipped out the door, knowing she didn't have much time because she was certain he would follow her.

"Coast clear?" Liana asked in the hallway.

"Temporarily. Let's go."

Moving quickly, they went outside and headed for the main gate. Just as Jessie had hoped they would, the reporters gathered there snapped to attention when they saw Liana coming toward them.

"Thanks again for doing this," Jessie said. "I know how much you hate them."

"If we can use them to do some good, it'll be worth it."

Shouted questions greeted them at the gate.

Several of Beck's men jumped between the two women and the mob.

Liana held up a hand to quiet the throngs as camera flashes exploded.

Blinded and sick with fear, Jessie scanned the sea of faces but all she saw was the residual blue light from the flashes.

"I'll answer a few questions," Liana said, "but first I need to ask a favor. My friend, Jessica Stone, is being stalked by this man." Liana took a copy of the mug shot Jessie handed her and held it up. "He's been spotted in this neighborhood. His name is Thomas Spector. He's a level-three sex offender and parole violator from New York."

Jessie handed the stack of flyers to the closest reporter. He took one and passed the pile on. She relaxed ever so slightly when it appeared they'd have their cooperation.

"If you see him anywhere near North Point, we ask you to please call 911 and notify North Point security. This man is considered dangerous, so don't attempt to capture him."

"Liana, are you and Travis North engaged?"

Liana's entire body went rigid with tension. "We are not."

"Any plans for a wedding?"

"Just the one we're holding here this weekend," she said lightly.

"Did you arrange for Jessica to hide out here?"

"I did a favor for a friend who was being pursued by a dangerous stalker."

"Jessica, how did Spector find out you were here?"

"That's a good question. We don't know."

"How long do you both plan to be here?"

"I'm going back to work on Sunday," Liana said.

"I'm not sure how long I'll be here," Jessie said.

"Will you see Travis again after you leave, Liana?"

"I sure hope so," Liana said with a wistful smile. "That's all for now. We appreciate any help you can provide in locating Thomas Spector. Thank you." She slipped an arm around Jessie's shoulders, and they turned away from the reporters to find two angry men waiting for them.

"What the hell do you think you're doing?" Peter grabbed Jessie's arm and steered her toward The Tower.

The rapid-speed click of cameras followed the foursome across the parking lot. No doubt they'd be all over the tabloids by morning.

"That was a damned stupid thing to do," Travis added. "What if they had rushed and trampled you?"

"They were very nice," Liana said, tugging her arm out of Travis's grasp.

"You wouldn't consider using me as bait," Jessie told Peter.

"So you pull a foolish stunt like that instead?"

"It won't be foolish if they help us find him."

"Let's go to my place," Travis said when they reached the lobby.

They rode the elevator in stony silence, emerging into Travis's penthouse.

Jessie watched Peter stalk across the living room to the patio. Fury rolled off him in great waves, sending a bolt of fear through her as she followed him. "I'm sorry you're mad," she said, "but I'm not sorry I did it. I had to do *something*."

He spun around to face her. "Why? Because I wasn't?"

Startled by his venomous tone, she took a step back from him. "I know you're doing all you can. This was something *I* could do."

"I might be doing all I can but it isn't enough, is it? I can't catch your stalker. I can't catch the vandals. What the hell am I good for anyway?"

Travis joined them. "Beck. . ."

"What, Travis? Are you going to say it, too? That I'm doing all I can? Do you think the guy lying in the hospital with second-degree burns is grateful for all I'm doing?"

Jessie had never seen him like this before and was frightened to realize her plan had sent him over some sort of edge.

"Peter, honey, listen to me."

He shook her off.

Jessie stared at his exhausted face as it sunk in that she had managed to wound his pride by taking matters into her own hands.

"You should find someone else for this job," Peter said to Travis.

Jessie gasped.

"I don't want anyone else," Travis said. "I already have the best there is."

Peter shook his head. "I'm not the best. Nothing I've done has worked. Maybe if you bring in someone else—"

"That's not going to happen," Travis said. "It's you or no one."

"I'm sorry, Travis, but I'm resigning."

"Peter!" Jessie cried. "You can't quit! You love this job."

He looked down at her with broken eyes. "You're right. I do love it, but he needs something I can't give him and so do you." Glancing at Travis, he added, "I'll stay through the wedding."

"Beck—"

Peter turned away from his friend and went inside. A minute later, they heard the ding of the elevator as he left.

Her eyes swimming with tears, Jessie turned to Travis. "What do we do? We have to do something."

"We need to give him some space," Travis said. "He's frustrated and he's tired. He'll come around."

Jessie wished she could be so certain.

Liana put her arm around Jessie. "Travis is right. Give him some time to settle down. We upset him with what we did, and he's acting out."

"You upset *both* of us," Travis added with a pointed look for Liana.

"I'm sorry to have caused all this trouble," Jessie said, her throat thick with tears. "I just needed to do *something* about this situation with Spector. Waiting for him to strike again was making me nuts."

"Hopefully, some good will come of it," Liana said, walking Jessie to the elevator. "I'll check on you later."

Jessie hugged her. "Thanks again for your help."

"I was happy to do it. It sure would be nice if the paparazzi proved useful to me for once."

Liana waited until the elevator doors closed before she turned to face Travis. "Don't say it."

"What shouldn't I say? That your plan was harebrained? That you put yourself in danger? That you put Jessie in danger?"

Liana pulsed with anger. "Let's see what you're saying if our 'harebrained' scheme actually works." She stalked away from him and went into the kitchen, her heart heavy because of the distance between them since they returned from the lake.

They were preparing for her imminent departure by withdrawing from each other. Liana knew she was doing it, too, which was ridiculous, because all she really wanted was put her arms around him and hold him close. She also felt bad about snapping at him just now and earlier, too, since she knew he was worried about her safety.

She filled Dash's bowl with dry food and refreshed her water. The dog nuzzled Liana's leg.

Liana crouched down to pet her. "I'm going to miss you, silly girl, and your daddy, too," she said, kissing the dog's face.

Dash replied with a swift lick across Liana's cheek.

Liana laughed and hugged her.

"You don't have to miss either of us," Travis said from the doorway.

Liana turned to him, and suddenly all she cared about was making it right again. "I didn't mean to be nasty. I know you're worried about me."

"I'm terrified for you, sweetheart. I'm afraid they're going to hurt you in their pursuit of the big story. And when I saw you out there at the gate with only a few of my guys standing between you and a mob. . ." He shuddered.

Her heart softened at his obvious concern for her. "Maybe it was harebrained, but Jessie was desperate, and I wanted to help her."

"I shouldn't have said that. Who knows? It could work. It just pains me to think of you leaving here and being totally vulnerable."

"I talked to Beck this afternoon, and he told me who to call about security. In fact, he offered to set it up for me."

"Thank you." Travis crouched down next to her and kissed her forehead. "Now I'll be able to sleep at night after you leave." Petting the dog, he added, "I meant what I said, Liana. You wouldn't have to miss either one of us—or worry about being safe—if you just stay."

"I can't do that. You know I can't."

He reached out to stop her from standing up. "You can do anything if you want it badly enough."

"And tie myself up in litigation for the next five years over broken contracts and disputes with disgruntled employees? No, thanks."

"Stay," he said with a pleading edge to his voice. "Stay with me."

"I told you from the very beginning that I would go, Travis. Please don't do this to me."

"You also said no strings and no emotions, but we both fell in love. Or at least I did. What do we do about that?"

"I fell in love, too," she said sadly. "And I wish I knew what to do about it."

"If you wanted me as much as I want you, you'd think of something. You'd find a way."

"You're being kind of unfair, aren't you? You expect me to turn my back on my career and my life, but would you? Would you sell this place and give up your dream to follow me around the world?"

His jaw clenched as he studied her. "If that's what it took to be with you, then yes, I'd do it in a minute."

Touched, Liana reached out to caress the tension from his face. "I'd never ask you to make such a sacrifice for me. And I don't want you to ask it of me, either. If one of us is going to give up everything it has to be done freely, or all that's good between us will be lost to resentment. I know if we're going to be together, it has to be me who walks away from the life I had before. All I'm asking for is some time to make sure that's the best thing for me. Do you understand what I'm trying to say, Travis?"

"Yes, I think so."

"We've known each other for less than two weeks, even if they were the two most wonderful weeks of my life."

"Mine, too." He sat on the floor and drew her into his embrace.

"It's still *only* two weeks." She rested her head on his chest. "I need some time to figure things out."

"How much time?"

"I don't know."

He tipped her chin up so he could see her eyes. "I want you to marry me, Liana." She shook her head. "Don't."

"Don't what?"

"Don't say that to get me to stay."

"You'll insult me if you accuse me of that. I *do* want to marry you, but I wasn't planning to ask you when we were sitting on the kitchen floor."

"Travis . . ."

"Wait." He silenced her with a kiss. "Hear me out." Caressing her face, he said, "I love you, Liana. I love you more than I've ever loved anyone. I want us to have a life together, and I'm willing to do whatever it takes to make that happen. You're telling me you're not ready for that just yet, so I'll wait. A year, two years, however long it takes. But I don't want you to leave here on Sunday and not know that I want us to have it all."

She combed her fingers through his hair. "In a perfect world, I'd love nothing more than to marry you and have children with you—a handsome dark-haired boy with his daddy's devastating grin—"

He looped a lock of her hair around his finger. "And a beautiful violet-eyed princess with her mommy's silky hair."

Liana's eyes filled with tears. "Don't," she whispered again. "Please."

"We can have it, Liana," he said urgently. "Anything and everything you want. I'd give you everything, if only you'd let me."

She punched his shoulder half-heartedly as tears cascaded down her face. "I knew I couldn't just have a fling."

He laughed softly and brushed away her tears. "I knew you couldn't, either."

"Then why'd you let me try?"

"Because I wouldn't have missed this time with you for anything, no matter what's ahead for us."

"I do love you, Travis," she said, looking up at him. "I know I've hurt you by not saying it more often."

"You've said it." He pressed his lips to hers. "That's all that matters."

"We're going to be late for dinner."

He stood up and held out his hand to help her up. "Do you think another half hour will matter?"

"I don't suppose so. Why?"

"I want to be with you right now, Liana," he said, his face serious and sad. "I need you."

She took his hand and led him into the bedroom where she undressed him, then shed her own clothes, and followed him into bed.

He held her tight against him for a long time before he even kissed her. When he pulled back from her, Liana was stunned to see tears in his eyes.

"Travis." She cupped his face, and brought his lips to hers for a soulful kiss.

"Look at me," he said as he entered her.

Liana shifted her eyes up to meet his.

"Tell me again, Liana," he whispered, holding his body still. "Just once more."

Steeped in the sensation of being filled by him in every possible way, she reached up to caress his face. "I love you, Travis. I love you so much."

"And I love you. No one else will ever love you the way I do." He began to move but didn't let her look away.

Forty-five minutes later, they sped away from North Point before the reporters could hop into cars that lined the access road and give chase.

Liana showed him a couple of shortcuts that bettered their lead, and by the time they reached Middletown, they were almost certain they had escaped.

"That gets the old heart pumping, doesn't it?" Liana asked, placing her hand on her chest.

"Sure does," he agreed. "I wasn't aware I'd be doing NASCAR driving when I bought this car."

Liana laughed and relaxed against the soft leather seat. She directed him to Memorial Boulevard, past First Beach and up the hill to Bellevue Avenue, the same neighborhood as Newport's famous mansions.

Travis whistled when they drove through a stone archway. "*This* is where they live? I knew they were loaded, but I never imagined this."

"The house has been in my Uncle Charlie's family forever."

"Was it weird for you growing up knowing she had so much and you had, well—"

"Less?" Liana asked with a laugh. "Not at all, because as snooty as Enid can be with other people, she's never pulled that crap with me. I wouldn't let her get away with it. I have the best memories of this house. We played fabulous games of hide-and-go-seek on the third floor and had tea parties and Christmas parties."

"It's funny how your uncle, who grew up with all this, is so normal," Travis said as he helped her out of the car.

"He's the loveliest man."

"I was always so relieved when he came to the pre-wedding meetings with Edith and Enid," Travis confessed.

Liana laughed. "Believe me, I know what you mean. He keeps them under control."

"He's the only reason I didn't kill the two of them before the wedding."

"Oh, you're *bad*," Liana said with a teasing grin. "That's my aunt and cousin you're talking about."

"Then I don't need to tell you."

"No, you certainly don't." She stopped him at the foot of the stone stairs and reached up to kiss him. "Thanks for coming tonight."

"Happy to," he said with a grimace.

Liana laughed and kissed him again.

The door opened, and Enid let out a squeal when she saw them kissing. "I've been reading about you two all over Europe! Quit that lip locking and get in here, will you?"

Travis nudged Liana to go on ahead of him.

She and Enid embraced at the door.

"You and I are *so* going to talk later," Enid said in what she considered to be a whisper.

"Liana doesn't kiss and tell," Travis said.

"She does to me," Enid informed him. "And how are you, Mr. North?"

"Just fine, Mrs. Littleton," he said, resorting to the phony tone he reserved just for her. "And you?"

She reached up to kiss his cheek. "I'm divine, but I have a bone to pick with you."

"Why? What did I do?"

"I just asked you to drive her home not create an international incident."

Travis laughed. "I believe you put a few other ideas in her head that went far beyond a simple ride home."

Liana blushed. "Travis . . ."

"I *sure* did." Laughing at her cousin's discomfort, Enid looped her arms through theirs and escorted them into the living room where the others were enjoying cocktails. One full corner of the room was piled high with wedding gifts waiting to be opened. Travis and Liana were greeted with hugs and kisses and handshakes.

"There they are!" Uncle Charlie said. "We were beginning to worry."

Travis and Liana exchanged guilty glances, and he smiled when her cheeks turned bright red.

"Sorry to worry you," Liana mumbled.

"We had a little trouble getting through the media's defensive line," Travis added.

"Well," Edith said when Charlie had fixed drinks for the new arrivals. "Let's have dinner."

CHAPTER 25

The first chance she got, Enid spirited Liana upstairs to her old bedroom and closed the door. "Was it sweaty?"

Liana flopped down onto the bed. "*Super* sweaty."

"It's about damned time!" Enid clapped her hands with delight as she lay down next to Liana. "Details. I need details. He's *so* sexy. If it wasn't for Brady, I would've wanted a go-round with him myself."

"You can't have him," Liana teased. "He's mine."

Enid studied her cousin for a long moment before she pushed herself up on one elbow. "Oh my God. You're in love with him."

"Completely."

"Oh, Leelee, *really?*"

Liana nodded and then began to laugh from the burst of pure joy that accompanied her confession.

Enid reached for her and hugged her. "I'm so glad to hear that. I knew he'd be perfect for you. You're going to quit modeling and come home to marry him, right?"

Liana shrugged. "I don't know yet. I mean he wants me to—marry him, that is—but I can't make life decisions based on two weeks. That would be foolish."

"You'd be foolish *not* to. It'd be the best thing you ever did. It's so obvious he's wild about you."

"I don't want to be pressured into anything." Liana got up from the bed and walked over to look out the window. "I need to make my own decisions."

"Liana, if you let this man go, you'll regret it for the rest of your life."

Liana turned to her. "I know that, but I don't want to have other regrets, either. I just want some time to figure it out." She threw her hands up with frustration. "Why does everyone think I'm being so unreasonable because I don't want to make life decisions after two weeks of great sex?"

Enid shook her head. "If that's all it was, you wouldn't be facing any life decisions, and you know it."

Liana sat back down next to her on the bed. "Don't look so disappointed in me. I can't stand it."

"I'm not disappointed. I just want you to be happy, Leelee. And I think you have a real chance for that with the oh-so-divine Mr. North."

"My true north?"

"Only you can know for sure." Enid's eyes sparkled with mirth. "But enough about all that. You *have* to tell me *something* about the sweaty stuff. Just one little detail."

"Travis was right: I don't kiss and tell."

"Oh, *come on!*" Enid said, giving Liana a push.

Liana nibbled on her lip as she mulled it over. "All right, but just one thing. That's all you're getting."

"I'll take it," Enid pulled her legs up Indian style.

"Tonight, just before we came here? That was when he told me he wants to marry me."

"Did he ask you?"

"Not officially, he just said he wants to. So anyway, we had a really intense conversation, and then he said he needed to be with me, you know . . ." Liana felt her face grow hot with embarrassment.

"Uh huh." Enid hung on Liana's every word. "In bed."

Liana smiled and nodded. "He asked me to look at him while we were . . ."

"Doing it," Enid filled in for her.

Liana laughed at her outrageous cousin. "Yes, but it was different this time. It was almost . . . spiritual. That's the only word I can think of to describe it."

"Wow," Enid said on a long exhale.

"Yeah, it was amazing. I've never felt as connected to another human being as I did to him in that moment."

Enid snorted. "You were connected all right."

"Enid!" Liana said, laughing as she pushed her cousin over on the bed. "Anyway, I guess we'll see what happens."

Enid reached for Liana's hand. "Don't walk away from him and think you'll find that connection with someone else, Liana."

"I have a lot to think about," Liana acknowledged. "There's no doubt about that. So what about you? Was it a sweaty honeymoon?"

Enid's eyes grew dreamy. "The sweatiest honeymoon *ever*."

Liana screamed and held up her hands to discourage her cousin from sharing the details.

Jessie paced from one end of her apartment to the other. What had felt spacious and open a few days ago had now become a prison cell as she hid from Spector and the threat he posed. Peter wasn't answering his phone, and he had asked her not to go anywhere without him. But how could she sit here wondering where he was and if he was serious about quitting his job?

As night fell over North Point, she couldn't take it anymore. Grabbing her key and the phone he had given her, she summoned the elevator.

Since his truck was parked in its usual place she asked for him in the clubhouse, but no one had seen him. They even called out to the gate to learn he hadn't been by in a couple of hours. A sick feeling settled in her stomach as she wondered if he planned to quit her along with his job. He couldn't. She wouldn't let him.

Wandering out to the boardwalk, she walked toward the beach hoping she'd find him brooding in the encroaching darkness. "Where are you?" she whispered.

The idea of returning to the life she'd led before she knew him was unimaginable. With one look, one touch, he had changed her forever, and she would do whatever it took to hold on to him.

Between the lights on the boardwalk, the inky darkness had her walking a little faster. Maybe being out here alone wasn't the best idea she'd ever had. Reaching for the phone, she was about to dial Peter's number again when something clamped down on her arm.

"Hello, Jessie."

A hand over her mouth muffled her scream.

On the way home, Travis held Liana close to him and brushed his lips over her hair. "So what did your bossy brat of a cousin get you to tell her?"

"Nothing."

"Why don't I believe you?"

"Because you have a suspicious nature?"

"Let me ask you just one question: Did the word sweaty come up at all?"

Liana was convulsed with laughter.

"I knew it! You *do* kiss and tell! I don't *believe* it!" He tickled her ribs, which sent her into another fit of laughter. "What did you tell her?"

Liana kissed his neck and then skimmed her tongue over his ear.

"Jesus," he muttered. "Are you trying to get us killed? I'm driving a car over here."

She did it again, but this time she also whispered what she wanted to do with him when they got home.

"Liana!" he sputtered. "*Stop.*"

But instead she got more descriptive and slid her hand up his thigh.

Travis sucked in a deep breath and veered the car off the road, into the parking lot at First Beach. The moment he had shifted into park, he reached for her. The kiss was almost violent, his tongue tangling with hers, and he was panting by the time he pulled back from her. "I just want to stop time. I don't know what I'm going to do without you for one day, let alone months on end."

"I never wanted to cause you that kind of pain, Travis."

"No regrets," he whispered. "No matter what, no regrets."

"None," she agreed, reaching for him again.

Several long, hot minutes later, he asked, "Now, what did you tell your cousin?"

Liana replied with a coy smile. "I never kiss and tell."

"You're as much of a brat as she is, but that's all right," he said confidently. "I'll get it out of you."

"Oh, I think I'm going to enjoy that."

When they had once again inched their way through the crowd of reporters waiting for them at the North Point gate, they were surprised to find two police cruisers parked outside the club.

"Wonder what's going on?" Travis said, a muscle in his cheek pulsing with tension.

Liana reached for his hand. "Beck would've called you if something was wrong."

"Yes, you're right."

They parked at the club and went inside, forgetting how anxious to get home they had been just a few minutes earlier. Holding hands with Liana, Travis went straight to his office where Beck was talking with two police officers.

"What's going on?" Travis asked, noting that Beck looked considerably better than he had a few hours ago.

"Oh, hey," Beck said. "I was just going to call you. They've made three arrests in the vandalism and the fire."

"The film we got from that photographer after the fire led us to two Portsmouth High School students," the police sergeant said. "Long story short, turns out they'd been hired by Jim Silvestri."

Travis's eyes widened with surprise. "The Town Council president?"

"The one and only."

"Apparently, this land used to belong to his family, and he was trying to buy it back," the other cop said. "He had almost raised enough money when you swooped in and beat him to it. He's confessed to everything—from putting roadblocks in front of your permits, to using his office to exert influence on others. When that didn't get rid of you, he hired two well-known local punks and set them loose over here."

"Whose idea was the fire?" Beck asked.

"His. The kids claim they had no idea anyone was in the house. They purposely waited until late on a Friday so no one would get hurt."

"How old are these kids?" Travis asked.

"One's fifteen and the other's sixteen."

"I don't want to press charges against them."

"But Travis—" Beck sputtered.

Travis held up his hand to stop his friend. "I want to see them here tomorrow," he said to the sergeant. "Can you arrange that?"

"They're going to be charged for the fire, Mr. North," the sergeant said. "The attorney general's office is prosecuting that case. You can request leniency, but they're going to face charges."

"I'd still like to see them."

"We'll arrange it."

"Are they in jail?" Travis asked.

"No, they were arraigned this afternoon and released on personal recognizance to their parents."

"What about Silvestri?"

"He's being arraigned tomorrow."

Travis reached out to shake hands with the cops. "Thank you very much for the time and effort you put into this. I appreciate it."

"We're sorry it took so long to crack this one."

"It wasn't for a lack of trying on your part," Travis said.

The sergeant's eyes shifted to Liana. "Without those photos, this would still be an open case. They led us to the kids who pointed the finger at Silvestri."

Travis exchanged satisfied smiles with Liana.

Beck saw the cops out a few minutes later.

"Unbelievable," Travis said to Liana when they were alone. "I can't get over that it was Silvestri and that those photos made the difference. We have you to thank. Who knows how long this would've gone on without your traveling band of photographers giving us just the evidence we needed?"

"I'm so glad for you that it's over." Liana looped her arms around his neck. "What are you planning to say to those boys?"

"Since they owe me a ton of money, I'll give them the chance to work it off around here."

"And maybe take them under your wing?"

He shrugged. "Maybe."

"You're a good man, Travis North, and I love you very much."

He caressed her face and leaned in to kiss her.

"Aww jeez, don't you two *ever* take a break?" Beck asked when he returned.

With a smile for Liana, Travis turned to his friend. "So I guess this means we can get back to normal around here."

Beck shrugged. "I still think you'd be better off with someone else running security."

"I don't agree. I need you here, Beck. I need someone with me who I can count on."

"I'll think about it."

"Have you talked to Jessie?" Liana asked.

"Not since I saw her earlier," Beck said.

"I know you're mad about what we did, but try to see it from her point of view," Liana said. "The waiting was getting to her."

"Still, to stick herself out there like that and to drag you along with her. . ."

"She didn't drag me anywhere I didn't want to go," Liana said. "Stop being a fool, and go talk to her."

Beck grinned at Travis. "Does she pull that with you, too?"

"Yep." Travis glanced down at Liana. "It's just one of the many things I love about her. Go find your lady and kiss and make up, will you?"

"All right, I'm going. In light of the arrests I'll be ending some of the surveillance on the property lines and focusing more people on the mob scene at the gate."

"Sounds good," Travis said. "See you in the morning, Beck."

"Have a nice evening," he said on his way out the door.

"We need to celebrate," Travis said as he led Liana from the office.

"What did you have in mind?"

"We'll start with the most expensive bottle of champagne I can find in the bar."

"Then what?"

He whispered the rest in her ear and laughed when her cheeks flamed with color.

"Stop it," she hissed.

"Be glad you weren't driving a car when I did that to you," he retorted.

She smiled at him, but her heart ached when she remembered they had just two more nights together.

CHAPTER 26

Beck practiced what he planned to say on the way to The Tower. Jessie needed to know he didn't approve of what she'd done, but he understood what had motivated her. He wondered if she was mad at him for leaving her alone all evening. At least he had some good news to share for once. The relief at knowing the vandals had been caught took the edge off his anger from earlier. He wished he could have been the one to snag them, but what really mattered is they wouldn't be causing Travis any more grief.

And how just like him to go easy on a couple of misguided kids. Sometimes Beck wanted to smack some sense into his kind-hearted friend. But Travis had excellent judgment, so Beck had to assume he knew what he was doing. If it had been up to him, he would've thrown the book at the punks who had caused them so much trouble.

He stepped off the elevator on the fifth floor and took a moment to prepare himself to talk some sense into Jessie. When he felt ready, he knocked on the door. "Jessie?" *Well, what'd you expect? That she'd be waiting for you? Yeah, kind of. Maybe she's asleep.* Using his key, he let himself in, but right away he could tell she wasn't there. In an immediate panic, he quickly searched the apartment and then reached for his cell phone to call the number he had given her.

She didn't answer, and he forced himself to calm down and remember the last time this had happened when he found her safe and sound in the gym. "She's probably there again," he said, using his radio to call to the clubhouse.

"She was here looking for you an hour or so ago," he was told.

An hour? "Can you check the gym?"

"I'm headed back there now, but the lights are off. I don't think anyone is there." A moment later, his colleague confirmed the gym was deserted.

Beck switched the radio frequency to one that encompassed every unit on the property. "This is Beck," he said, struggling to keep the panic out of his voice as he asked if anyone had seen Jessie. After a series of negative replies, he said, "I need every available staff member in the clubhouse conference room in five minutes."

He left her apartment and summoned the elevator, dialing 911 on his cell phone. As the elevator deposited him on the top floor, Beck finished calling in the report to local police. He knocked on Travis's door. His friend answered a minute later wearing only a pair of gym shorts, and Beck could tell he had gotten him out of bed. "Jessie's missing."

Jessie fought to stay calm as Spector dragged her through the dark to the south end of the North Point property where the smell of fire lingered. Knowing Peter had regular patrols of the property scheduled around the clock, she prayed someone would find her before Spector could harm her.

"How did you get in here?" she finally asked when she had regained the ability to speak.

"Took a long walk on the beach," he said with an oily smile that made her skin crawl. "You and your sexy friend Liana McDermott were so cute out there today talking to the media about me. It was good of you to confirm you were right where your 'bodyguard' said you'd be."

Jessie gasped. One of the men who'd brought her here had told him? That wasn't possible! Artie had hired the top security firm in New York City to transport her. "They didn't tell you. You're making that up. They were professionals."

"Everyone can be bought, my sweet." His fingers dug into her neck as he steered her along the dark path.

"Where are you taking me?" Jessie asked, her heart pounding with fear and adrenaline.

"To our own secret hideaway where no one will bother us."

"Peter will find us. He's already looking for me," Jessie said with more bravado than she felt. She had no idea if he even knew that she'd been taken or if he planned to check in with her after their argument.

"He's been real effective at catching the vandals," Spector said with a harsh laugh. "He doesn't scare me."

Jessie was reminded of the mindless fear of being attacked by her stepfather and vowed to get through whatever Spector had planned for her the same way she had gotten through the hell of her home life—by mentally removing herself from what was happening to her. She had perfected the art of slipping out of the moment and into a safe place where nothing could harm her. It had been years since she'd needed the safe place, but she took comfort in knowing it was still there.

She stumbled in the dark, and he dragged her roughly along with him, no doubt bruising her arms. Imagining Peter taking Spector apart piece by piece also brought comfort. He would find her. She had no doubt. He would find her.

"How do you know she's missing?" Travis asked, running a hand through his hair in an effort to bring order to it.

"She's not in the apartment or the club. They said she was over there an hour ago looking for me. No one's seen her since."

Tying a silk robe around her waist, Liana joined them. "What's wrong?"

"Beck can't find Jessie."

Liana gasped.

"Cops are on their way," Beck said. "And I have our people gathering in the conference room. I could use your help."

"You have it," Travis said.

"Thank you," Beck said, his voice catching. "He has her. I know it."

Liana reached for his hand. "Stay calm. She needs you to stay calm and do what you do best."

Beck sucked in a deep breath as he nodded. "Yes." He made a huge effort to pull himself together and focus on finding Jessie. "You're right. I'll see you over there?"

"We'll be right there," Travis said.

As he made his way to the clubhouse, Beck struggled to take Liana's advice. The night was extra dark since clouds covered the moon, and Beck could only imagine how terrified Jessie must be. *I promised her this wouldn't happen, and then I left her alone for hours because I was mad with her. I may as well have delivered her right to Spector.*

Pushing those thoughts aside lest he go mad with recriminations, Beck stood outside the main door to the club and watched flashing police lights come down the long entrance road for the second time that night.

The same sergeant from earlier emerged from the car along with a patrolman.

"Got some more trouble, Mr. Beck?"

Beck quickly filled them in, and tried to not to panic when the sergeant radioed for additional back up.

"Normally, we require twenty-four hours on a missing adult, but since she's had a history with Spector and you've seen him in the area, we'll waive that," the sergeant explained.

"I appreciate it. We have to find her before he can rape her." As Beck said the words, his heart ached as he remembered what she'd gone through with her stepfather. "We have to find her."

"We'll do everything we can," the sergeant assured him.

Hand-in-hand, Travis and Liana came running across the parking lot as Beck showed the cops inside to where most of the North Point security staff waited for them.

Within fifteen minutes, they had teamed up North Point staff with police to cover every inch of the property and a half-mile beyond the property lines.

"He had to have come in on foot," Beck said. "There's no way he got through our gate."

"That works to our advantage," Travis said. "He can't get as far on foot."

"He's got a significant head start on us," Beck reminded him, the cold fear settling in his gut as he grabbed a flashlight.

"You don't know that," Liana said. "He could've grabbed her right before you went looking for her."

"That's true," the sergeant said.

"Where are you going?" Travis asked Beck.

"To look for her. I can't just sit here and wait."

"I'll go with you," Travis said, glancing at Liana.

She nodded in encouragement.

"You said she has a cell phone?" the sergeant asked.

"That's right, but she's not answering."

"Does it have GPS capability?"

For the first time since he'd discovered her missing, Beck's spirits lifted. "Jesus, how could I have forgotten that?"

"You're not thinking with your head right now." Travis rested a hand on Beck's chest. "This is about the woman you love." He turned to the cop. "Can we track it?"

"If it's on, we should be able to get a reading. It'll take an hour or so, but we'll see what we can do."

"Thanks," Beck said, shoving a handgun into the back of his shorts.

"Let's go," Travis said, grabbing another flashlight. To Liana he said, "Call us if they get a signal."

"I will," she said, stopping him for a kiss. She squeezed Beck's arm. "Be careful."

Spector shoved Jessie into a small wooden shack where the scurry of bugs and rodents made her want to shriek. The smell of old fish and bait had her choking back a gag. He lit a candle, illuminating a grungy cot in the corner and two dilapidated wooden chairs.

The glow of the candle off his doughy face had Jessie stepping back in fear until she reached the far wall of the cabin. As she realized there was nowhere else to go, that the man she had feared for months had her all to himself, and that Peter probably wasn't going to find her before Spector harmed her, Jessie began to cry.

"Oh, now, is that really necessary?" he said in a sickeningly sweet tone. "You and I should be old friends by now. None of this would've been necessary if you had just talked to me the way I asked you to. I asked nicely, didn't I? I sent you nice letters asking you to have coffee with me. That's all I wanted—some coffee, some conversation. Would that have been too much for you to give one of your biggest fans?"

"No," she said softly.

"So why did you ignore me? Why did you make me come after you this way?"

"Because I don't know you."

"The police told you I did bad things to those other women, didn't they? Well, they ignored me, too, so they had to be punished." He took a step toward her. "Just like you do."

"No," Jessie said. "Don't touch me."

"Too good for me, Jessica Stone, the supermodel? Prancing around in your panties for all the world to see. You ought to be ashamed of yourself." He reached up to free the top two buttons on her blouse.

"Please," she whispered, her legs trembling. "I'll give you money. I'll give you anything you want. Just don't touch me."

"Your money means nothing to me." He took another step until he was so close she could feel his breath on her face. "That's not what I want from you."

She turned away from him and closed her eyes. If this had to happen, she didn't have to look.

He unbuttoned her blouse and pushed it off her shoulders.

"Mmm," he said as he fondled her breasts through her bra.

Jessie felt herself slipping away as she imagined they were Peter's hands squeezing her nipples. He was her new safe place. A sense of peace came over her as she thought of him, of the life they had planned, the family they would have together. His baby could be growing inside her right this minute.

As if someone had slapped her face, that thought filled her with rage and snapped her out of the placid state of acceptance. In the past, she'd had no choice but to lie there and take it. But she wasn't twelve years old and defenseless any more. She was a grown woman who knew how to fight back.

If Spector planned to rape her, he'd have to kill her.

Beck moved quickly down the boardwalk.

Travis had to jog to keep up with him. "Talk to me. What're you thinking?"

"That if he rapes or kills her, I'll have myself to blame."

"How do you figure?"

"I let my stupid pride cloud my judgment. I left her alone for hours. *Hours*, Travis. What the hell was I hoping to prove?"

"That you're human just like the rest of us, that you were pissed at what she did today—and with good reason."

"So I had to go off and lick my wounds while a fucking psycho grabbed her?"

"I don't know where you got the idea that you're supposed to be more than a mortal man, Beck."

"What the hell is that supposed to mean?"

"You blame yourself for everything—for the vandalism, for Jessie, for what happened to your partner all those years ago. I hate to break it to you, pal, but you're not God."

Fuming, Beck stopped and turned. "Easy for you to say when everything you touch turns to gold, while everything *I* touch turns to shit."

"Is that what you think? Jesus Christ, Beck, I've worked my fucking ass off for *years* to get this place off the ground. I couldn't control the people who tried to stop me any more than you could. I wish you'd quit holding yourself up to these impossible standards that no one could live up to. You're in for a whole shit load of disappointment if you can't admit you're just as human as the next guy."

Beck's free hand rolled into a fist that he would've loved to plow into Travis's sanctimonious face. "So you're saying I'm a jerk because I feel bad about what happened with the vandals? That I'm a jerk because I feel bad that I left my fiancée alone and her psycho stalker snatched her?"

"No," Travis said softly. "That's not what I'm saying. I'm telling you it's not your fault, you idiot. None of it is your fault." Travis sighed with frustration. "Does it ever occur to you that maybe Silvestri would've achieved his goal of shutting me down if not for everything you did to stop him? Does it occur to you that your partner still would've gotten shot even if you hadn't gone to call for backup? Does it occur to you that Jessie could've been snatched off the streets of New York and no one who loved her would've known to look for her? You're not God, Beck. You can't control these things."

As Travis's words sunk in, Beck's eyes filled with tears. "I left her alone, Trav, knowing that guy was out there. I left her alone because I was mad that she defied me, that she didn't trust me to take care of her."

"We're going to find her, and when we do, the only thing she's going to care about is that you found her." He put his arm around Beck's shoulders. "Come on. Let's keep looking."

CHAPTER 27

Jessie bided her time. She'd stood silently compliant as he stripped her naked. Watching his every move, she noticed a tremor in his hands and a wild look in his eyes. He didn't expect her to fight back, and that's where he'd made his mistake.

His eyes never left her as he undressed himself.

She wanted to gag when his stumpy erection flopped free of saggy boxer shorts. It was all she could do not to tell him how pathetic he was next to what she'd become accustomed to. Thoughts of Peter kept her from losing it as she waited for her chance.

Spector tugged her toward the bed.

Jessie resisted.

Thrown off balance, he overcorrected.

She kicked him squarely in the balls.

Howling, he collapsed, and she bolted for the door.

His hand clamped around ankle.

Jessie went down hard on the wooden floor. Something tore into her knee. The pain was vicious, and she fought back a wave of nausea.

"*You bitch,*" he growled.

She twisted her foot out of his grasp and hauled herself up. Her knee throbbed with pain as blood streamed down her leg. Using her good leg, she kicked him in the face. Without waiting to see if she'd succeeded in knocking him out, she made for the door.

"Help!" she screamed as she limped naked into the darkness. "Help me!"

"Do you hear that?" Travis asked.

"What?"

"Listen."

Off in the distance, they heard Jessie's cries for help.

"That's her!" Beck said, sprinting toward the voice in the dark as he radioed for back up.

They thrashed through weeds. A branch slashed Beck's cheek, and a hot stream of blood ran down his face. "Jessie! *Jessie!*"

"Peter!"

Aware of Travis following close behind him, Beck ran until his heart threatened to explode in his chest from exertion. "Where are you, baby?"

"Here!"

It was so dark he had to follow the sound of her voice to get to her. And then there she was. He could barely make out her naked, huddled form. He whipped his shirt over his head and helped her into it before he wrapped his arms around her. "I've got you." He buried his face in her fragrant curls, feeling as if he could faint from the sheer relief. "I've got you. You're safe now."

Sobs shook her petite frame as she clung to him. "I knew you'd come."

Swallowing a surge of nausea, he said, "Did he. . ."

"No. I kicked him in the balls before he could."

"That's my girl," Beck said, filled with pride. "Where is he, honey?"

"There was a smelly shack." She pointed. "That way."

"The old fishing shack," Travis said.

Beck knew of the place, about a half-mile south of the North Point property line.

"I hurt my knee," she said, moving her hand to show him the wound.

Travis shined the light on it.

Jessie took one look at the ugly cut and passed out in Beck's arms.

Beck glanced up at Travis. "Will you stay with her?"

"Beck, wait for the cops. Let them do it."

"Will you stay with her or not?"

"Of course I will," Travis said, dropping to his knees next to Jessie.

Beck transferred Jessie's head to Travis's lap and stood up.

"Don't kill him," Travis said. "Think of her, and *do not* kill him."

With a long last glance at Jessie's pale, beautiful, lifeless face, Beck stomped off through the woods. Even in the dark, he knew exactly where he was going. Running, it took him less than ten minutes to reach the cabin, and he marveled that Jessie had gotten so far on a badly injured leg. He tugged the gun from the back of his shorts and kicked the door open. Spector lay on the floor in all his glory, weeping. Blood streamed from his nose, and his balls were grotesquely swollen

Beck swore with disappointment. He'd wanted the guy to put up a fight so he would have an excuse to beat the shit out of him. But rather than give in to that urge, he reached for his radio.

Beck paced in the emergency room hallway as he waited for the doctor. They had whisked Jessie away, telling him he had to wait out here because he wasn't her family. He'd be rectifying that as soon as he could. He would be her family, and she would be his.

Travis and Liana arrived with a bag of clean clothes for Jessie.

Beck had grabbed a shirt from his office before jumping into the ambulance to accompany Jessie. It had taken six stitches to close the wound on his face.

"Any word?" Travis asked.

"Not yet. I don't know what's taking so long."

Liana reached for Beck's hand and urged him to sit next to her. "She's safe, she's alive, and she's in good hands. What else matters?"

He nodded, knowing she was right.

Travis took a seat on the other side of Liana.

They waited for almost an hour before a harried nurse called Beck's name.

He jumped up.

"Ms. Stone is asking for you."

Beck followed her through a maze of hallways.

"They want to keep her for twenty-four hours, but she wants out of here."

Beck laughed at Jessie's feistiness. "If I promise to take excellent care of her, can I take her home?"

"Fight it out with the doctor." She gestured him into a room where Jessie sat on the bed with her bandaged knee elevated on a pillow. Her cheeks were flushed, her blue eyes hot with temper. Beck had never loved her more.

"Oh good, you're here." She held out her hand him. "Will you please tell him you're my fiancé, and you can take care of me?"

Startled to hear the word fiancé from her for the first time, Beck stared at her. "Peter?"

"Yes," he said, tearing his eyes off her to look at the doctor. "That's right. I'm her fiancé. I'd like to take her home."

"The wound was deep, and we can better manage her pain here," the exasperated doctor said. "It's going to be bad when the local wears off."

"Can you give her something for it?" Beck asked.

"Yes, but it won't be as effective as I.V. medication."

"Could we have a minute?" Beck asked the doctor.

"Sure. I'll be back."

When they were alone, Beck leaned down to kiss her. "Maybe he's right, honey."

"Take me home, Peter. Take me to your home where we'll live together."

Weakened by her bottomless blue eyes and pale face, he could deny her nothing. "What am I supposed to say to that?"

"How about okay?" she asked with the smile he couldn't resist.

He brought her hand to his lips. "Okay."

They pulled up to his place in Common Fence Point just as the sun began to peek over the horizon.

"It's on the water," Jessie said with a contented sigh.

"It's a work in progress, so don't expect too much," Beck said as he scooped her up to carry her inside.

"Wait," she said when they reached they door.

"What?"

"Kiss me before you carry me over the threshold."

He laughed as he indulged her. "That shot they gave you made you goofy."

"I'm not goofy." She tossed out her arms and nearly threw him off balance. "I'm free of all worries, and I'm in love. I've never been happier in my whole life than I am right now. Right in this moment."

"Neither have I," he said, his tone hoarse with emotion as he stole another kiss. "Ready to go in?"

She nodded.

He deposited her on the sofa and turned on the lights. Propping a pillow under her injured leg, he said, "It's better during the day when you can see the water."

"It's beautiful."

"No, honey," he said with a smile. "Your place at The Tower was beautiful. This is just a house."

"This is going to be our *home*." Her face went soft with emotion. "We'll put the Christmas tree right there by the window."

"Whatever you want." He couldn't take his eyes off her as he realized how perfectly she fit in his place. He wondered if he should pinch himself to make sure he hadn't dreamed her into his life.

"Come by me."

Moving to the coffee table, he sat facing her and reached for her hand. "I just want you to know that I'm really proud of you for the way you defended yourself against that animal."

She studied him for a long moment. "I was going to let him. . . you know. . . the way I used to let my stepfather. It never occurred to me back then that I could resist. But I thought of you and of the baby we could be having. . . You gave me the strength to fight."

His eyes blurred with tears. "I love you so much. I'm sorry I didn't do a better job of protecting you. I never should've left you alone all night—"

She stopped him with a finger to his lips. "I didn't do what you told me to. I took foolish chances, and I paid the price. If I'd listened to you, Spector never would've gotten close enough to grab me."

"But who knows how long this madness would've gone on? Thanks to you, it's over, he's in jail, and he'll never harm you or anyone else again."

"I put a *hurt* on him."

"You sure did," he said, laughing. "How's your knee?"

"It's just fine."

He decided not to remind her that it would hurt like hell once the drugs wore off. "I never got a chance to put away my Jessica Stone swimsuit calendar, so don't be surprised to see it hanging in the kitchen."

Her mouth fell open. "You do *not* have that!"

"Wanna bet? I was in love with you even before I met you."

She cradled his hand against her chest. "You aren't going to quit your job, are you?"

"I guess not. Besides, Travis won't let me."

"That's good, because one of us needs to work."

"Travis is super generous, but we'll never be rich. Not like you would've been as a model."

"Since I'm always anticipating disaster—or I used to until I met you—I saved most of what I made. I'll be bringing a pretty decent dowry to the table."

"Will you now?" Needing to hold her, he stretched out next to her on the sofa. "So I'm marrying money?"

She giggled. "Some." She worked a hand into his shorts pocket.

Beck jolted when she brushed against his package. "What're you *doing?*"

"I need your phone."

"Well, jeez, honey, just ask me."

Giggling again, she said, "It was more fun this way."

He handed her the phone. "You're loopy on drugs."

"I'm loopy on *love.*"

Rolling his eyes, he asked, "Who are you calling?"

"My agent."

"Now?"

"Uh huh."

Beck watched her fumble through the dialing and wondered if he should be letting her do anything important when she was high as a kite.

She tipped the phone so Beck could hear, too. "Artie! Wake up! It's Jessie! You aren't going to believe it! I caught Spector! All by myself. I kicked him right in the *balls!*"

Beck laughed at Artie's exclamations.

"I have good news and bad news." She attempted a sober tone that failed miserably. "The good news is I'm getting married! The bad news is I'm quitting the business."

"But you have commitments," Artie sputtered. "Obligations."

She directed a sly grin at Beck. "Tell 'em I'm knocked up. Thanks for everything, Artie. Mostly thanks for sending me to Peter. He took *very* good care of me."

"Yes, apparently. Well, darling, I wish you all the best. If you ever change your mind, you know where I am."

"I won't change my mind. Bye, Artie."

Beck slipped an arm around her waist and nuzzled the curve of her neck as she ended the call. "Are you?"

"What?" she asked.

"Knocked up?"

She shrugged. "Don't know yet, but I figure if we get it on two or three times a day, I will be before anyone can sue me for breach of contract."

"I can get onboard with that plan."

Cracking up, she brought him in for a kiss. "Starting now?"

"No time like the present."

Travis and Liana followed the sleepless night at the hospital with a Saturday full of wedding preparations and mini-crises. Liana handled each one as it arose, and by late afternoon all she wanted was a nap. Instead she went to the condo, took a long bath to calm her frayed nerves, and got dressed in the same gown she'd worn to Tom and Justine's wedding the week before.

As she was putting on her earrings, Travis rushed in to get changed.

"I was just staring to wonder where you were," she said.

"Sorry, sweetheart." He kissed her. "I got hung up in a meeting. You look beautiful, as always."

"Thank you." She looked away from him when her eyes flooded.

"Hey, what's wrong?"

"I can't believe it's already been a week since I teased you about my friend Marco and this dress. I'm not ready for our fling to be over."

He drew her into his arms. "It's not over. It's just getting started."

"I don't want to go, Travis. I don't want to leave you."

"I know." He glanced over at her two suitcases in the corner. "You're all packed, though, huh?"

"I didn't want to waste the time we'd have together later packing. I left your Stanford shirt, the shorts you loaned me, and the North Point jacket on the bed."

"Keep them—the shirt and the jacket, that is. The shorts were way too big for you, as I recall. I'd like to think of you sleeping in my shirt when you can't sleep with me."

She held him for another minute before she reluctantly released him so he could shower and change. As they walked hand-in-hand from The Tower to the club,

Liana was hit with a sense of déjà vu. But this time, Travis didn't stop and kiss her for the photographers. This time they kept their heads down as they struggled with the storm of emotions her impending departure was stirring up in both of them.

A North Point staff member named Chloe waited for them in the club.

"We have a small problem," she said, biting her thumbnail as her eyes darted from Travis to Liana.

"What kind of problem?" Travis asked.

"Um, the bride has cold feet. She's saying she wants to cancel the whole thing."

"Is she in the lounge?" Liana asked, referring to the room set aside for brides. Chloe nodded.

"I'll take care of it," Liana said with a quick kiss for Travis. "Don't worry."

Travis watched her go, filled with pride at the way she had blossomed over the last two weeks into a confident, productive, sensual woman. Curious as to how she would handle the jittery bride, he followed her to the lounge and listened at the door.

Inside, Liana approached Lucy's teary-eyed mother. "I don't know what to do with her," the frazzled mom said.

"Do you mind giving me a few minutes with her?" Liana asked.

"Be my guest."

Travis ducked out of the way as the mother of the bride emerged from the room.

"You look lovely, Lucy," Liana said.

Lucy fiddled with the lace on her veil. "Thank you."

"What's the matter?"

"Everything just feels wrong. I can't explain it."

"Are you maybe a little scared?"

Lucy shrugged.

"I know I'd be scared if I were you," Liana said, tuning into Lucy's shyness. "All those people looking at me and having to smile for hours." Liana shuddered.

"Yes," Lucy said, brightening. "That's it exactly."

"What about Ben?"

Lucy's blue eyes filled with tears. "I love Ben."

"And he loves you. That was so obvious to me the other day at our meeting. Did you notice that he never took his eyes off you?"

"He didn't?"

"Not once." Liana took a deep breath to calm the ache in her own heart. "If I had a man who looked at me like that, I'd want to marry him. And I'd just grit my teeth to get through the wedding so I could have the rest of my life with him."

Lucy twisted her hands in her lap as she thought about that.

"It's just a couple of hours, and then it's you and Ben forever. You can do that for him, for your future, can't you?"

"Yes," Lucy said with a firm nod and a smile. "I can do that for him, for us. Do you know anything about the big surprise he has planned for me?"

"As a matter of fact, I do." Liana clutched Lucy's hand. "And it's not something you're going to want to miss, believe me. Your guests are gathered at the gazebo, the judge is ready, Ben's here, and you got a beautiful, perfect summer evening. What do you say we go get you married?"

"Okay. Thank you, Liana."

Liana led Lucy from the room and was startled to find Travis outside the door.

Their eyes met, and she knew in an instant that he had heard everything she'd said to Lucy—and misunderstood it. "Travis . . ." she said haltingly.

He forced a smile. "Let's get this gorgeous bride to her wedding, shall we?"

CHAPTER 28

Still smarting from what he'd overheard, Travis sought out a quiet corner off the kitchen to hide out while appetizers were being served in the tent. *I can't believe she said that—if I had a man who looked at me the way Ben looks at you, I'd marry him. Have I not had my heart in my eyes every time I've looked at her for the last two weeks?*

He sat down on a stack of beer cases and rested his elbows on his knees. *Was there anything else I could've done or said to show her how much I love her?* For a long time he sat there and contemplated that question and several others cycling through his tired mind. Clearly, he hadn't done enough.

With most of the waiters working in the tent the kitchen grew quiet, and Travis tuned into a conversation two teenage girls were having as they assembled salads.

"She's so amazingly beautiful, isn't she?"

"And a lot nicer than you'd expect her to be."

"Yeah."

"I read in the *Enquirer* that she's going back to work soon. I wonder if she'll ever come back here again."

"Why would she? If I were her and was lucky enough to have the life she has, I'd never come back to this two-bit town again. There isn't even a movie theater or a McDonald's. This place sucks."

"But Mr. North is *so* gorgeous."

"Ew, he's *old!*"

Travis suppressed a groan. He'd just turned thirty-six!

"He's still gorgeous."

"Well, it's not like she's going to marry him. Why would she want to give up the life she has for this place?"

"I love it here."

"Not me. As soon as I graduate, I'm so outta here, and I'm never coming back. She won't either. Wait 'n see."

The girls worked in silence for a few minutes.

Travis heard the click of high heels entering the kitchen.

"Excuse me, have you girls seen Mr. North?" Liana asked.

"Um, no, Ms. McDermott. He's not in here."

"If you see him, will you please tell him I'm looking for him?"

"We will."

"Thank you."

After Liana walked away, the more opinionated of the two girls said, "She *won't* be back."

They soon moved on to another station, and their voices faded out of earshot. It was just as well. Travis had heard more than enough.

As the waiters served cake, Travis wandered into the tent to check on things. He saw Liana consulting with the groom on the other side of the tent, their heads bent together. Travis watched her hand something to Ben and then leave him with a quick hug.

She noticed Travis standing at the back of the tent and signaled for him to stay there.

The eyes of every man in the tent were drawn to her as she cut through the dining area to where he waited for her.

"Everything going all right?" he asked.

"Yes, fine. Travis, what you heard me say to Lucy . . ."

"Don't worry about it."

"But . . ."

The band called the bride and groom to the stage.

"What's going on?"

Liana turned toward the stage. "Watch."

Ben helped an astounded Lucy onto a stool and adjusted the wireless microphone Liana had given him. Then Ben nodded to the band, which launched into "Unchained Melody."

Liana leaned back against Travis, who looped his arms around her waist.

"Wow, he's good," Travis whispered in her ear just before he began to softly sing along with Ben.

Liana turned to put her arms around his neck and look up at him.

His entire body riddled with tension, he shifted his eyes away from hers, reached for her hands, and removed them from his shoulders.

"Travis? What is it?"

"I'm sorry. I just can't do this."

He left Liana standing frozen in place and walked out of the tent.

More than an hour passed before the wedding ended and she could go after him. No one had seen him in the club, so she walked to The Tower and took the elevator to the apartment, which was dark when she arrived. "Travis?" she called. He didn't answer, so she went into the bedroom and flipped on the light. His tuxedo jacket and bow tie were on the bed, but there was no other sign of him.

Out on the patio his white shirt caught her eye from the living room. Opening the glass door, she stepped outside where he leaned against the safety rail that encircled the patio. "Travis? I've been looking for you."

He turned to her. "You found me."

"You didn't want me to?"

He shrugged.

"I'm sorry for what I said to Lucy, but I was only trying—"

"Stop, Liana." He held up his hand. "Please. Just stop."

The hard set to his face filled Liana with fear and turned him into someone she barely recognized.

"Let me ask you something," he said.

"Anything."

"After you leave tomorrow, are you ever coming back?"

"I want to. I wish I could say what you want to hear . . ."

He smiled, but his eyes were hard. "You've told me how unhappy you are in your career, how much you hate the media and the rest of it."

"I do."

"Then the only conclusion I can reach is you don't love me enough to give it up, or worse yet, you think I don't love *you* enough."

"That's not true! I don't think either of those things. You're putting words in my mouth!"

"If what we had together was going to be enough for you, Liana, you'd know it by now. There wouldn't be a decision."

"I absolutely *refuse* to be pressured into making the biggest decision of my life without taking the time I need to think it through."

He shook his head with dismay. "We were deluding ourselves by pretending this was more than a fling."

"But," she stammered, "what you said last night . . . You said you wanted to marry me and you'd wait for me. I don't understand. What changed?"

"I took my head out of the clouds for a few minutes and didn't like what I saw. That's all."

"And what exactly did you see?" she asked in a small voice.

"Me sitting here like a chump waiting forever for you to come back when you probably have no intention of ever coming back."

"I never said that. I just asked for a little time to figure things out."

"Well, now you don't need it. I'm letting you off the hook."

She closed the distance between them and rested her hands on his chest. "I don't want to be let off the hook. I love you, Travis."

"You don't belong here, and I don't belong anywhere else."

She looked up at him with tears in her eyes, but his face was unreadable. "Did you think I didn't belong here when you asked me to work here with you? I thought we made a good team."

"We've had a taste of what our life together could be like, and you don't like the life you're leading now. What's left to decide?" Travis grasped her shoulders and seemed to be making a huge effort not to shake her. "You say you love me, you like working here with me, your family lives in town, you hate modeling. *What is there to think about?*"

"It's just . . . I can't . . ."

With a deep sigh he dropped his hands from her shoulders and took a step back. "We had a good time, and I appreciated your help with the weddings. You did an excellent job. I really hope that working here showed you what you're capable of. But let's not torture ourselves by wishing for something that can't ever happen between us. I think it would be best if you went to your mother's tonight."

Tears rolled down her face. "Why are you doing this?" she whispered. "Why are you forcing me to decide everything right now?"

"Because it's better we face facts now rather than months from now. I just can't put myself through the agony of waiting for something that's not going to happen."

"If that's how you want it . . ."

"It is."

"Do you love me? Or was that just fling talk? I'm sorry if I don't know the difference. I've never had a fling before."

"I loved you."

His use of the past tense wasn't lost on her, and even when she reached up to caress his face, his expression didn't soften. "I had a wonderful time," she said. "Thank you." She went up on tiptoes to kiss him one last time before she went inside to get her bags. In his bedroom, she was struck by the memory of her first time in that room, when she had been desperate to get out of the horrible bridesmaid dress.

She brushed away tears, put the keys he had given her on his dresser, and squatted down to hug Dash. "Be good, sweet girl." She kissed the dog's pretty face and, grabbing her bags, went to summon the elevator. As the doors closed she took one last look at Travis on the patio, his head bent and his shoulders stooped.

Leaving her bags in the garage, she walked over to the club to find Beck and asked him for a ride to her mother's house. She was grateful when he didn't ask any questions about why she was leaving a day early.

They drove through the North Point gates, but Liana didn't look back. "How's Jessie?"

"A little better."

"Thanks for coming in tonight. I know you didn't want to leave her."

"She insisted I come. She refuses to be fearful."

"Good for her," Liana said in a dull, flat tone, wishing she could be as fearless as her courageous friend. Liana was relieved to find no reporters at her mother's house. They had apparently given up on finding her there.

Beck pulled into the driveway and turned to her. "Your new security team will meet you at the airport in the morning. I think you'll like them."

Liana reached out to squeeze his hand. "I appreciate all your help with that."

"I was happy to do it. You'll be glad you have them."

"I know." She hated to even think about the major change in her life that their presence would represent.

Beck helped with her bags. At the door, he rested a hand on her arm. "He can be really stubborn. I don't know what happened tonight, but he loves you—really loves you. I just thought you should know that."

She kissed his cheek. "Thank you, Beck, for everything. I wish you and Jessie all the best. It was a pleasure knowing you."

He hugged her. "The pleasure was all mine. Take care of yourself, Liana."

She nodded and went inside.

Except for quick trips to let Dash out, Travis didn't leave his apartment for two days after Liana left. He wanted some time to prepare himself to face the rest of his life without her, but it didn't take long to realize her essence had permeated every corner of his world. The home he had once loved was now a storage place for painful memories. He had a sick feeling he would encounter the same problem on the boat, in his office, and throughout the club when he finally ventured back to work.

Late on the second day, he went into his bedroom and stretched out on the bed. Turning on his side, he came face to face with the box of condoms on the bedside table. Pulling open the drawer open to put them away, he discovered the panties he had taken from her in the movie theater. As he reached for them and bunched them into his fist, it finally hit him.

"Oh my God," he whispered. "What've I done?"

Dash jumped on the bed, curled up next to him, and rested her head on his chest.

Travis welcomed the comfort and rolled his face into the dog's soft coat. "I sent her away, Dash. I was so awful to her."

Dash whimpered and licked his chin.

"What am I supposed to do without her? Everywhere I look I see her. I can still smell her perfume on the pillow. How long do you think that will last?"

The dog nuzzled his face.

"I messed things up with her, and all because I was so afraid of losing her. Well, now I have, and let me tell you, it hurts every bit as much as I thought it would." He ran his fingers through the dog's fur. "I wonder how she's doing."

Travis took a deep breath. "Do you think she misses us? Nah, probably not—not after the way I treated her. I wanted to be different, you know? Different from all the guys who are so caught up in her fame and her beauty. So what did I do? I got her to fall in love with me, and then I turned her away. I really blew it," he whispered. "Big time. But there's nothing I can do about it now."

Dash lifted her head and whined.

"Believe me, girl, if I thought she'd want to see me I'd go after her. But I was a jerk to her, and she's through with me. She can have any guy she wants. She doesn't need one who treats her like crap."

Dash barked sharply to express her dismay.

"You'll never leave me, will you, girl?"

Dropping her head to his chest, Dash sighed. She'd done what she could.

Travis was attempting to get some work done in his office when Chloe came in to tell him he had a visitor.

"Who is it?"

"Horse face," Chloe whispered.

Travis groaned.

"What do you want me to do?"

"Show her in, Chloe. Thanks."

"Good luck," Chloe whispered on her way out.

Enid breezed into the office, bringing with her a cloud of French perfume. She tossed her alligator purse onto the chair in front of his desk and stood with hands on bountiful hips.

Travis raised an eyebrow. "Something I can help you with, Mrs. Littleton?"

"You're an ass."

Travis kept his expression neutral. "Anything else?" He shuffled some papers on his desk. "I'm kind of busy here."

"I repeat: You. Are. An. Ass. Do you think I'd let just *any* man get near my cousin?" She rested her hands on the desk. "I thought you were worthy of her."

"I guess you thought wrong."

"No, I didn't. I thought exactly right. So what the hell happened?"

"I'm sure you've heard the whole story."

"Travis North, you're going to tell me what happened." She moved her purse and flopped down in the chair. "I'm not leaving until you do."

"Suit yourself." He picked up the phone.

Enid launched out of her seat and pressed the hook. "Tell me what changed, Travis. One night you want to marry her, and the next night it's over for you. *Why?*"

Travis's jaw ached with tension as he passed the phone receiver back and forth between his hands. "I heard her talking to the bride."

Enid nodded. "And she said if she had a man who looked at her the way Ben looked at Lucy, she'd marry him."

"She *had* a man who looked at her like that."

"She *knew* that, you idiot."

"Then why did she say what she did?"

"She was doing the job *you* asked her to do. Let me ask you this: Did that bride go through with her wedding?"

"Yes."

"Then I guess whatever she said to that poor girl worked. The wedding went perfectly, and you have Liana to thank for it, but you're too stupid to see that."

"You've got a lot of nerve coming into *my* office and calling me every name you can think of."

"I've got plenty more where they came from. Liana tried to tell you she only said what she thought Lucy needed to hear, but you didn't let her."

Travis hung up the phone and sat back to brood.

"There must've been something else."

He sighed when he realized she wasn't going to give up. "There were these two girls talking in the kitchen," he said, aware of exactly how stupid *this* was going to sound to her. "They were saying they couldn't wait to get out of here when they graduate, and that if they had Liana's life they'd never come back to a town that doesn't even have a McDonald's."

Enid rolled her eyes. "And of course Liana's known for her love of a good Big Mac. So let me get this straight. You let a couple of disgruntled teenaged girls convince you to walk away from the love of your life?"

He grimaced. Her words were like a dagger in his heart.

"You're an even bigger idiot than I give you credit for being."

"I'm starting to agree with you," he murmured. "I just needed her to want me as much as I wanted her. Is that so unreasonable?"

"She *did* want you that much. Why was it so impossible for you to give her a little time so she could feel like she was making an *informed* decision rather than an *impetuous* one?"

"Because I couldn't bear the idea of being without her for even that long," he confessed.

"So is this better?"

"No," he said sadly. "This is hell."

She stared at him for a long, disconcerting moment.

He finally wilted under the heat of her glare. "What?"

"I'm trying to decide if you deserve a second chance. You so totally blew the first one."

Travis got up and came around the desk. "Enid, please. I want to fix this. *Help* me."

"You look like shit."

"I haven't slept in more than a week. *Please.*"

She picked up her purse. "You broke her heart, Travis. Into a thousand pieces. If you hurt her again, I'll kill you. Is that clear?"

"Crystal."

"My Aunt Agnes always knows where she is. Don't make me regret telling you this."

"You won't."

She headed for the door.

"Enid?"

Turning back to him, she raised an eyebrow.

"Thank you."

With a curt nod, she left.

Travis flopped into his chair. He sat there for a long time letting the music from the club's sound system lull him as he thought about what Enid had said.

He tuned into the unmistakable sound of Neil Diamond's voice, singing "The Story of My Life." Travis had heard the song a hundred times before on the loop they played in the club, but this time he was riveted by the haunting words about a life that began the day a certain someone walked into it and ended the day she left.

In that moment, Travis understood that losing Liana would ruin his life and no amount of time would ever be enough to fix it. He reached for the phone to call Agnes

CHAPTER 29

Liana's feet burned in the hot sand, but she didn't move a muscle as the makeup artist reapplied her lip liner for the third time—and it was only nine o'clock. The Costa del Sol, known for hot sunny days, was living up to its reputation on this morning, and Liana began to droop from the heat. She wanted nothing more than to dive head first into the foamy waves that crashed against the sugar-white sand in the south of Spain.

"Feet," she said without moving her lips.

"What?"

"Feet burning."

"Oh! Why didn't you say so?" The makeup woman hustled Liana to the cooler wet sand. "Sorry about that."

A wardrobe assistant followed them and readjusted Liana's white string bikini. When the woman grabbed Liana's breasts like they were two hunks of meat, it was all Liana could do not to smack her. Instead she did what she always did—she stood still and let them manhandle her. Whatever it took to get the job done so she could get back to her hotel and be alone.

Usually, she looked forward to the *Sports Illustrated* shoot. Often she saw other models who had become acquaintances over the years, and in the past, she had enjoyed the camaraderie. But this year there were a bunch of fresh new faces, many of them so caught up in their own hoopla Liana couldn't be bothered with getting to know them. That, like everything else since she left Rhode Island, would take too much effort.

She was in hotter demand than ever after all the media attention her relationship with Travis had generated. Artie had her heavily scheduled well into next year, and that was fine with her. She had discovered being busy was preferable to idleness, which gave her too much time to think.

Artie had finally told her more about the "tidbit" he had mentioned during her vacation. He was in negotiations with the world's top cosmetics company to make Liana "The Face of L'Élégance." Artie was ecstatic about it, most likely because he would make a fortune in commissions on the deal. He was disappointed by her lackluster reaction to the plum offer, but Liana told him to work it out. She didn't care about the details.

Standing on the sidelines watching Liana intently as the makeup artist gave her face one last thorough inspection were two of the four men who now accompanied her everywhere she went. They were nice enough and did their best not to be overly intrusive, but Liana was always aware of them. The media had been so relentless in their pursuit of her, first in Milan and now in Spain, she'd been grateful to have the bodyguards. She knew the paparazzi were salivating for just a scrap of information about the status of her relationship with Travis, but she wasn't talking and was confident he wouldn't either.

As she did so many times every day, she thought of him and wondered if he missed her anywhere near as much as she missed him. Over and over again she replayed that last conversation with him, asking herself each time why she couldn't have just given him the guarantee he'd needed. But then she remembered how unyielding he had been, and she got mad all over again.

She hadn't appreciated his ultimatum. *I wasn't ready to make a commitment based on just two weeks together, and it wasn't fair of him to pressure me the way he did.* But after spending more than a week without him she wished she had that last night to do over. Right about now she'd give him anything he wanted if it meant she could be with him again.

"Are you ready, sweetheart?" the photographer called.

A spike of white-hot pain seared Liana. "Don't call me that," she snapped.

Unaccustomed to such a sharp tone from her, the shocked photographer, makeup artist, and wardrobe assistant stared at her.

"Let's get this done." Liana walked to where the surf met the sand and struck the pose the photographer wanted, pretending not to hear him mutter, "Fucking bitchy models." She didn't care what any of them thought of her. Not anymore.

By the time the day finally began to wind down, Liana ached everywhere. She dreamed of a hot bath, room service, and her king-sized hotel bed.

"Okay," the photographer called. "That's a wrap for today. Noon start tomorrow. Thank you, everyone."

Liana relaxed her pose and bent in half to knead her burning calf muscles. Her feet were wrinkled like raisins from the hours of standing in the surf, and her neck had kinks that might be permanent. She took a last yearning look at the surf, wishing she had the strength to dive in the way she'd wanted to all day. But even that would take too much effort.

Her personal assistant handed her a robe.

"Thanks." Liana tossed the robe over her arm as she walked slowly up the beach to where she'd left her flip-flops and tote bag.

Stopping for one big stretch before she continued on to the car that waited to return her to the hotel, Liana looked up and gasped when she saw Travis watching her from the top of one of the huge hills that lined the beach. Her heart began to beat faster, and her breath got caught in her throat as he made his way down the rocky path. Wearing khaki shorts and a long-sleeved white shirt rolled up over his tanned forearms, he had never looked better to her.

As he approached, Liana's bodyguards closed ranks around her.

"It's all right, you guys," she said softly, and they backed off. Liana resisted the urge to jump into his arms. "What are you doing here?"

"I, uh . . ." He glanced over his shoulder to where everything had come to a complete stop with all eyes focused on them. "Is there somewhere we can talk? Without an audience?"

Liana studied his handsome face for a long moment and was struck by how exhausted he looked. "I have a car and driver waiting for me. Do you want to come with me?"

"Yes," he said with visible relief. "I very much want to go with you." He took the robe that still hung over her arm and held it for her.

She turned back to him as she tied it around her waist.

He freed her long hair and let it slide through his fingers.

The longing on his face was almost enough to undo her, and had there not been so many people watching them she would have reached for him right then and there.

In the parking lot, Travis handed his rental car keys to one of Liana's bodyguards, who would follow them. The other bodyguard got in next to Liana's driver. Photographers with long-range lenses recorded her every move from a roped-off area. They had gone crazy when they realized who was with her.

When they were settled in the backseat, Liana turned to Travis. "I can't believe you're here. How did you know where to find me?"

"I asked your mother."

Liana raised an eyebrow. "I'm surprised she told you. The last time I saw her she wasn't too happy with you."

"Suffice to say I had to use a considerable amount of charm to get her to tell me what I needed to know." He reached for her hand. "How'd you get so tanned?"

"It's fake."

He ran a hand over her arm as if to see if the tan would rub off. "Wow, it doesn't look fake."

"You know what the best part of the fake tan is?"

"I can't imagine."

"No tan lines."

He swallowed hard, and his eyes never wavered from hers.

"Travis . . ."

He kissed her hand. "We'll talk, sweetheart. When we're alone."

Thrilled to see him, Liana realized she had been dead inside without him. Just a few minutes with him, the feel of his hand wrapped around hers, and hearing him call her sweetheart brought her right back to life. He *was* her life. That was suddenly so obvious she wondered how she ever could have questioned it.

"I never had any idea how hard you work," he said after a long period of silence during which neither of them was able to look away from the other.

"How long were you up there watching?"

"A while. How do you hold a position for so long?"

"Painfully," she said with a grimace. "I'm aching from head to toe at the moment."

He shook his head with dismay. "And you have to do it again tomorrow."

"Not until noon, thank God."

"As least you're in a beautiful place for all this torture."

"Have you been here before?"

He shook his head. "Luckily, I've been to South America a couple of times, so I had a passport, but I've never been to Europe."

"Never?" she asked, her eyes wide with amazement.

"We can't all be globe-trotting supermodels."

"You could've been," she teased, remembering their discussion about how well he wore an Armani tuxedo.

"I'd rather live out of the back of a Pinto."

They shared a smile that warmed Liana all the way down to her tired bones. "How are Beck and Jessie doing?"

"They got married the day before yesterday at North Point. It was very sweet and touching, just the two of them, me, and a J.P. We all wished you were there."

"Just think," she said with a dreamy smile, "they're married because of our fling."

"They got their happy ending. Will we get ours?"

"I hope so." She squeezed his hand. "I really do."

The driver pulled into the palm tree-lined driveway at the Hotel Duques de Medinaceli in downtown El Puerto de Santa Maria, and the driver and bodyguard got out of the car.

Travis stopped her when she started to go out the door the Spanish driver held for her. "I came right from the airport in Jerez to find you. I need to see about getting a room."

She reached for his hand. "No, you don't."

"I don't want to be presumptuous, especially after the way we left things the last time."

"You're not being presumptuous. Get your bag, and come with me."

As she led him through the luxurious hotel, the bodyguards followed at a respectful distance. "Do you know what I love about Europe?" she asked.

"What's that?"

"Everything is so old. In this very city is the palace where Christopher Columbus waited for King Ferdinand's approval of his journey to the New World. It makes me realize just how young our country really is compared to the rest of the world."

He gazed at her with eyes full of love.

Her cheeks heated from the intensity of his expression. "What?"

"I missed you," he said. "I missed you so much."

"I missed you, too."

At the doorway to her suite, Liana held Travis back while the bodyguards opened her door and checked to make sure the rooms were secure.

"We'll be right next door, Ms. McDermott. Let us know if you wish to go anywhere."

"I'll be staying in tonight. Please relax and enjoy your evening."

The larger of the two bodyguards gave Travis a suspicious once over. "You, too. We'll see you in the morning."

When they had walked away, Travis released a sigh of relief. "Christ, I thought he was going to demand a body cavity search."

Liana laughed as she closed the door. "You were the one who wanted me to have security."

"Not to keep you safe from *me*." He sobered all of a sudden. "Although, that might've been a good idea."

"Travis," Liana whispered as she finally allowed herself to do what she had wanted to do since he first appeared on the beach. She wrapped her arms around his neck and rested her face against his chest. "Tell me why you're here."

He held her tight against him. "First things first," he said, tilting her chin up to kiss her lightly.

Combing her fingers through his hair, she skimmed her tongue over his bottom lip.

Travis groaned, lifted her off her feet, and devoured her. "Liana," he said when they came up for air, "I'm sorry. I screwed things up so royally. I was an idiot. I was so afraid of losing you that I drove you away, thinking somehow that would be easier. But it wasn't. It was awful. I love you so much—"

"Shh," she said, silencing him with another passionate kiss.

"Is it too late for us?"

"No, it's not too late." She winced when she moved her sore neck.

He picked her up and carried her to the high four-poster bed with red sheers draped over the posts. Tossed across the foot of the bed was his Stanford T-shirt.

She noticed him staring at the shirt. "It's a poor substitute," she said, reaching for his hand to bring him down next to her.

"You're so tired, sweetheart," he said, dropping soft kisses on her face, her neck, and the triangle of skin on her chest left exposed by her robe.

She traced her finger over the stubble on his jaw. "You look exhausted yourself."

"I haven't had a full night of sleep since you left." He brushed the hair off her face. "I reach for you in my sleep, but I can't find you. I wake up looking for you."

Pressing her lips against the inside of his wrist, she said, "I've done those same things. I never thought I could get used to sleeping with someone so fast. I dream I'm with you, and when I wake up alone, it hurts so much it takes my breath away. I'm afraid I'm going to wake up now and find out I dreamt this."

Overwhelmed, he dropped his head to her chest.

She ran her fingers through his hair. "I love you, Travis."

A deep sigh rattled through him. He looked up at her with eyes full of love. "All the way over here, on that endless flight from Boston to Madrid, and then from Madrid to Jerez, the only thing I could think about was what I would do if you didn't love me anymore."

She caressed his face. "I'll always love you."

His kiss was full of love and hunger and passion.

Liana put her arms around him, urging him on top of her. "Make love to me."

"That's not why I'm here, Liana."

"I know," she said, sliding her hands under his shirt.

"Wait, sweetheart. We need to talk."

"We will," she whispered against his lips. "After."

"I see you haven't lost your enthusiasm for make-up sex," he said, kissing her ear and sending a shiver through her.

Liana laughed softly and massaged his back. "It's still the best kind—especially when you think you've lost the most important person in the world and then he suddenly reappears."

"I'm sorry for what I put you through, Liana. I lost my mind when we ran out of time."

"I know."

He rolled over and brought her with him. "What's this?" he asked, reaching for the frame on her bedside table. "Oh . . . the night we met."

"I had all the negatives you got from Enid's photographer developed, but there wasn't one with a full view of your face. I was so sad about that. I framed that one of us dancing because it was the best one of you."

He put the frame back on the table and held up the page she had torn from the tabloid. "You kept this?"

"It's an amazing picture."

He smiled. "You were so mad when I did that."

"Not after I saw the photo. Now it's just one of many beautiful memories."

Returning the page to the table, he put his arm around her, and ran his hand up and down her back. "I was wrong to pressure you to make a decision you weren't ready to make. I know that now. I was just so desperate to keep you with me. I'm sure that's not how it seemed to you that last night, but it's the truth."

"Travis—"

He brushed a finger over her lips. "Hear me out, sweetheart. I want to ask you something, but I don't want you to answer me now, okay?"

Her heart pounding with anticipation, she nodded.

"Liana, my love, will you marry me? Will you live with me and have a family with me and work with me?"

Her eyes filled, and her heart overflowed with joy.

"Your mother is getting married at North Point on Christmas Eve. I want you to take the next few months to think it over, and when you come home for her wedding you can give me your answer."

"But, Travis . . ."

He shook his head. "I realized after you left that I have no life at all without you, so we'll do it your way. If you don't want to get married, we don't have to. I'll visit you. You'll visit me. We'll work it out. But it occurred to me that I told you I wanted to marry you, but I never actually asked you. So now I have." He kissed her softly. "I love you, and I'll wait for you. No matter how long it takes. I'll wait."

Touched to her very core, she whispered, "So what do we do for the next few months until my mother's wedding?"

"I'll leave you alone so you can think."

"But the last ten days have been so awful, Travis. I don't want to go months without talking to you or being with you."

He took her hand and brought it to his lips. "It'll be different this time, sweetheart, because you'll know I love you and I'm waiting for you. You'll know you have me—any way you want me."

"I can't believe you're willing to do this."

"I don't think you were even in the elevator when I realized what a terrible mistake I'd made by letting you go. After you left, I saw you everywhere. The emptiness was worse than anything I've ever experienced. I love you. My dog loves you. She's been so depressed since you left."

"Aw, my poor sweet girl. Who's watching her while you're here?"

"Your mother."

"*Really?*"

"Uh huh. It was part of the large package of concessions I had to make to get her to tell me where you were."

Liana laughed. "Made you work for it, did she?"

"I suggested she consider law school when she finishes college. I also received a thorough ass kicking from your cousin, which included a threat to my life if I should happen to hurt you again. I'm quite certain she meant it."

"I can assure you she did."

"She's not just a brat, she's mean, too," he said with a pout.

"Oh, baby," Liana said in little girl voice. "Did she hurt your feelings?"

"She called me names. Bad names."

Liana dissolved into laughter.

"You think it's funny?" He rolled on top of her and tickled her ribs.

She screamed with laughter.

A sharp rap on the door startled them into silence.

"Ms. McDermott!"

"Shit," Travis whispered. "It's your security."

"I'm fine," she called out.

"I need to see you."

Travis dissolved into laughter.

Liana swatted at him as she got out of bed and reached for her robe. "Shut *up.*" She ran her hands through her messy hair and opened the door. "Hi there," she said in a cheerful voice. "Sorry about the noise, but I'm okay."

The same big man who'd checked out Travis earlier peered around Liana to look into the room.

From the bed, Travis smiled and waved at him.

He scowled at Travis and returned his attention to Liana. "You're sure everything's all right?"

With a glance over her shoulder at Travis, Liana said, "Yes, everything's just fine."

CHAPTER 30

Throughout that long, endless autumn, Travis lived for only one thing: the weekly postcards he received from Liana. They came from Madrid, Milan, the Bahamas, New York, London, and Paris, and all of them contained the same one-word message: THINKING. Travis tacked the cards up on the bulletin board in his office, and by the second week in December the board was nearly full.

He had done his best during their long months apart to ignore the tabloid coverage of her every move. As badly as he craved the slightest detail, he was wary of tabloid lies. He refused to let gossip screw things up for them. Not after they had gotten this far. And in all his meetings with Agnes about her wedding, neither of them had ever broached the subject of her daughter or what had transpired between Travis and Liana in Spain.

Four days before Agnes's Christmas Eve wedding, an item in the *Wall Street Journal* caught Travis's attention. His heart stopped when he read the headline: "Supermodel Liana McDermott Named Face of L'Élégance." Travis read and reread the article that outlined the multi-year, seven-figure deal that would make Liana the cosmetic giant's top public persona.

Stunned by the news, he tossed the paper aside and sat back in his chair. "She's not giving it up," he whispered. "She's not going to choose me." Glancing up at the collage of postcards, Travis hurt like he never had before. He had been so sure. After their time together in Spain, he'd been so sure she would come home to him. "I can't believe I was such a fool."

He thought he was ready to see her again. But as he watched her come down the aisle in a burgundy silk gown that hugged every curve, he realized he was utterly unprepared to see her and even more unprepared to say goodbye to her. The fake tan was gone, and she carried a bouquet of Christmas flowers as she went through her duties as her mother's maid of honor. As a bridesmaid, Enid wore the same gown as Liana. Agnes, stunning in a beaded floor-length ivory dress, glowed with happiness.

After a brief hello and a kiss to Liana's cheek in the receiving line, Travis, who was there as Agnes's guest, did his best to stay out of the way so Liana could attend to her mother. But right after dinner when the dancing started, she came looking for him.

"What are you doing back here in the corner?" she asked with amusement dancing in her violet eyes. "My mother invited you to sit with the family."

"I didn't want to be in the way."

Her eyebrows knitted with confusion. "You wouldn't have been in the way. Will you dance with me?"

He studied the hand she held out to him, wondering if he had the wherewithal to hold her one last time and then let her go if that was what she wanted. "Sure." Taking the hand she offered, he followed her to the dance floor.

Holding her in his arms and remembering the way she fit so perfectly against him made Travis breathless with longing. "You look so beautiful tonight."

She smiled up at him. "This time I got to pick the dress."

"I like the color."

"I knew you would," she said. "I missed you."

"Me, too."

"Something's wrong."

He shook his head.

With her finger on his chin she brought his eyes back to her. "I know you, remember?"

"I remember everything."

"Let's get out of here."

"You can't leave your mother's wedding."

Liana glanced over to where her mother danced with David. They were so caught up in their joy they might have been the only two people in the room. "I don't think we'll be missed."

Travis let her lead him from the dance floor and into his office.

She shut the door and leaned back against it, zeroing in on the bulletin board full of postcards. "You kept them all!" she said with a delighted smile.

He shrugged.

"What's wrong, Travis? Have you changed your mind about us? Did I take too long to think about it?"

"No."

"Then what is it?"

He reached for the folded newspaper on his desk and held it up for her to see. "This. This is what's wrong."

She crossed the room to take the paper from him. "Oh," she said, wincing. "You heard about that, huh?"

"Yes," he said through gritted teeth. "I heard about it."

"And you think I've chosen my career over you."

"Haven't you?"

Liana put the paper down on his desk and walked over to look out the window. "After you left Spain, do you know what I did first?" She turned to him. "I called my agent and told him that as of the twenty-fourth of December I'd be retiring from modeling."

"But what about—"

"Wait, Travis. It's your turn to hear *me* out."

Frustrated, he ran his hands through his hair and leaned back against the desk.

Liana went to him and rested her hands on his chest. "I was so relieved to see you in Spain—that you had come all that way to see me and to fix things between us. . . ."

Travis looped his arms around her waist.

"And that you were willing to give me as much time as I needed showed me how much you love me. I knew before you left Spain that there was nothing left to decide. So I used the time you gave me to fulfill outstanding obligations. I dissolved my company and gave my employees plenty of money to go quietly so the press wouldn't jump all over me—well, anymore than they were already, that is. I worked twelve, fourteen, sixteen hours a day for months to get free so I could come home to you."

Filled with hope, Travis dared to ask, "But what about L'Élégance?"

"Ah, yes, L'Élégance," she said with the smile that had made her an international sensation. "I agreed *only* to a print campaign, and they offered me seven million a year for two days a month. I thought the businessman in you might see that as a pretty good deal."

Travis gasped. "Are you *shitting* me?"

"Would I shit you?" She slid her arms up around his neck. "I didn't think you'd mind too much if I spent two days a month in New York, that is if you're willing to let me out of my duties here at North Point. I hoped you might even come with me once in a while."

"For seven mil a year, I think we can arrange a few days off." He bent his head and found her lips. "Are you sure, Liana? Really sure?"

"I love you, Travis, and I love being here at North Point. Remember when you told me this place spoke to you when you first saw it?"

He nodded.

"When I came through the gates tonight it felt just like coming home."

Overwhelmed with emotion, he hugged her, drinking in the distinctive scent he'd missed so much.

"Now, I don't want you to get too excited about all that money." She trailed kisses over the light stubble he had left on his jaw for her. "I'm donating half of it to the cause I've agreed to lend my name to."

He was busy kissing her neck. "What cause is that?"

"The National Down's Syndrome Society."

Travis froze mid-kiss and pulled back to look at her.

She reached up to brush the hair off his forehead. "I told them my future brother-in-law has Down's and I'd like to help. They asked me to be their national spokesperson, and they want to announce it at a press conference after the holidays." Her mouth lifted into a shy smile. "I'd love for you and Evan to be there with me."

"Yes," he whispered as he kissed her. "We'll be there. Thank you, Liana."

"No, thank *you*—for showing me I could do and be anything I wanted and for giving me the courage to take control of my life."

"You always had it in you, sweetheart."

"What I want more than anything else, though, is you." Her cheeks flamed with color, and Travis had never loved her more. "Is that question you asked me in Spain still on the table?"

"Hold that thought." He left her with a light kiss and went around his desk. Opening the top drawer, he reached for a jeweler's box and returned to her. "I bought this the day I got home from Spain." He opened the box, withdrew the ring, and held it out to her. "Will you marry me, Liana?"

"Yes." She wiped away the tears that spilled down her cheeks. "Yes, I'll marry you, Travis." Launching herself into his arms, she held on for a long time.

When she finally released him, Travis slid the ring onto her left hand.

"It's beautiful," she whispered, taking her first good look at the shimmering emerald-cut diamond.

"So are you." He kissed the hand where she now wore his ring. "I'm going to do everything I can to make sure you're never sorry you chose me."

"I chose *us*, and in the end, it was the easiest decision I've ever made. I know I'll never be sorry."

"Oh," he gasped. "Listen. This song . . . I heard it after you left this summer." He put his arms around her and looked down at her. "You *are* the story of my life, Liana. I hope you know that."

"And you, Travis, are *my* true north."

"Welcome home, sweetheart."

Check out the True North Readers Group at facebook.com/groups/TrueNorthBook/.

ABOUT THE AUTHOR

Marie Force is the *New York Times, USA Today* and *Wall Street Journal* best-selling, award-winning author of more than 25 contemporary romances, including The McCarthys of Gansett Island Series, the Fatal Series, the Treading Water Series and numerous stand-alone books. Her new series, Green Mountain Series, is coming in 2014. While her husband was in the Navy, Marie lived in Spain, Maryland and Florida, and she is now settled in her home state of Rhode Island. She is the mother of two teenagers and two feisty dogs, Brandy and Louie. Subscribe to updates from Marie about new books and other news at *http://marieforce.com/*. Follow her on Twitter *@marieforce,* and on Facebook at *www.facebook.com/MarieForceAuthor.* Join one of her many reader groups! View the list at *http://marieforce.com/connect/.* Contact Marie at marie@marieforce.com.

Other Contemporary Romances Available from Marie Force:

The Treading Water Series
Book 1: Treading Water
Book 2: Marking Time
Book 3: Starting Over
Book 4: Coming Home

The McCarthys of Gansett Island Series
Book 1: Maid for Love
Book 2: Fool for Love
Book 3: Ready for Love
Book 4: Falling for Love
Book 5: Hoping for Love
Book 6: Season for Love
Book 7: Longing for Love
Book 8: Waiting for Love
Book 9: Time for Love

The Green Mountain Series
Book 1: All You Need is Love, Feb. 14, 2014

Single Titles
Georgia on My Mind
True North
The Fall
Everyone Loves a Hero
Love at First Flight
Line of Scrimmage

Romantic Suspense Novels Available from Marie Force:

The Fatal Series

Book 1: Fatal Affair

Book 2: Fatal Justice

Book 3: Fatal Consequences

Book 3.5: Fatal Destiny, the Wedding Novella

Book 4: Fatal Flaw

Book 5: Fatal Deception

Book 6: Fatal Mistake

Single Title

The Wreck

CPSIA information can be obtained at www.ICGtesting.com
Printed in the USA
LVOW04s2009240814

400678LV00029B/1546/P